ALICE GAMES

MICHELLE R REID

To David
Find the magic everyday!
Michelle R Reid

HEART DREAMS PRESS

Alice Games

By Michelle R Reid
Published by Heart Dreams Press

Cover Designer: by Cover Couture

ISBN: 1-942000-31-0
ISBN: 978-1-942000-31-0

CHAPTER ONE

HOW COULD I concentrate on the campus tour when I was being distracted by a white Playboy bunny?

The tour had been going so well. I'd figured out where my future dorm was going to be, snagged a bus schedule, made almost two pages of helpful notes, and managed not to draw too much attention to myself as I geeked out over my surroundings. My future. The campus, with its Victorian gothic style red brick buildings almost buried in the rich foliage, was exactly like the picture on the Cornell website. We had just barely entered Milstein Hall when I saw the bunny woman.

She was just barely visible out of the corner of my eye, ghost-like in her all-white outfit and flesh tones in a humanoid shape with ears flopping over her fluffy, white hair. She walked right in front of the group just as I looked up to the sweeping concrete ceiling so high above our heads.

Had I really just seen that? I did a double take, turning my head to follow where she'd gone—and looked right into a blank concrete wall. She was gone. Completely. And the rest of the almost twenty people in my tour group were acting like nothing happened. So, either scantily clad women were common at Cornell and I missed the memo, or no one else saw her? Was this a joke to see how long she could do it before someone noticed? There had to be a better way to relieve the stress of finals. Like studying more.

I barely had time to think about it, though, because the sounds of my tour's feet slapping on the concrete floor was fading as they kept going without me. I hurried and caught up, missing my chance to really study my surroundings as the tour headed up the two flights of stairs to the mezzanine.

Just then, out of the corner of my eye, there was a blur of white humanoid. I whipped around, right in the middle of the stairs, to catch her—and my mouth dropped open. She was floating almost ten feet off the side of the mezzanine, and twenty feet in the air. No ropes or strings that I could see. I looked at my classmates, waiting for their reaction, but no one seemed to notice the woman. I turned back, and she was gone.

What was going on? *How* was it going on?

Determined to catch her this time and unravel this joke, I spun to the left, ignoring the looks my fellow tour members gave me. My gaze went down to the cold, hard concrete twenty feet below and my stomach twisted. Why had I looked down? I let out the air frozen in my lungs and forced my heart to slow.

The rest of the tour attendees weren't having any problems. They filled the narrow mezzanine corridor and hung over the thick concrete railings, pointing at the university students below or looking out of the panoramic glass walls.

I gripped my packet of books and mentally shook my head. Honestly, my mind was playing tricks on me. Maybe I was the one that was stressed. Determined not to squander any more precious time, I focused on the tour again.

"The Milstein Hall is one of the newest buildings to Cornell University," said Becca, the tour guide, voice echoing around us. There was a perfect perk in her step and bounce in her ponytail. She turned and beamed with pride, her red school shirt as bright as her school spirit. At least the color made her easy to spot. "This is part of the AAP, or Architecture, Art, and Planning College. I think there are a couple future attendees with us now, right?" She pointed to two gangly guys whispering ecstatically to each other and gazing around in awe.

I had to admit this was an impressive building. It looked like a giant piece of origami, made out of concrete, steel, and glass. Everything was oblong—the railings, the beams, and even the glass panes on the walls. But then there were artistic aspects, like the ceiling that arched down until it touched the ground, with recessed lights that followed the curvature.

Bubbles of excitement fluttered in my stomach like fireworks. In five months, I'd get to call Cornell University home—though not this exact building. No more high school classes pretending to be college courses and kids whining about how their parents pushed them into it. This was going to be real.

I saw white out of the corner of my eye again and turned. And came face to face with another girl on the tour.

She stood so close that her white knit top almost brushed the sleeve of my worn t-shirt. She blinked green eyes, heavy with mascara, confused when I stared her full in the face.

Her friend cut off her babble about boys and gawked at me too.

I stepped back to a comfortable distance, trying not to fidget. My hands gripped the tour packet I had been folding and unfolding. "Ah, sorry." What was I going to say if she asked why I turned? Or could they see the bunny-woman too, but were sophisticated enough not to react?

The girl waved her hand in dismissal. "It's okay. I'm Kristin. What are you going to major in, ah ...?" She stalled for my name.

Relief bloomed inside. She was actually asking about something I could talk about all day. "Ali. I'm going into botany, with a minor in zoology."

Her eyes went blank, interest dying. "Oh, what's that?"

"It's the study of plants." And obviously not something *she* could talk about all day. "What about you?"

"Communications." She tossed her pretty black hair.

I nodded slowly, trying not to wince. My worst subject. Sometimes I forgot that Cornell had non-science majors. Well, now what was I supposed to do? She was the kind of person I'd planned to hide from in the science lab.

Some people go to college to 'get a life' or something. Party all the time and wake up hungover every morning. Not me. I just wanted to get in, get done, and get out. When I go to South America after graduation to find some new species and put my name in the history books, any friends or boyfriends I had would be left behind anyway, so why even try to develop deep relationships?

I reached up and toyed with the thin, white gold chain resting on my collarbone, then forced my hand to grip the straps of my shoulder bag instead as I tried to come up with something to say.

Kristin's friend bumped her shoulder. "Hey, we're moving on." She grabbed Kristin's arm and dragged her away. Their shoes clicked on the gray concrete.

"Okay!" Becca the guide gushed as she walked. "We're going to make a quick stop at the Milstein's student lounge before lunch. You'll love it! It's fifty feet in the air, extending right over University Avenue. And after that, we're going to visit the counselors, so while you eat think of questions you want to ask them. If you've already been accepted to Cornell—congrats by the way—you can set up your class schedule at that point. Now would be a good time to beat the crowd before all the good classes are filled."

A rush of excitement tingled the top of my head and made my heart pump fast. That was it. The reason why I was even on this tour. University seniors had already picked their classes, the rest was first come, first served. Having the right class schedule was vital. One class out of order could be the difference between graduating in three years or four. For eight years, I'd worked so hard for this next step. I had the scholarship set up, board included, and now all I had to do was make sure nothing went wrong.

I melted into the back of the small crowd. Until lunch was done, the back was fine. As much as I wanted to be front row and learning more about my future, I didn't know how I would explain getting into someone's face like that again. No one else seemed to notice that bunny-woman as she popped in and out of sight, either. Was someone playing a joke on me?

White flashed.

I spun around and found nothing. Again. This time I was determined not to look down. A frustrated yell was on the tip of my tongue, but I bit it back. It was bad enough that I knew my annoyance was starting to show on my face. I didn't need to be the center of attention, too.

I took a deep breath. I shouldn't be so upset over something like this. Either the bunny-woman would show herself, or she wouldn't. I had to concentrate on what was important. A young woman running around in a scanty white suit wasn't.

The sounds of my group faded. I looked around, alarmed when I saw the last of them disappearing up the top of the stairs leading to the student lounge.

"This is getting out of hand," I whispered. I hurried after them, making sure to stay in the exact middle of the mezzanine. I came to a stop at the bottom of the stairs.

They were two stories high. The textured steel of the stairs and handrails gleamed in the sunlight streaming in through the massive glass wall. The stairs were anchored into the wall with minimal steel support, giving them a pretty—horrifying—floating effect.

A couple passed me and started up the stairs.

My brows pulled together, and I took a breath for what seemed like the millionth time in twenty minutes. No big deal. *People go up and down every day.* And I needed to catch up. Staying exactly in the middle of the wide planks, I kept my eyes on the landing platform and ran up the stairs. It wasn't until there were only two stairs left that my curiosity got the better of me.

I glanced down. With nothing to obstruct my view, the concrete was very visible between the steel steps. And very far away.

I froze on the step as bile rose in the back of my throat. Why did I look down? I knew better. Sucking in a shallow breath, I forced my eyes back to the landing.

And gasped.

There she was. After twenty minutes of torture, the Playboy bunny was standing in full view on the landing right in front of me.

I was shocked enough to almost forget I was four stories high.

The beautiful woman was at least six feet tall, not counting her white, six-inch stilettos. Her hourglass figure was squeezed into a white leotard that showed off her long legs. Her lips were frost pink. The base of her white floppy bunny ears was cleverly hidden in her fluffy, bleached blonde curls.

Her head cocked to the side and she smiled, dark eyes pleasantly happy. "Hello, Alice. You were quite hard to find." Her voice was low and mature despite her youthful appearance.

I blinked at her, mouth open. "What? How do you know my name?" Or at least, my real name. I threw my hands in the air. "Never mind. Listen, I'm busy right now. This is important—"

"Yes, I know. Very important. We've been expecting you." The bunny kept smiling brightly as her hands shot out and hit my shoulders, shoving me backwards.

CHAPTER TWO

I SCREAMED as I pitched backward into the air. My bag slid off my shoulder and hit the stairs first with a thump. For a second, all I could see were the curved lights above.

Then wind swirled around me, ripping at my hair and clothes so hard and fast that I choked. My mouth closed and my arms came up to shield my face. I was falling. I knew I was falling, and I had two flights of steel stairs to go down.

But it didn't feel like I was going down. It was like being in a wind tunnel, the cold air spinning around and around, offset by random hot blasts. It spun me in circles like a human bullet. I tried to keep my eyes open, desperate to see what was going on, but the wind blinded me, drying out my eyes and making them water. The world spun by in a blur of green. My stomach churned, and I closed my eyes, waiting for the pain.

It never came.

The breath whooshed out of me when I landed flat on my stomach, head on my arms. It hurt, but it wasn't as jarring as I expected a twenty-foot fall to be. For all the force I felt, I could have just tripped over my feet.

"Alice?" a soft female voice mumbled.

I lay on carpet, thick enough to bury my fingers in. Was that right? I should be lying on cold concrete. There wasn't anything this homey in the Milstein building. Instead of the sterile smell of concrete and steel, the scent of wood, old books, and roses wafted over me. How was that possible?

"Alice?" It wasn't the voice of the woman who'd pushed me; it was too sweet and dignified. "Open your eyes, please."

Could I? I didn't know that I wanted to. I opened my eyes a little bit, expecting to see a lot of people—the paramedics, students, police, and random bystanders taking pictures on their phones—but there were none of those. Just one girl.

Well, she was the height of a girl, but in every other way she was a woman. Her perfectly beautiful, heart-shaped face held the look of eternal youth, but her petite figure wasn't girlish. She wore a multicolored dress any Disney princess would envy. The trim bodice had a square neckline, and the sparkly skirt flared out until the base was wider than she was tall. Her sleeves, made out of the same sparkly material as the skirt, puffed into balls at her shoulders. Thick, curly brown hair fell to her waist.

I blinked at her, completely confused. "You definitely don't look like a nurse." Was I dreaming?

Her rose-red, perfectly shaped lips curved up in a smile. "No, I'm not. Hello, Alice. My name is Red Queen. Nice to meet you."

I shifted into a sitting position.

We were in a den. A large wooden desk took up most of the wall to my right. The other walls were covered in bookshelves that outlined an elaborate fireplace, where a warm fire crackled. That fire was the only visible light, but still the room was brighter than I expected.

The only explanation I could think of was I had hurt myself falling and this was a dream my mind created to cope with the injury. It must be a dream, because there were no irises in Red Queen's huge brown eyes. At all.

"Ali," I mumbled, my mind still trying to connect the dots of how I got here. Unfortunately, there were way too many gaps for me to come to a conclusion.

Her black lashes fluttered in a blink. "Pardon me?"

"Call me Ali. Alice is my mother's name." Her introductions finally registered in my head, distracting me from my surroundings. "Did you say 'Red Queen?'?"

She bobbed a tiny curtsy and delicately touched a cute little crown on top of her dark curls. A large ruby gleamed from twisted golden cords in the firelight. "Yes, Alice—ah, I mean, Ali. I am the ruler of—"

"Let me guess," I said in a flat voice. My whole life, people have teased me about white bunnies and red roses. It doesn't matter that I don't even look like the classic Alice, with my brown hair and brown eyes. "Wonderland or Underland or whatever." First a white Playboy bunny, now this? What was going on?

Her brows wrinkled. "No." Her right hand came up and cupped her cheek. "I've never heard of Underland, although several other Alices have called this world Wonderland. Its correct name is Oz."

I stared at her for a whole minute. Where did I start with the questions? Other Alices? As in, there'd been lots of them? It seemed safer to stay on subject. "Oz? Like Dorothy and the Wizard?"

She frowned and looked at the ground. My question

obviously troubled her. "I don't know what a *dorothy* is, but here in the Ruby Castle, we prefer not to talk about White Wizard. He is ... well, we like to keep things peaceful here." Her voice wobbled. She pressed her lips into a tight line and began to pace, tapping her fingertips together. Did she look a little paler in the firelight?

This was crazy. "I can't believe I came up with such a weird dream." I dropped my face into my hands. Please tell me I was in a hospital bed, hallucinating from some medication. "I don't have time to be dreaming, I have to pick out my classes." The sound of Red Queen's dress as it swooshed across the carpet stopped in front of me. She waited until I looked up, then reached out and pinched my cheek. Hard.

"Ow!" I jumped and covered my cheek with my hand, alarmed on so many levels. You can't get hurt in dreams, right? I was no dream expert, but doesn't that just wake you up? However, despite the way my cheek throbbed, I was still staring at this tiny woman. But that wasn't possible.

"Ali." She stared at me very seriously. "This isn't a dream. It's a game." There was nothing girlish about her now. "One that will affect the lives of everyone in Oz." Red Queen paused, looking intently into my eyes. "It will undoubtedly affect your life too." Suddenly, she smiled as bright as the sun. "So, let's get dressed."

"Dressed?"

"Of course. You can't possibly go to the party in those—ah." She pointed to my pants. "Whatever those are."

"Jeans?" I fingered the well-worn material. "I'd rather stay in them."

"Don't be silly." She laughed my comment aside, then reached out and tugged my wrist as if to assist me.

I stood up without her help. Instantly I felt oversized.

She was about four and a half feet tall. I was average height, but next to her I was a giant.

Keeping her hold on my wrist, Red Queen walked me to the door. "It's too dangerous for you to keep any articles from your world."

Dangerous? They were just clothes. Nothing flashy, just comfortable. I debated arguing with her, but decided to see how this played out first.

On the other side of the door was a rectangular room full of dresses hanging on poles. Each dress was as puffy and colorful as the one Red Queen wore. I eyed her warily as she let go of me in the middle of the room and wandered off, humming. If she thought I was going to pretend to be an overdressed prom queen, she was crazy.

In all the stories I'd heard, the Red Queen was evil, with the whole "off with their head" thing. This tiny woman didn't look malicious—she seemed like a rather likable and gentle person. Then again, I wasn't exactly here by choice. Had she brought me here? Was she really the good guy? She obviously seemed to think so, but hers was the only opinion I had.

"What's so bad about the White Wizard?" I crossed my arms, careful not to touch the brightly colored materials around me.

She poked her head out of a pile of dresses. "He is a denizen of chaos. When he has the rule, Oz is in an endless winter." She shivered. Her hand lingered on a dress as her gaze dropped to the floor. "And the Cheshire Cat is loose." Her voice was so quiet, I barely heard it.

"The Cheshire Cat?" I frowned, envisioning a roly-poly striped feline with a wide smile. "What's so bad about him?"

She shook her head, an unreadable expression on her face. "I promise I'll try to keep you away from him as much as I can." She looked to the side and brightened. "Oh, that's it." She pulled out a dress taller than she was.

I jumped when the door on the other side of the room flew open. Maids—lots of maids—bustled through. They all wore pale-blue dresses with puffy skirts and white ruffled aprons. Each woman had platinum-blonde, curly hair, trimmed like a cotton candy ball and topped with white, frilly caps. Like Red Queen, their blue eyes had no irises. Every single one of the fifteen maids looked exactly the same. As if that wasn't odd enough, two off-white leather pieces were attached to the underside of their hats and hung down like a pair of, I don't know ... ears?

Two maids carried a linen sheet over to Red Queen and held it up like a shield. The rest of the maids attacked me, ripping my clothes off so fast I couldn't prevent it. I yelled and tried to defend myself, but some of their determined hands held me still while they rest made quick work. They even went so far as to strip my bra, underwear and necklace.

As fast as my clothes came off, they put more clothes on. First, lacey red undergarments. Next a black slip, then a corset that they tightened brutally. They settled a hoop slip around my waist then pulled the actual dress over my head. Two maids buttoned me up while another held my hips steady as three more shoved heels on my feet. Two others applied blush to my cheeks and a pink cream to my lips.

As suddenly as they had appeared, they all hurried out, closing the door behind them. It was like they had never been there at all.

I was left in a purple dress, its full skirt almost as wide as Red Queen's. The tight, long-sleeved bodice ended in a square neck. Matching gems lined the wrists, neckline, and waist.

My mouth hung open, and I breathed hard. "What just happened?" I looked around, the cool silky material brushing against my hot skin. "Where are my clothes?"

Red Queen smiled with gentle amusement, as if this wasn't the first time she'd seen this happen. "As I said, it's time to go to the party. A lady must always look her best, especially when being viewed by the world." She walked toward the door on the far side of the wall.

The world? My stomach twisted with anxiety. How many people did she expect me to meet? She hadn't even told me what was going on. What did she expect me to do?

Something glittered out of the corner of my eye. I turned toward it. My necklace lay on the floor just at the edge of my skirt, the white gold barely visible. One of the maids must have dropped it. Quickly I scooped it up and stuffed it in my lacy bra, where it would be safe. I didn't care about how Red Queen said my stuff was dangerous. This was *my* necklace. The only thing I had left of sanity.

"Ali," Red Queen chimed from the far door, making me jump. She must not have seen me pick up the chain, because all she did was smile. "Come along."

I stared at her, arms crossed in front of me.

Her smile stayed in place but her brow wrinkled in worry. "I understand that you're confused. But you will never go home if you stay in this room. I will help as much as I can. Bunny took such a long time to find you, and now there isn't much time left."

I frowned at her. "No, you don't understand. I can't be in another world. Earth doesn't have the advanced technology to send someone to another world. Or dimension or whatever." I glanced at the chandelier and the candelabras on the walls with the dripping wax candles. Then I plucked at my skirt. "And it looks like you don't have the technology, either."

She gave a tiny giggle. "Oz doesn't need science to bring an Alice here."

"What, you mean magic?" I shifted my weight to the right, annoyed. She was barking up the wrong tree if she thought she'd make me believe in something I couldn't touch or see.

But you are here, seeing her. And you can feel the fabric on your skin and ground under your feet, a very unhelpful voice whispered in the back of my head.

She nodded. Her fingers twisted together in front of her. She tried to keep a smile on her face, but the anxious lines returned to her brow. "There have been several Alices who refused to acknowledge the evidence in front of their eyes and continued to insist this is a dream. You would be wise not to fall into that category."

I shook my head but went with her.

We entered a circular room lined with numbered red doors, twelve of them in total. Our shoes clicked on the white-and-black tile as Red Queen led me through a door on the far side labeled twelve. On the other side was a small room with a huge, red, velvet curtain on the right side. Many muffled sounds and voices came from beyond the thick material.

I reached up to touch my necklace on my collarbone for reassurance. When my fingers found only bare skin, they tugged on my hair instead. "What is this party about?"

"This is the Last Night of Peace Ball. And as the Alice, you are our honored guest," Red Queen said pleasantly. She stood right in front of the curtain. "It's called 'Night' but there's only an hour left."

A jolt went down my spine. "The Last Night of Peace?" That didn't sound very good. "What does that mean?"

She stared at me, face calm and collected. "At midnight, White Wizard will be released from the Diamond Castle, and everything begins again."

CHAPTER THREE

THE CURTAIN WHOOSHED OPEN, and the sounds it had been blocking assaulted my ears in full force. I flinched. The smell of warm bodies wafted over with an odd afternote—it reminded me of a zoo.

We were at the top of a huge staircase. Below were hundreds of people, all dressed in gowns and suits right out of the Renaissance era.

Red Queen delicately held out her right hand. A bright red wand appeared in her delicate fingers.

I rolled my eyes. Of course, she had a wand. She was a regular little Glinda, wasn't she? It was an impressive sleight of hand, but I hoped she wouldn't start singing.

The crowd went silent.

Red Queen smiled, her pretty face full of love. She looked like a jewel shining in the spotlight. "People of Oz, I present to you," she motioned to me with her free hand, "Ali of Alice!"

What was that about? I shook my head. The crowd erupted in applause, and I raised a hand in an awkward wave, wishing I was anywhere else. Like back at Cornell. They cheered, but most of them wore worried expressions.

A man in the front of the crowd scratched the brown dog ears poking out of his head and leaned over to whisper to a woman with peacock feathers pluming out behind her. The woman's feathers flared out in response to what he said.

My hand slowly lowered. What the ...?

She reached behind and smoothed them back into place.

The man with dog ears smiled, a tail attached to his trousers wagging.

Next to him, a short, fat man with a pig snout for a nose snorted in admonishment. The couple glared at him, and he wiggled his nose and glared right back.

Shock settled over me, like a cold egg being cracked on my head and dripping down to my toes. Their animal parts, they were just too real. Way too real. Make-up and mechanical costumes weren't that sophisticated. I searched the crowd. Those three had to be a fluke.

But no—every single person had animal traits. Literally. There were people with elephant ears flapping and taking up space, cow horns poking out of hats, and horse tails flicking around. They weren't costumes; they were real and mobile. The maids that dressed me—the leather beneath their hats must have been actual ears. *Sheep* ears, based on their curly white hair. So, the ears on the Playboy bunny had been real?

But humans don't have animal parts. Red Queen doesn't. I don't. So how did these people get them?

Red Queen spoke, drawing my attention back from the animal people below. "Let the Last Night of Peace commence!" Her voice rang out like a bell. "For the Alice Games begins anew!"

This game, whatever that meant, was called the Alice Games? If it was anything physical, they were in for a surprise. I sucked at sports.

The people cheered again.

My hands clenched at my sides. This was getting out of hand. "Red Queen, what is going on? I really don't have the time for any of this. Games? Are you kidding me? I was on my way to plan out the next three years of *my life*. If I don't get to that meeting, it'll be a waste of the last eight years of hard work." I crossed my arms.

She took a deep breath and clasped her hands together in front of her, then spoke in a low voice. "I know you don't understand, and honestly you don't really have to. All you have to know is that you are special. And you, the Alice of Alice, have come to Oz to choose the next ruler—me or White Wizard."

She was nuts. Beyond crazy. I snorted and waved my hands in the air. "What? Me? What do I know about this place and these people? Can't I just pick you and go home right now?"

Bothered more than I should be, I looked out over the people milling about below us. As much as I was in a hurry, Red Queen had said this 'game' was going to impact the life of every single one of them and more people who I couldn't see. A decision like that shouldn't be taken lightly. But I didn't know them, and I didn't completely believe they were real. How could I know who I should pick? I'd barely met Red Queen, and I didn't know anything about White Wizard at all, other than Red Queen's opinion. And I still didn't know if she really was as kind as she seemed or if it was a farce. This was too huge a decision for a complete stranger to make.

Red Queen's smile was small and sweet, her brown eyes warm with amusement. "If only it were that simple. But the decision can't be made until you are at the Emerald Castle at False Dawn on noon the second day. If you make it there, then you can choose and go home."

She said "if you make it there" heavily, like I might not.

Quickly, I added up the numbers in my head. "Wait, that's in thirty-six hours. I can't be here that long! I have things to do in my world!" I'll miss the councilor's appointment, my flight home, and maybe even my English final. Forget not getting classes at Cornell, I won't even graduate High School at that point.

She waved a hand, brushing off my problems. "Your world and Oz move at different times. I'm sure it won't be an issue. As long as you get to the Emerald Castle by False Dawn. I can't promise anything after that."

I frowned at her. She was sure, but she didn't know for sure. "So I was teleported or whatever to the Ruby Castle? Why wasn't I just simply taken to the Emerald City—ah, Castle?"

She blinked in surprise, like she'd never been asked that question before. Every other question I'd asked, she always had a quick answer—like she was expecting the question and already had a speech ready for it. But this one stalled her. "Because I'm the current Queen—until midnight. So Oz brought you to me."

"And if White Wizard was the ruler, I'd be taken to him?" I finished.

She nodded slowly. "Yes."

I sighed, wondering if his place was close to the Emerald Castle. "And I have to do this? It's really the only way?" At this point, I was willing to do almost anything to get out of this crazy place and get back to Cornell as fast as possible.

"Yes." Red Queen nodded and motioned to the room with her wand. "Now, there are people I really must introduce you to. Shall we?" She floated down the stairs as if gliding down a cloud.

Trying not to clop like a horse, I followed her. The temperature rose with every step.

People turned and greeted the tiny queen as we got to the bottom. Despite 'not having much time left,' she paused and exchanged words with everyone who greeted her. I would have preferred to skirt around the sides of the crowd next to the star-filled windows that framed the entire right wall from floor to ceiling, but she plowed right through the middle.

She knew the name of every person and greeted each as if they were the most important person in the world. At her side, I watched in amazement and confusion, trying to comprehend caring about this many people. She couldn't be more opposite of me. I'd hate to stand there and talk to so many people. I wouldn't know what to say or how to relate to them. But she glowed under their devotion. I would have given anything to be a wallflower on the side of the room. It was hard enough to breathe with the corset, and the hot, sticky, animal-scented air didn't help.

I didn't pay much attention to what they were saying. Instead, I studied their faces and actions as I tried to get used to being surrounded by so many people.

It was easy to see that everyone here loved Red Queen. Animal ears perked up, dog tails wagged, and bird feathers ruffled and fluffed with pleasure when she spoke. They were vocal about their support, clasping her hands and gushing about how wonderful she was and how they wished she would always be queen.

Those particular words were aimed at me, as were their anxious looks. It seemed that as much as they adored their current queen, they feared me. Hardly anyone tried to exchange words with me, instead they just talked in my general direction. Red Queen didn't try to force me into any conversations. In fact, she acted like their behavior was completely normal.

"Why are they so afraid of me?" I finally asked. I had expected them to be overly courteous and overwhelming, since I was supposed to pick their next ruler.

Red Queen opened her mouth, then she looked over my shoulder. Her face lit up with pleasure.

A man's tenor voice answered from right behind me. "Well, you are from another world."

I jumped and whirled around.

"And you can ruin our lives until the next Alice comes," a second man said in a deep voice, right beside the first.

They were like a comedic pair right out of a Renaissance fair. The man on the right was long and skinny. He wore a sand-colored shirt over black pants and soft leather boots. Dull brown hair parted perfectly to the side and smoothed around a pair of foot-long, brown rabbit ears. His pupil-less eyes were solid gray.

The huge, handsome man next to him had big muscles that rippled under his off-white, long-sleeved shirt, tucked into a pair of, well, golden pants. His golden hair stuck out in all directions, leaving the round ears on top of his head barely visible. A thin, golden, lion tail swished lazily behind him. In the room full of hot bodies, he still smelled like a pleasant, musky cologne.

Red Queen stepped beside me, her brows dropping in a

frown. "Gentlemen, that wasn't very kind." She cleared her throat. "Some introductions are in order. Ali, meet Lional and Hareson. They will assist you when I'm not available. Gentlemen, this is Ali."

"Ah, hi." I forced a smile and nodded. If this was anything like the stories, I was meeting the Cowardly Lion and the March Hare. Not very encouraging. Lional was rather impressive looking. Hareson just gave off the impression of a straight-laced butler. Oh, boy.

The men exchanged looks.

"Ali, huh?" Lional rumbled. Like the other people, he wasn't talking to me. His eyes were fixed on Red Queen like she was the only person in the world. "That's different. I thought my ears were failing me when I heard you say 'Ali of Alice.'" The fluffy tip of his tail twitched.

The rest of his words faded out as I began to ignore him as much as he was me. Immediately, I became interested in the tail bouncing behind him. I knew enough about animal anatomy to guess how his skeletal structure accommodated the appendage. A person with a real tail was way more interesting than CGI, and most everyone in the room had one. So why didn't Red Queen and I have animal parts? Was it because she was a queen and I was from another world?

A bit of bright color caught my attention, and I glanced down. I was standing in the middle of a yellow circle about four feet in diameter. Directly in front of my toes, a foot-wide yellow line led out five feet in the shape of an arrow before fading into nothing.

I nearly jumped out of my skin. I took a big step to the side, wobbling in my high heels, but the circle moved with me. No matter how I moved, the circle stayed centered on me, and the arrow continued to point in the same direction—out the huge windows on the south side of the room.

The three people around me exchanged glances again.

"My, my, an Alice has found the Yellow Path by herself," Hareson muttered. His nose twitched. "How odd."

I glanced at him, struggling to keep my voice calm. "Yellow Path? Is that what this is?" I pointed at it. For some reason, it was fine—interesting even—that the people here were different. But the idea that something from this world would attach itself to me made my skin crawl. "What does it do?"

Hareson sniffed, and one of his ears flopped to the side as he finally spoke to me. "I could only assume it's the Yellow Path. We can't see it. Only an Alice can see it."

Red Queen nodded. "It will show you the path you need to take."

So, it was like a GPS? Concerned, I motioned to them. "I thought that's what you guys are for. Why would I need something like this if you'll be there?"

They exchanged glances again, having an entire conversation without words in that one second. The men looked away.

Red Queen turned back to me. "We will be there. In just a minute, Hareson and Lional will escort you to your room where you can sleep nice and safe. In the morning, we and a group of selected others will take you to the Emerald Castle. But as a precaution, Oz has provided you with directions. And there are Domains you have to visit. You and I won't know where until the Yellow Path takes you there."

"What's a Domain?" I asked.

Hareson startled and pulled a pocket watch from his breast pocket. "Ah, my Queen ..."

Red Queen jolted and slapped a hand to her cheek.

"Oh, no. I lost track of time." She looked at me closely as if wondering something. "I guess it's just going to have to happen here."

I tensed. "What's going to happen?"

Instead of answering, her chin tilted until she looked up at a huge elaborate copper clock above the staircase. She sighed in a sad, wistful way, her perfect face as lovely as ever. Her hands clenched around her wand possessively. "It begins."

I turned to the clock just as it struck twelve. The first chime rang out.

Instantly my stomach twisted painfully, like my insides were in a blender. Gasping, I grabbed my stomach and bent over, face tight.

Red Queen turned and watched me. There wasn't any alarm in her expression at my sudden pain, just open curiosity.

Hareson, Lional, and the rest of the room all reacted in the same way as I did, clutching their stomachs and moaning in pain.

A tingling and twisting sensation ran through my body, starting at my toes and working up to my spinning head. Eyes wide, I looked down at the fingers clutching my stomach. They were shrinking! Not only were they shrinking, but fine, dark brown fur was starting to cover them in a silky coat. All my limbs were shriveling, and my waist was thinning rapidly. As I shrank, my clothes evaporated into nothing. I yelled in fright as my line of vision lurched forward with the rest of my body. I landed on all fours, far shorter than I used to be.

The tingling sensation stopped.

While the clock chimed again, I gasped and examined my body.

"Holy mother of hairballs!" I shrieked. "I'm a cat! I'm a cat! Why am I a cat?" Dimly, I thought that I shouldn't be able to talk out loud if I was a cat, but there were more pressing matters to worry about. I jerked this way and that, clawing at the dark brown tail attached to me.

"Ali! Ali, stop!" Red Queen crouched over me and stopped my movements with a firm hand. "A brown cat," she muttered to herself. "How surprising. I wonder what that means."

I looked up at her, still freaking out. "What's happening?"

Any desperate hopes that this was a dream shriveled and died. I really was a cat in another world called Oz.

"You have to play by the rules," Red Queen explained. "During the Alice Games, the dark belongs to White Wizard. From sunset—or midnight on the first day—until dawn, the citizens are animals. It's chaos."

The clock rang again. Number ten, I thought dimly. "That's—that's stupid!"

The wand in Red Queen's hand disappeared in an explosion of red sparkles. She frowned, her eyes worried and overly bright. "Stay with Hareson and Lional in the Ruby Castle where it's safe. We'll talk more in the morning. I hope."

"What are you talking about?" I yelled.

The clock struck twelve.

Red Queen vanished in another shower of sparkles.

The clock went silent and all the lights in the room blinked out.

CHAPTER FOUR

"RED QUEEN?" I called out into the dark room. Well, I'd call it dark if I were human. With my newfound feline eyesight, the moonbeams streaming though the high windows gave plenty of light.

Another new sense woke up with a vengeance. The ballroom reeked like a rank zoo, so strong it was almost nauseating. I sneezed and tried to cover my nose with a furry paw. "Red Queen?"

Lional's voice rumbled next to me. "A cat, huh?"

I jumped and turned, almost stepping on my tail in the process. It was so strange to be able to feel every hair on my body stick up and feel the muscles in my back arch my spine high.

"You are a weird Alice," he said. "Don't bother calling for her. Red Queen can't hear or help you right now–she's in the moon."

My mouth almost dropped open as I stared up at him from below. Far below. Lional the lion was so much bigger than I was. He stood proud, and took a second to shake out his long, bronze colored main. He looked down at me with flat golden eyes. I remember standing in a zoo and watching a lion eat a cow leg right next to the enclosure's windows and thinking that, regardless of how fascinating, I never wanted to meet a lion face to face without a fence between us. I thought the same thing now.

However, there was intelligence in his eyes instead of simple bloodthirst. That was reassuring. Sort of.

"The moon?" I repeated.

"Remember she told you the night is White Wizard's time?" Hareson stepped up to me. Sure enough, he was a hare about the same size as me. His long brown ears rested against the gentle curve of his back. "She's locked up during the night just as he is during the day." It was odd hearing his stiff voice come out of something that looked so soft and fluffy. It didn't help that his nose twitched with every word he spoke. His ears lifted, flopping behind him then perking up again.

Suddenly I was overcome with an overpowering temptation to reach out and swat Hareson with my paws. Disappointed with myself, I shook my head and looked around for a distraction. I might be smooshed into a cat-shaped box right now, but that didn't mean I had to act like a cat.

Every single person in the room was an animal, the same type as the body part they displayed while human. Besides Lional, I was the only feline in the room.

Taking a deep breath, I turned to my guides. "Okay. What do we do now?" My tail twitched, distracting me. I didn't mean to move it, but apparently the appendage had a mind of its own, flicking and swishing across the yellow colored ground, revealing the anxiety I wanted to hide.

Hareson stood on his hind legs and looked out the windows on the right side of the room. "Like Red Queen said, it's time to retire to bed. It's far too dangerous to travel right now."

I followed his gaze and gasped. Giant white snowflakes fell heavily past the window panes. "It's *snowing*?" I swear it wasn't snowing a couple minutes ago.

A large yowl echoed through the ball room, vibrating off the walls and echoing in my tight chest.

The crowd in the room gasped and screamed with terror.

I jumped and looked at Lional to make sure he wasn't the one who'd made the sound. He looked as alarmed as everyone else. His mane bristled and tail stilled as his bulking muscles bunched with anticipation. His great head jerked around, golden eyes blazing with fury. His mouth dropped open, panting to taste the scent of the air and hone his search.

The tension radiating from him was nerve-wracking. I took a couple steps closer to Hareson. The hair on my back bristled.

Hareson trembled. His ears were erect, and his nose twitched wildly. "Was that *inside*?" he whispered in alarm. "How? White Wizard's taint shouldn't be able to get in Ruby Castle."

The animals around us shifted and shook in fear, emitting frightened animal noises. "Cheshire Cat! It's the Cheshire Cat!" Someone began to sob.

My heart kicked up a beat as their emotions saturated my own.

Another yowl sounded from somewhere in the rafters.

"He's inside!" someone screamed.

It was like a dam broke. The animals around us exploded in panic. They bolted this way and that, running into the walls and windows in their haste. Hareson, Lional, and I were pressed together in the chaos. I hissed and jerked out of the way of a horse's hoof. It missed me by an inch. Lional stepped forward until he was standing over Hareson and me, protecting us. He grunted when animals rammed him, but stayed in place.

Two of the windows exploded in showers of glass from all the bodies hitting them. The animals flooded through the snow-filled holes, pushing and shoving each other. Larger animals stepped on the smaller ones, and the smaller animals used the large ones as bridges. Every once in a while, random throws of dust exploded into the air.

Their panic was like a drug, kicking up my fight or flight response. My heart pounded and my ears flicked around madly. Instinct demanded that I run out of the room with the rest of the crowd. But the fear of getting trampled mixed with the rational, human part of my mind, reminding me I was supposed to stay with Hareson and Lional, and that kept me still.

Why hadn't we left yet? Were they waiting until the animals were gone and it wasn't so dangerous to move? Or did they think the Cheshire Cat would follow the panicking animals? My question was answered when most of the animals had disappeared through the hole.

Lional raised his head and yelled out, "Cheshire Cat! Show yourself! Today, I will take my revenge!"

My jaw dropped in disbelief. "Please tell me you're joking." I thought we were supposed to spend a safe evening, sleeping, then travel to the Emerald Castle as easy as a daisy in the morning. Nothing like this was ever mentioned in the plans.

Even Red Queen said that the Cheshire Cat was dangerous. What was Lional doing, challenging someone the rest of Oz was terrified of? Maybe Lional was that good;

Red Queen did think he could protect me. There weren't many animals that could take on a full-grown male lion. But if he was strong enough to take on the Cheshire Cat, why did all the other animals run away? Wouldn't they be safer with Lional?

I stepped out from under the lion, absentmindedly noting how weird it was to walk on all fours. Thank goodness this new body instinctively knew how to move.

"Shh! Lional, don't!" Hareson hissed. "We have to get out of here. What if those monsters can get in too?" His eyes were wide enough that I could see the whites. He couldn't stop looking around, rising up on his hind legs, then squatting down again. "We need to find somewhere safe and come up with a new plan."

A merciless laugh echoed in the room. "Really, Lional?" The threatening male voice growled from the top of the stairs.

Lional snarled. "Cheshire Cat!"

My ears perked straight up and I looked over my shoulder. My stomach clenched in terror and I felt sick.

The Cheshire Cat was nothing like any of the stories. There was no round-faced, roly-poly British Shorthair cat standing at the top of the stairs. He was a massive white tiger. At least eleven feet from nose to tip and well over six hundred pounds, he stood on the stairs like he owned them.

The few animals left in the room emptied out quickly, until the only ones left were me, Lional, Hareson, and the Cheshire Cat.

Hareson trembled more than ever. He nudged me with his nose, herding me toward the window.

Logic would say Hareson had the right idea, but for some reason my legs felt frozen to the ground. Dimly I was aware that my body was shaking as much as his. Why did they call him the Cheshire Cat if he was a tiger? It was obvious that he was dangerous, or else the animals wouldn't have acted like that. I knew I should run, but my mind was on overload from the shock of this world, turning into a cat, and the possibility that someone was trying to kill me.

Lional bounded toward the tiger, snarling like the lion he was. He did look impressive with his pluming mane and deep noises, but a male lion was still smaller than a male tiger. "Today, you curse of Oz, I will kill you!" He roared, the sound echoing like a pounding drum deep in my chest.

The white tiger flashed his teeth and leapt down the stairs. I don't know how he did it, but he cleared the space of the room in seconds. He moved faster than my eyes could follow.

The huge cats clashed in the middle of the ballroom. Roars and snarls echoed, the acoustics of the room amplifying the sounds. They exchanged bites and slashes in raw feline fury.

Hareson pushed harder than ever. "Go, Ali! Go!" he pleaded.

I was paralyzed, horrified by the scene in front of me. There was nothing thrilling about watching these two majestic cats try to kill each other. The tiger reached out and ran his massive claws over Lional's flanks, leaving a gash in his wake. Lional roared in pain. Only there was no blood.

In fact, in spite of all the injuries both cats sported, there wasn't a single speck of blood on them or the ground.

It wasn't until my paw landed on something cold that I realized Hareson had pushed me almost out of the room. I glanced down at the snow spilling onto the marble floor.

Just then, Lional gave a truly horrible scream. I turned to see the Cheshire Cat lunge in and clamp his jaws around

Lional's throat, cutting Lional's yell off. Suddenly, Lional exploded into a cloud of dust.

I screamed in shock. He killed him! The Cheshire Cat killed Lional!

Breathing hard and showing his big teeth, the white tiger turned toward us. His cold gaze landed on me, sending chills as cold as ice down my spine.

"Run!" Hareson yelled. "Run!"

This time, I didn't need any urging. I whipped around and bolted out of the broken window as fast as I could. Thick snow clung to the sides of the ruby red castle walls and spread out until it was eaten up by the black forest. Any sign of the animals that had already run away was smothered by snow that fell in fat, heavy flakes. I was jumping more than running just to get through the belly deep snow, but it didn't matter. Anything just to get away.

The one lucky break I got was the fact that the Yellow Path wasn't affected by the falling snow. It floated atop like a beacon, pointing alongside the Ruby Castle's red wall, towards the front.

Hareson hopped beside me. "Follow the Yellow Path," he gasped between hops. "Just follow the Yellow Path." He sounded like he was reassuring himself as he was me. "Why is this happening? Never in any Alice Game has—"

He cut off when two huge mounds of snow rose up in front of us, straddling the yellow line. I skidded to a stop, snow bunching around my chest, and gaped as the snow grew almost seven feet tall. In a snap, the snow collapsed in on itself and hardened, taking shape. In seconds, two huge ice sculptures towered over us. They were humanoid with triangular chests, long arms, and hands tipped with long talons.

Then they started to move. In unison, they looked down at me, glowing holes where their eyes should be.

"What are those?" I gasped in fear, blinking at the snow in my face.

A sound echoed across the ground behind me. My ear twitched back, bringing the sound more into focus. It sounded like snow crunching. I looked over my shoulder just as the Cheshire Cat sauntered out of the broken window. His white and black coat blended into the cold environment perfectly and complemented the gleaming, red castle walls. His cold eyes were fixated on me.

"Go!" Hareson yelled. He leapt up. With a dull thump, he kicked one of the ice monsters in the chest with his hind legs.

The ice monster didn't even flinch. It reached for me with a hand bigger than my whole body.

Fear washed away all my thoughts. I turned and bolted to the side, barely getting out of the way as the monster's hand thudded against the ground. I paid no attention to Hareson or the Yellow Path—that pointed between the legs of those monsters. I simply ran as fast as I could to the closest cover that was available. The forest.

The trees might be bare and scary looking, but not as frightening as what was behind me. Hareson yelled something, but I couldn't understand him over the blood pounding in my cold ears. I breached the tree line and darted around the giant trees and bushes, trying to get lost in the foliage. Anything to make myself harder to follow.

Moments later, the sounds of branches and wood breaking echoed behind me. I glanced over my shoulder as an ice monster shoved aside a tree branch so hard it snapped right off. My gut twisted painfully. If it could do that to a branch almost three inches thick, what would it do to me?

And still the Yellow Path pointed back, directly at the monsters.

I don't know how long I ran or where I was going. My sense of smell wasn't any use—everything just smelled like a crisp winter night. The rest of my cat's physique wasn't helping either. The snow was only six inches deep, which would have been fine if I were a human. As a cat, it froze my stomach, and my new fifth appendage was freezing its fur off. Tails weren't all they were cracked up to be.

Everything looked the same. An icy hell with frost-covered trees, random snow pits that came up to my ears, and slick patches of ice. All the while, I could hear the sounds of those things crashing through the trees behind me. I couldn't hear any sounds that indicated Hareson or the Cheshire Cat.

Even so, I couldn't run forever. My limbs were freezing and burning at the same time, trying to lock up painfully. The fur that should have kept me warm was soaked from the snow falling from the sky and the powder I was clawing my way through. The air was so cold, it hurt my lungs more than it helped.

Think, Ali, I ordered myself, *think of something. What do I do?* I was a cat—no thumbs. No way to make any form of defense. I didn't know anything about Oz, and I knew less about the monsters chasing me. Ice shouldn't be moving like this—shouldn't be moving at all.

My mind cleared slightly. There was something I did understand about my situation. I was a small cat. I knew the basics of feline anatomy, and the color of the trees around me were almost the same color as my fur.

I jumped onto a thick fallen log and looked around, trying to find a good place to hide. Not far away was a thick, branchy bush with a pile of snow on top. I hopped down and darted under it. It wasn't comfortable. The sharp little branches stabbed me from all directions, but there was enough space and a small gap in the snow that I could look through and see my surroundings.

Where was Hareson? Wasn't he supposed to help me now that Lional was gone? Though really, what could a hare do against a tiger that a lion couldn't? There was a reason the food chain existed. Food chain. Oh man, what if the Cheshire Cat had eaten Hareson?

The sound of snow crunching under heavy feet on the other side of the log marred the silent air. My ears perked up and turned that direction as I forced my breathing to become shallow, soundless.

Out of the darkness, the ice monsters appeared and stopped at the other side of the log. They tried to step over it but couldn't raise their knees high enough. Their jaws moved up and down, making a clicking sound against their skulls as ice hit ice, and they swung their arms around in agitation. Instead of walking around or jumping over it, their mouths dropped open in a silent roar of anger and they started to tear at the log, their massive claws taking it apart, chunk by chunk.

I was left watching in horror at the sheer violence from under my bush just feet away. But there was something else that I noticed. They couldn't seem to jump or make noise. They must be made out of solid ice, there were no muscles that could expand and contract. In the right situation, that could give me an advantage. Maybe I'd get a chance to use that when they walked past.

At least the Yellow Path wasn't pointing at them anymore, but it was still indicating that I needed to go back the way that I came. Back to the Ruby Castle. But to do that, I'd have to go around the monsters.

With a crack, the log split in two. The monsters shoved the pieces apart and walked forward, the snow crunching under their heavy feet.

I gritted my teeth together and squatted closer to the ground, enough that my chin sank between my two paws. Adrenaline pumped through my veins, adding tingles to my already shivering skin.

Go away, I thought. *You can't see me.* I was a brown cat, hiding under a bush covered in snow, in the night. They shouldn't be able to see me.

They walked right up to my bush and looked down right at me.

One bent over and reached both hands out for me. My heart stopped. I lunged out of the bush a second before its hands clapped together, crushing the whole bush into splinters. I turned tail and ran as fast as I could in the opposite direction.

How did they find me? It was like they knew I was there.

The monsters clicked their jaws sharply and thudded after me again.

The yowl of a tiger up ahead made me freeze in my tracks. Just hearing it, the wet fur on my shoulders rose in alarm, letting more cold air against my skin. I couldn't see him, but I knew that sound. That same haunting sound that echoed in the rafters in Ruby Castle and scared everyone so badly. I could barely get away from the monsters, now I had to worry about a tiger too?

I swallowed and looked around. What could I do against a tiger? It was ten pounds against six hundred. Not a fair fight.

There was a break in the trees to my right. I glanced over and let my breath out. I'm not going to die here. Gray peaks of a small river gleamed in the moonlight. Along the shore was a tree, heavy with snow and with several low hanging branches reaching most of the way across the water. I was light enough, I could walk along the branches and jump the rest of the way. The monsters couldn't jump, and they were made out of heavy ice. They wouldn't be able to get across the water. I had to count on that.

Granted, it wouldn't be a problem for the Cheshire Cat, but I needed to solve one problem at a time. Maybe I'd get lucky and he wouldn't be able to find me.

I turned and ran over to the tree. My ears flicked back as I considered my options. Choosing the thickest branch, I hopped up and crept carefully across. It was slow moving, worming my way around the offshoots that jutted out of the main branch. Only a foot below, the river rushed, its tinkling sound echoing loudly in my sensitive ears. Little flecks of water jumped up at me as the water parted around rocks.

Halfway across the branch, I heard the heavy thuds of the monsters get closer and stop. I looked over my shoulder and gasped when I saw them right next to my tree and reaching for me. All the hair stood up on my body and I half ran a couple steps farther across the branch. Their clawed fingers closing sharply with *clank*s in the cold air, missing my tail by inches. I let out a satisfied breath and turned back to hurry across.

My branch gave a hard lurch.

A feline yowl escaped my lips and I grabbed onto the branch, claws flexing to dig into the wet bark.

I glanced over my shoulder just as one of the monsters swung its huge claws at my branch again, leaving giant gashes in the bark. The limb bounced around in the air, me with it, my claws the only thing keeping me on. Alarmed, I glanced down at the water rushing under me. I needed to get across. Now.

I let go and scrambled over the branch, heart pounding faster than ever. The limb began to slant down, my weight affecting it now. It was time to jump. I wasn't a pro at cat jumps, but hopefully I could make it across the remaining three feet of water to the shore. I leaned down, bunching up my muscles and prepared to jump. The limb lurched violently again, the thinner part whipping me up and down hard enough to disorient.

My front paws slipped off the wet bark and my gut tightened painfully as I realized I was falling. My yell of fright was cut off as I splashed face first into the icy water. I hit the bottom of the river and kicked off it, towards the surface. I broke through with a frantic gasp. The current grabbed me and swept me away.

Sputtering, my paws clawed at the water in desperation, barely keeping my head above the water. My body wanted to freeze up from the intense cold, but I kept paddling. The water was only about two feet deep. If I were human, I could just stand up. Instead, I was tossed to and fro like a rag doll. If I didn't get out of this water soon, I was going to die.

My surroundings and the monsters were swept past, replaced with more black trees that flew by at a dizzying pace.

A thick, fallen branch rested half in the water ahead, with the bulk of the wood on the shore. I yowled in relief and tried to position my body in line with it. My teeth gritted in effort. It was so hard, fighting against the current with these tiny paws. "Get ... there."

The branch got closer.

"Ah!" I reached out a paw and clawed at the soft, wet wood.

The undertow of the eddy tried to drag me under, but I reached out my other paw and dug my claws in. It felt like they were being ripped out, but I wasn't going to let go.

"I am not going to die in this crazy world *as a cat*!" I pulled as hard as I could.

My freezing muscles screamed in pain, but slowly the water gave way enough that my back claws could reach the wood. Coughing and suddenly sleepy, I worked my way out of the water. I don't know what was wobbling more, me or the branch, but I kept going across until I fell off and collapsed onto the snowy shore.

I had to keep going. Had to get out of the snow and somewhere dry or I'd get hypothermia. I would freeze to death if I stayed here.

But my body wouldn't listen. My arms tingled and grew heavier and heavier. I tried to raise my head, but I couldn't.

No, stay awake!

My blurry eyes weren't listening any more than my body.

White faded into black.

CHAPTER FIVE

SO WARM. Humming contently, I snuggled closer to the body pillow.

Man, what a crappy dream. Wonderland, Oz, and I should never be mixed in the same sentence—never mind the same world. What a bad combination. I still didn't get how cats were involved, but who could ever understand dreams?

The blanket was heavier than normal. As unwilling to wake up as I was, one of my eyes cracked open to a flesh colored blur. It was shaped like an ... arm? What ...?

"Aah!" Panicked, I pushed myself off the ground. I squeaked when I stepped on my skirt and fell flat against—what was a wall doing here? My mind raced, and I looked around, trying to make sense of my surroundings.

I was in a short, wooden shack barely taller than me with no windows, just a short door. In the opposite corner stood a stone fireplace with a cheery, crackling fire under a hole in the roof. Next to it lay a crumpled pile of material that looked like my dress, the corset, and the hoop slip.

Alarmed and horrified anew, I looked down. I was definitely human again, which thankfully included clothing. Sort of. I was in my last layer of slip, with cap sleeves and a square neckline. Fortunately, the black silky material wasn't see-through, but its length was at least three inches past my toes.

Relieved I wasn't naked, I turned my attention to the most concerning thing of all. The object I'd been cuddling with was a man, sleeping right in front of the door.

He appeared to be a couple years older than me. His shirtless body was long and lean with well-toned muscles in all the right places. His hair was, well, orange. Popping out of that orange hair were cat ears of the same color with white tips. An orange tail with a white tip stuck out of his gray pants. Maybe the fact that he had animal parts should have made him less appealing, but that wasn't the case.

He turned his handsome face toward me and cracked open solid, deep brown eyes. "You are really loud in the morning," he observed, voice groggy with sleep. His tail twitched in irritation.

"Sorry," I muttered out of reflex. Then I shook my head. Why was I apologizing? "I mean, what's going on? Where am I?"

"This is an abandoned Munchkin shack in Cheshire Forest." He closed his eyes and relaxed back to a comfortable position. "And what is going on is that I'm sleeping."

"Wait, who are you?" My arms wanted to cross in front of my stomach, but I couldn't let on how nervous I was. Was this person a friend or someone else who wanted to kill me? Instead I made fists and forced them to stay at my sides.

"Ace," he muttered with his eyes still closed. "Look, I just found a half-drowned cat and decided to pick it up to see if it was alive. That's all. Now be quiet until I wake up."

I stared at him. He was seriously just going to go back to

sleep with me here? Wasn't he worried? It's not like I could do much to him, but still? "Hang on, why is my dress—"

"It was cold and wet. Now, *shh.*" His breathing deepened. After a couple minutes of further silence, I deemed him asleep.

I ran my hands through my hair as my mind raced. What should I do now? I was in a short shack with a cat-man. Weren't there horror movies that started like this? He didn't seem particularly threatening. At least, I couldn't see him trying to hurt me if he was content to sleep by me. On the other hand, he was sleeping right in front of the door. There was no way out without waking him.

So, I was stuck here. With a sigh, I sank down the wall and tucked my legs up against my chest. I rested my chin on my knees and fidgeted with all the material around me. The slip's long skirt was meant to go with heels. Who knew where they were right now? Being shoeless wasn't a big deal to me. While most of my classmates spent their summers in the mall, I spent mine roaming the streams and hillside barefoot with my brothers and friends. But how was I supposed to move in this slip?

Move where, anyway? I stared down at the yellow glow on the floor and lightly brushed at the color. It was supposed to lead me to where I needed to go. Right now the path led to the door. Big surprise. And where to after that? Red Queen had mentioned something about the Emerald Castle where I was supposed to choose the next ruler of Oz. By False Dawn, but I didn't even know what time it was now. And the only person I knew of the small selection was Red Queen. Was she really the most loved ruler? I needed to find more information.

But how? The people were scared of me. How could I make them talk to me?

I glanced at the sleeping cat-man. He wasn't scared of me. Frowning, I watched his tail twitch. Briefly I wondered what breed of cat Ace was. There were no stripes on his tail. Probably just an orange tabby.

I really should be leaving. Not only was I being hunted by ice monsters and a man-eating tiger, I didn't have that much time. What if I'd wasted half a day sleeping? How far behind was I?

Disregarding Ace as much as he was disregarding me, I stood up and pulled at my skirt. I couldn't move quickly with the length. I tried to tie it up in a knot at my knees. When I was done, the knot was the size of a basketball, and I was barely more mobile than before.

This was ridiculous. Maybe I could rip the material? I'd heard it wasn't as easy as books and movies made it sound, but I could give it a try. I was not going to run around in lacy red underwear, after all. After working the knot out, I sat back down and pulled at the slippery silk. How did they make this thing? There wasn't a single seam in the entire slip, and it was not tearing.

"What are you doing?"

I jumped and nearly fell over.

Ace sat cross-legged, watching me with interest. His gaze was level, but a wild gleam showed in his eyes.

I looked down and tugged at my skirt. "I'm trying to make this shorter. I can't move with it this long." My fingers slipped off the fabric again. "Wish I had some scissors or something. A knife, maybe."

Something thudded into the wooden wall right next to my head, and I gasped. I turned to find a knife protruding from the wall several inches from my face.

Mouth working, I glared at him. "What was that?"

He shrugged, and a half smile touched his lips. "You said you wanted a knife." His eyes twinkled.

Wow, he was hot when his eyes lit up like that. Trying not to let his smile distract me, I looked him up and down. Where did the knife come from? I knew from first-hand knowledge that he didn't have any knives strapped to his bare torso. There wasn't a single place he could have kept it, was there? Then again, it's not like I'd checked his pants.

"Thanks," I muttered. "Next time, just hand it to me." I pulled the knife out of the wall. The blue handle fit perfectly in my hand, and the silver blade slid through the material like it was warm butter.

I glanced at him and found him watching me. Amusement was still the primary expression on his face, but there was something else just behind it. Curiosity? Confusion?

"You haven't asked my name yet," I said slowly, proud of how nonchalant my voice was. Did he care?

He flashed another smile. "I know your name. Everyone in Oz knows your name."

"Really? How would you know?" I stopped cutting my skirt, waiting for his answer. Fame wasn't always good.

He shrugged and tugged the wrinkles out of his pants, completely at ease. His ears twitched. "It's not hard. Your scent, for one. You don't smell like an Ozian."

I frowned. Should I be offended? The last time I'd been awake, I was a drenched cat-sicle, but the smell couldn't be that bad, right? "What do I smell like?"

He laughed. "Not like an animal, that's for sure. Most Ozians carry a trace of their animal form even when they're human. You don't. I don't even know the name of what you smell like." His nose twitched. "But it's nice," he added quickly.

Despite the situation, I felt like laughing. That was

totally a guy answer. I bit my lips and swallowed to stay cool and collected. "It's just soap. Nothing special. Thanks, though." I went back to cutting the skirt. Was my scent what kept giving me away last night while I was hiding? Those monsters seemed to always know exactly where I was. "What else sets me apart?" If I was going to be hunted, it was best to know so I could change it.

"Your eyes. They have the black things in there."

"Pupils," I corrected absentmindedly. I couldn't change that.

"Oh, and the dress." He motioned to the one piled on the ground. "I took it off so you would actually dry. It has Red Queen all over it. Colorful, sparkly, and poufy." He smiled, and his eyes softened with fondness.

I stared at him. Whether or not he meant to, he was showing honest emotion. He genuinely liked Red Queen. Did that mean he was a good person? If he liked her, then he was aligned with her, right? "You seem to know a lot about her." I sliced at the back half of the skirt.

He blinked as if startled out of his thoughts. "Sure. About as much as anyone in Oz." He shrugged off my comment. "She's pretty open about herself."

His answer sounded like a half-truth, or an easy way out of a tough question. I nodded, accepting that for now. "The people seem to really love her."

Ace shrugged. He leaned back against the door and laced his hands behind his head. His right ear flicked back as if listening to something on the other side of the door, then it came forward. "Of course. She's Red Queen. The people love her and she loves them. Don't you?"

"I only met her for an hour or so. That's not long enough to form a true opinion." And trying to get answers from her was like trying to wring water from a rock. "Yet apparently I'm supposed to make an important decision. I can't do that without finding out more about what the people want." I shrugged.

When Ace didn't say anything, I glanced at him. He stared at me with an unfathomable expression, as if I was something new and different, but he didn't know what to make of me.

"Well, what do you think of White Wizard?" I prompted.

He snorted and shook his head. "If you had fun last night, pick him."

No, I couldn't say that last night was fun. It had been the worst night of my life. "Why did everyone turn into animals?" The terror and confusion I had felt was still so fresh on my mind, it was hard to keep my voice steady.

The tip of Ace's tail twitched and slapped at the floor. His brow set in a hard line and the smile slipped from his face. "That's how White Wizard views the people of Oz. As animals, stupid and pointless. So that's what they become when he's in charge, since he's the only one important enough to be human."

That sounded awful. "The snow and the snow monsters?" Was it still snowing outside? The fire in the corner made it warm in here, and bright light shone through the hole in the ceiling. "Was that the White Wizard, too?"

Ace nodded to the side. "Fun, huh? Brainless, giant brutes." His nose wrinkled in disdain. "White Wizard likes to make sure that people can't tell him no. He's a black and white kind of guy."

His reaction made me pause. He seemed just as familiar with White Wizard as with Red Queen. His tone lacked the warmth, but I could tell he knew White Wizard. Well.

What was with this guy? I wracked my mind to place

the name Ace somewhere in the Wonderland and Oz stories, but nothing rang a bell. Red Queen, Hareson, and Lional were easy. I even understood White Wizard. But Ace? How did he fit in?

"You're staring at me," he said with a sly smile.

I blinked. My cheeks went up in flames, burning beyond control. "Oh, sorry. I was ... thinking." I cleared my throat and looked down at my skirt. It was done. Standing up, I turned this way and that, examining the knee-length hack job. It was as straight as I could get it without a ruler. As long as I could move, it was fine.

"Good enough." I walked over to Ace. "Thanks for letting me borrow this." I held out the knife.

A part of me wanted to keep it. Hide it somewhere in my skirt, make a makeshift tie, strap it to my thigh and hope I didn't cut myself with it. If I was being hunted by a tiger, having something to defend myself would be helpful. But it's not like I knew how to use it, anyway. I was just as likely to hurt myself as I was the Cheshire Cat.

Ace was slow to take it. "You are an odd Alice." His dark brown eyes bored into mine. "You seem very logical and smart, but you're giving back a form of protection. For that matter, you're stuck in a room with me and even asking my opinion on a serious subject."

I shrugged. "What other choice do I have? It's not my knife, it's yours. You'd get it back from me if you wanted it. And I'll have to ask everyone's opinion on the rulers. It's important to know all the facts before making a judgment."

I walked over to the dress on the floor and picked it up. It was then I noticed a wide-necked, sleeveless shirt underneath it. It was plain white except for a three-inch-wide gray band that went across the chest. Given the size, it could only belong to Ace. Did he protect the dress from the dirt because he knew it belonged to Red Queen?

Carefully folding the dress and leaving the shirt where it was, I turned back to him. "It's Ali, by the way. My name is Ali."

His brows rose. "Ali, huh?"

His reaction was the same as everyone else's. I waved a hand. "Really, my name isn't that odd. It's actually a rather common name where I'm from. What's odd to me is hearing Alice used in plural form. You're not the first person to mention multiple Alices. Why is that?"

Ace's brows rose high on his forehead as he smiled in amusement. "This is called the Alice Games, right?"

I sighed. "You know, this doesn't feel like a game to me. What part of it is a game?"

"I know that you showed up late, but they really didn't explain anything to you, did they?" He stretched his arms up and arched his back in a full body stretch. "The game is if Red Queen can get the Alice to the Emerald Castle or not. White Wizard doesn't need you to pick him at the Emerald Castle, but that's the only way Red Queen can win."

"What happens to me if I don't make it to the Emerald Castle by False Dawn?" Could I just stay here until that time then go home?

He was quiet for a second. "There's only ever been one Alice that didn't make it in time. No one knows what happened to her. She was just whisked out of Oz. If she survived, I don't know what state she's in. For all I know, she could still be stuck in In-Between." His tone was grave.

"What's In-Between?" I shifted, uneasy.

He took a breath and reverted back to a playful air, hiding whatever he was thinking behind a smile. "The space between your world and Oz. Oz created the Emerald Castle to bring the Alices through safely. But outside that building ..." He left the negative experience hanging.

So I couldn't just hang around. The only way home was to play the game and get to the Emerald Castle on time. I didn't want to get whisked into a space void any more than I wanted to be found by the Cheshire Cat.

I could try to find the Emerald Castle alone—I had the Yellow Path. I'd done things alone so far, though not by choice. Having the help of Red Queen, however that played out, would be a benefit. It sounded like she wanted me to make it as much as I wanted to. She even mentioned an escort to take me to the Emerald Castle. That sounded a thousand times better than walking the whole way, since it seemed like a sizable distance.

Still, there was one more thing I wanted Ace to verify. Okay, there were a lot of things, but I really needed to get back to Red Queen. "So, a girl named Alice comes here and the games start? How many Alices have there been?"

Ace scratched his chin. "You're number twenty-seven."

My eyes widened. *Twenty-seven*? Twenty-six other girls from my world had come to Oz? How long had it been like this? "Did they come back-to-back?" When he shook his head, I gaped at him. "How many years has it been since the Alice Games first started?"

This time he looked at the fire crackling in the fireplace. For a second, the light hit just right to reflect off his eyes. "Too long." His voice was soft, barely audible. "So very long."

For a moment, I stared at him. There was something about the way his head was tilted and the gleam in his eyes that made him look dangerous. Not threatening, but he seemed like someone you don't want to cross. I shook my head, trying to understand what he meant. "That's crazy. That many girls, and none of them have been able to fix the problem?"

It was his turn to pause. He blinked quickly out of his stupor and focused back on me. "Problem? Why do you call it that?"

"Well, isn't it?" It really was time to go. I'd stalled long enough. Should I bring the hoop skirt and corset too? I picked up the hoop skirt and frowned. It would be really cumbersome to carry, and there was no way I was getting back into that corset. "If there wasn't a problem that needed to be fixed, all those Alices wouldn't have been brought here. The question is, what's the real problem and how do you permanently fix it?" The hoop skirt would definitely stay here. I set it down and faced Ace.

He still lounged against the door, examining me.

I took a couple steps toward the door and motioned for him to get out of the way. He didn't budge. "Are you going to move or not?" It was time to figure out what his play was.

His eyes lit up with mischief. "Why?"

"I need to get out. I can't spend the whole day here, no matter how nice this chat has been."

"All right, all right," he laughed. "At least you said I was nice to talk to. However, you're forgetting something."

"What's that?"

He rose and closed the gap between us in one smooth step. "You haven't paid me yet." He was tall enough that his orange hair brushed the ceiling of the shack even though his back was slightly bent.

My heart leapt and danced at his sudden nearness. What was wrong with me? I still hadn't decided if I could trust him. "Pay?"

His ears twitched toward the door again, but his calm

manner didn't change. "Of course. I saved your life, so you owe me. Pay up."

His logic wasn't all that farfetched, but there was one problem. "Uh, I don't have anything to pay you with. Unless you want the dress. But it's not mine, so I don't think I should give it away." I rolled the wad of material in my hands. It must be worth a fortune, since it was covered in gems. Red Queen already admitted they weren't scientifically advanced, so they most likely didn't have the technology to manufacture stones.

Ace rocked back on his heels and tucked his thumbs into the waistband of his pants. "No, I don't want that. It has to be something of yours."

Something of mine? What did I have that was mine still? I had a kiss, a sneaky voice in my mind whispered. My whole body froze as my cheeks warmed a little. That was absurd! Even if he was downright sexy. I took a breath and shoved that thought aside. They had thoroughly stripped me earlier, so what did I have?

"Ah." I frowned. I did have something that was mine still. I glanced at him, then turned my back. Face redder than ever, I reached into my bra and pulled out the necklace I'd hidden there. It was warm. My hand clenched over the last piece of sanity I had left. But if it was the only way to get out of this room, I didn't have a choice.

"Um, I have this," I mumbled, then turned and offered him the necklace. I could tell I was failing miserably at controlling my blush. Honestly. As if the situation wasn't bad enough.

Ace's grin was instant. "A necklace, huh? That will do." His fingers lingered on my hand as he took it from me.

His touch was like liquid fire, melting into my skin and shooting through my veins, making my blood run hot and my heart pump harder. What was so attractive about him? He was just a cat-guy. He shouldn't be so appealing, he should be weird.

I cleared my throat and tried to take control of the situation. "So my debt is paid? I can go now?"

For a second, he looked like a cat watching a mouse run away, then he nodded and stepped back, revealing the door with a gentlemanly wave of his hand. "Follow your Yellow Path through the flowers. Red Queen should be waiting on the other side."

I tore my gaze away from the door and back to him. "How would she know where to find me?" I thought I'd have to spend all day looking for her.

"All Role Players know where you are." He reached out and casually opened the door. Blinding light exploded into the small, dark room.

I blinked rapidly as my eyes tried to adjust.

Ace slid an arm around my waist and walked me out the door. My eyes were still watering like crazy as he ushered me through.

A sudden sneeze attack assaulted me and I stepped away from him, trying not to sound like an elephant trumpeting. "Excuse me," I mumbled and wiped my wet eyes. "Ace, what's a Role Player—" I blinked and looked around.

He was gone.

CHAPTER SIX

FROM THE DOORWAY of the Munchkin shack, I could see that Ace's shirt was gone. The fire in the fireplace was out, with little wisps of smoke rising up. If it weren't for my shorter slip with its jagged edges, I would have thought I'd dreamed the whole thing. Still confused, I turned and looked around.

I was in the middle of a tropical forest—the Cheshire Forest, according to Ace. A light mist hung in the air, melting between trees as thick as cars. Beams of light broke through the thick canopy, casting spotlights on smaller plants that bloomed in vibrant colors.

The smell of the damp, rich soil was like a balm to my soul, relaxing and invigorating at the same time. With a big sigh, I dug my toes into the spongy dirt and breathed in the humid air. This was my dream. To stand in a jungle, surrounded by plants and dirt, and know that I could discover a new plant form. Find some mystery in the world that no one else has ever discovered before. Cornell University was simply a stepping stone—the biggest one I needed to take to get there.

Yet, here I was. In a jungle that Earth knows nothing about. Everything was a new discovery.

The Yellow Path might lead to the left, but it could wait a short moment. I couldn't resist letting out a tiny squeak of excitement as I practically danced over to the closest tree and examined the giant leaves. They were bigger than a sheet of paper. Fascinated, I noted the multicolored veins that ribbed the leaves. The effect was subtle, but where one leaf overlapped another, the rainbow veins glowed. Feeling like a kid at Christmas, I moved the waxy leaf around carefully, just to make the colors of the lower leaf pop more.

"Phosphorescent lights on a tree this big?" I squealed and ran my fingers over the veins. "What kind of protein creates these colors? Oh, what I wouldn't give for a microscope and a notebook and camera right now," I said aloud. "I need a whole lab."

A voice—or two? —whispered from somewhere low to my right. It was so soft, the sounds jumbled together obscurely.

The hair prickled on the back of my neck. "Hello?"

There was no response. The dark foliage was beautiful but silent. Aside from myself, I couldn't hear another living thing. No birds, bugs, nothing. Eerie.

I didn't imagine the whispers, did I?

Something white gleamed on the ground. The bright stark shade seemed off from the natural colors around me. I walked over to it, stepping over high roots and around leafy bushes. Whatever it was just lay there, shining between the thick blades of a patch of green grass. Perplexed, I parted the foliage and crouched over it. The object, roughly twelve inches long, gleamed like white crystal, and was shaped like ...

"A footprint?"

Bursting with curiosity, I brushed it with my fingertips. Icy shots of pain went from my fingers all the way to my toes, numbing my hand for a second and covering my whole body in goosebumps. Gasping in pain, I stumbled back and landed on my butt.

I rubbed my fingers against the material on my stomach and stared at the footprint. It was ice, dry and biting. And it wasn't alone. From this angle, I could see more of them spaced evenly apart, leading off into the forest. Only I'd never seen footprints that were raised pieces of ice. Biting my lip, I followed their direction with my eyes. My fingers still hurt from the ice burn. When I touched the ice, it was like I could feel the owner's emotions. I don't know how I knew, but this person was full of hatred, as cold as the dry ice. Did the prints belong to the Cheshire Cat?

I scrambled to my feet and turned to hurry the other way—the way the Yellow Path was leading me. I couldn't help but pause to look around. I was dying to stay and study everything about this place. Only the burn on my fingers was a sharp reminder that I shouldn't. Not only did I not have the time, I might not exactly be safe here. The safest place, and most time effective travel method, was with Red Queen—after all, nothing bad had happened till she disappeared. Ace said she was on the other side of the flowers. I didn't know what that meant, but I bet the Yellow Path did.

I followed the arrow past the Munchkin shack and the building quickly disappeared behind thick forest. The Yellow Path glowed brightly over the moss and dirt. The forest was so thick, I had to push aside huge leaf after huge leaf just to walk forward. Sometimes I swore a tree shifted just to stick its leaves in my face and catch at the wadded dress with its branches. I normally didn't believe in disturbing nature, but after a while I would have given anything for a machete.

All at once, the leaves and trees were gone. I stumbled to a stop and stared, open mouthed. So, this is what Ace meant when he mentioned the flowers. A huge field covered in flowers stretched to the right and left as far as the eye could see. They looked like chest-high sunflowers, except with white petals instead of yellow.

Another forest lined the other side of the wide field, but the trees looked to be temperate, not tropical. Odd. How could there be jungle on one side of a flower field and deciduous trees on the other? It shouldn't be physically possible. Mountains, oceans, and wind patterns decided if forests became tropical or temperate, and the change was never this drastic. There was no wind, and I couldn't see a mountain or ocean around. Just a lot of white flowers, like a dividing barrier.

It screamed *wrong*, but there wasn't time to consider the physical problems with this picture. I mean, in Oz people also turned into animals and hot guys with cat ears that could disappear into thin air.

The Yellow Path didn't point directly ahead, but angled to the side. Following it with my eyes, I saw a small path through the flowers. A sigh of relief escaped me. The path was narrow, only about two feet wide, but it seemed to go all the way across.

I was twenty feet in when I heard, somewhere off to the right, something that sounded like water hitting the ground. I paused. When there wasn't another sound, I moved forward again, slowly. With everything that had happened to me since I came to this world, my heart started to race in anticipation.

Another splash of water hit the ground on my left.

This time I stopped completely and stood up on my toes. There was nothing but flowers for as far as I could see. Warily, I continued walking.

My hand brushed against a flower on my right. A geyser of water exploded out of the black center and smacked the side of my face. Gasping with shock, I stumbled off the path and into the flowers. They went off all around me. Jets of water hit other flowers, and they detonated in a domino effect.

Unsure what else to do, I hugged the dress to my chest to protect it and shielded my face as the flowers pelted me over and over with water. Blindly, I stumbled toward the path.

Something grabbed my wrist and I screamed. Puffing, I looked up through the water dripping over my face.

Ace stood in front of me, ears perked up in attention and his laughter barely contained. A huge grin split his face and his brown eyes danced. "Not that way! This way!" he yelled over the sound of water slapping the ground. "Run!"

He tugged on my wrist, his hold gentle but insistent, and I followed. He flinched away from a water spout, laughing, and began to run. He kept his pace slow enough that I didn't fall behind. Water exploded around us as we ran, showering us and soaking the path. I didn't know if he was doing it on purpose, but Ace's tail brushed the flowers as we ran, causing more to erupt. Ace kept glancing over his shoulder at me, his smile playful and eyes alive with the fire of an exciting game.

It wasn't long before I was grinning with enjoyment as much as he was. We stumbled down the path, laughing and slipping on the wet ground. Ace's hold on my wrist slipped down until we were hand in hand. The warmth in his grasp and his long, strong fingers were as distracting as the water hitting me in the face, and it made my heart race as much as the running did.

We broke out of the flowers, into the temperate forest. I staggered to a stop and bent over, breathing hard. I wrapped an arm around my aching sides, hugging the soaked dress against my stomach. When was the last time I'd gotten so wet fully clothed and loved it? I was normally that girl who brought a book to the pool while the others played in the water.

I looked up at him. I was drenched head to toe, my hair plastered to my face, but all I could do was smile.

He was just as wet, smiling just as big.

My eyes dropped to our joined hands. My cheeks turned red, and I slipped my hand out of his. I cleared my throat and looked back at the field, still breathing hard. "I've never experienced flowers like that before."

"What, the water lilies?" Most of the laughter left Ace's voice, replaced by a more subdued tone.

"You call these water lilies, huh?" I crouched down right next to them, tucking the dress in my lap. It might be ruined already from the water, but I didn't want it to get muddy too.

I glanced at Ace to find he had taken off his shirt and was staring at it rather intently as he wrung the water out of it. When it stopped dripping so much, he untwisted the shirt and shook it a couple times, then draped it over my shoulders. It was large enough to cover me from the shoulders to the ground in this position.

It was only then that I realized how revealing my attire must've been. The slip was fine when it was dry, but when wet, it clung like a second skin. My face went up in flames as my arms snaked through the large armholes. The shirt smelled nice, like cinnamon and earth. "Thanks," I said, touched at his chivalrous actions.

As soon as I was properly covered, his smile came back. Just like before, he seemed at ease in his pants and shirtless attire. He looked over the field. "Yes, these are water lilies. They're my favorite flower."

"Hmm." I turned back to them. "There are water lilies in my world, too. But they don't look like these. They live in ponds and lakes with just their flowers floating on top." My fingers inched forward to brush a flower. But the thought of what we'd just gone through stopped me. "How does it shoot water?"

Now that I wasn't getting wet from the water lilies, they were the most fascinating plant I'd ever seen, and I was dying to know how they worked. Forget Red Queen's claim about magic. There had to be a scientific explanation to all of it.

Ace crouched down next to me. I wanted to lean into his warmth, but I didn't dare. He grabbed the stem of a flower and, before it had time to spray, cut it off with a knife I never saw him take out. With another sleight of hand, the knife disappeared. He offered the flower to me as water dribbled out of its cut stem.

I blinked. "Oh, you didn't have to do that." I took the flower, fingering the surprisingly stiff stem. "I could have just looked at it still attached. Observation and discovery don't have to happen only through handling—"

"You're the first girl I've ever met who doesn't like to get flowers. Most girls just melt at the sight of them." Ace shook his head, chuckling.

My whole body went up in flames. What was wrong with me? "Ah, no. It's not that," I stammered. "I do like getting flowers. What girl doesn't, like you said? I was just thinking academically. Not, you know, like *that*. I just ... like plants," I finished lamely. Where was a tree that I could bang my head against? *Honestly*!

His warm brown eyes danced, and he tried not to smile too wide. "I like plants too. What do you think of Oz's water lilies?"

I went back to the flower. In my element now, my body relaxed as my mind went to work. "Well, it's really different." I cupped the flower, breathing in its faint, sweet scent, while measuring the size with my hand. "For a flower this size, the petals wouldn't normally be as thick and strong as card stock. Yet they are so soft. Like felt." I brushed the white pieces and rubbed my fingers together. There wasn't any pollen residue. I frowned and peered closely at the flower. "Weird. It doesn't look like there are any stamens or pistils. Or any reproductive parts whatsoever. How can the species thrive without them?" I pressed my index finger into the velvety black center. It indented, then reformed like a sponge. "Hmm. How does this work?" Were the reproductive parts hidden somewhere else? It didn't seem logical.

I flipped the flower over to examine the stem and received another shock. It was as hollow as a straw, which explained why it felt like one. The walls of the stem were completely solid, like plastic. "There's nothing inside," I exclaimed. "How does photosynthesis happen? There's no chloroplast or anything. How does this plant survive, reproduce—or anything?" My firm resolution that science could finally explain something in this world was losing its grip.

"It's magic," Ace said, looking over the field. "Oz wills the flowers to live, so they do."

There was that M-word again. Magic. "You make it sound like the land is actually alive. Not just the plants but the dirt and air."

Ace blinked and turned to me, one brow raised and a half smile on his lips. "Of course, it's alive. Oz is alive. It feels, breathes, cries, and has its own opinion. It also has rules that it expects to be followed."

I shook my head. There was always a logical explanation in my opinion. Still full of doubt, I looked back at the flower field.

And saw something that could be called magical.

In the morning air, random water streams gleamed like arcs of glitter above a white petal carpet. Mist hovered above the flowers and reflected circles of rainbows, dozens of them, everywhere. Surrounding the field was a green jungle backdrop, trunks and vines half shrouded in white gray mist.

Since I came to Oz, I'd been forced into a dress, turned into a cat, and chased through a frozen hell by ice monsters and a bloodthirsty, murderous tiger. Even in the Cheshire Forest, something was off. But here, I could relax and simply think.

"How beautiful." I didn't realize I'd said the words out loud until they echoed in my ears.

Ace grinned down at me. "You sound surprised." His eyes drank in the view as if he couldn't get enough of it. Did he know how gentle his eyes got when he talked about Oz? I could tell he had a special love for this land.

But there was a sad flicker on his face, despite the smile. He rested a hand on his hip, his chin high with pride. The only thing missing from the picture, besides a shirt, was a sword.

He blinked as if pulled from his thoughts and looked down at me. "Why are you smiling?"

I jumped. Was I smiling? I hadn't even realized it. "Ah,

oh. Nothing." Man, my face was burning up again! "Just, well, a funny thought."

"What thought?" He grinned.

I shouldn't have said anything. "It's dumb, really."

"Tell me anyway. Then I can share the laugh."

My gaze dropped to the flower in my hands. I played with it, using my hair to hide my blush. "I just thought, well, right there you looked like a knight. Looking over his kingdom." I smiled up at him, expecting him to laugh.

He didn't. His eyes widened, and his full lips parted in shock. Suddenly his face smoothed blank, like he was nothing but a mannequin in a store window. He took a breath and turned away from me toward the flowers.

Did I say something wrong? I was just teasing, but what if I had hurt his feelings somehow? How was I to know it was the wrong thing to say, when I didn't know anything about him? This is why I sucked at working with people. I always said the wrong things around them. "Ace—"

He grinned down at me in his usual mischievous way. "You're an odd Alice. Or should I say, girls named Ali are odd?"

I let the topic drop. I didn't want to put my foot in my mouth any more than I already had. Instead, I scowled. "People keep calling me weird. But I'm not. It's this place that's weird. Nothing about this world makes any sense. There's no logic in any of it."

"There's plenty of logic in Oz. As long as you follow the rules."

"What rules? That's twice you've mentioned rules, but no one else has ever explained any."

Ace started to answer me but stopped. He blinked and lifted his head, then closed his eyes and took a breath. "The wind changed." His voice was full of disbelief. He glanced down at me, his face unfathomable.

"Huh?" I looked around, noting some leaves swaying in the breeze. It was so slight that I hadn't even noticed there was wind at all. "What about the wind?" I turned to him.

He was gone. Just like before. He was there one second and gone the next.

"Ace?" I stood up, tucking the dress in the crook of my arm and looking around. I hadn't even heard him move, and he had been right next to me. What was going on? Bothered by my sudden aloneness, I twisted my fingers in the hem of his shirt to reassure myself.

A bush just behind me rustled, and I turned toward it, thinking it was him.

A young woman stumbled out of the bush with a distressed bleat.

I blinked at her, recognizing one of the maids that dressed me last night.

She huffed at the bush and straightened her blue dress, smoothing the white apron down until it was perfect. She was just tucking her hair back in place when she finally glanced around and saw me. She gave another startled bleat and jumped.

This was not who I was thinking I'd see first. "Um, hi?"

She looked me up and down, taking in my attire with something between horror and incredulity. Then she took a breath and forced a smile on her face, but kept her eyes on the ground at my feet. "Hello. I'm Shirley. We've all been waiting for you, Alice of Alice." She curtsied then motioned behind her. "Red Queen is this way."

"Thank you," I muttered, her nervous actions making me all the more awkward. Connecting with people was hard enough, how was I going to learn everyone's opinion if they all acted like this around me?

She jumped like she was touched with a live wire then turned and started trekking through the woods—which involved plowing straight through the bush she just came out of.

Perplexed, I cradled my flower in my hand and tucked the ball of wet material under the other arm. After one more look around for Ace, I walked around the bush and followed Shirley down the Yellow Path. From her body language I decided she wouldn't want to walk side by side, so I trailed behind. Bemused, I watched her stumble through the forest. She was a lot clumsier than I thought someone who grew up without modern technology would be.

Wishing it was Ace I was walking with, I distracted myself with my surroundings. The conifer trees, as thick as I was tall, were lovely with a red tint to their bark and bright green needles. Rather than green leaves, the deciduous trees had red, gold, blue, and pink foliage that popped with gusto between the towering pines. I stopped right next to a lavender-leafed tree and had to touch it. The leaves were still thick with glucose, instead of drying out as the tree prepared for winter. These were the natural colors? How pretty.

The bushes didn't have the rainbow veins of colors or huge leaves like the Cheshire Forest, but the simple structure of the multicolored leafy plants was just as lovely. The ground was harder but smooth on my bare feet, a light maple color against my yellow marker. Even stranger, the foliage parted around me to make walking easier—unlike the Cheshire Forest trees that took every chance to make my journey harder.

"What is this forest called?"

Shirley glanced back. "This is the Rainbow Forest." Her voice was curt.

How original. But at least she spoke. That was enough to break the ice, right? I ran my thumb up and down the stem of my flower, enjoying the smooth texture, then took a breath. "So, who do you think I should pick?" I asked Shirley.

She stopped fast and turned around, completely complexed. "What did you say?"

I shrugged and shifted the dress. "Well, I need to pick the next ruler, right? You work at the Ruby Castle. What do you love about Red Queen?"

Her brow wrinkled more than ever. She glanced around, then said softly, "You know, Alice of Alice, you don't have to pick out of just the obvious Queen Candidates. There is someone else." She stepped closer to me, her pale eyes wide and intense.

Just then, a man called out, "Who's there?" The bushes parted and a man in shining red and bronze armor stepped through.

Shirley jumped like she was having a heart attack. "It's me, Shirley the maid. I brought the Alice of Alice." She motioned to me.

The guard looked over Shirley's shoulder at me. He stiffened and glanced just above my head. "Ah, yes. The Alice of Alice. Good job, maid," he muttered, without looking at her. "You may go. I'll take it from here."

Shirley curtsied and hurried unevenly past him, disappearing through the tall shrubs.

"Ah, thank you for showing me the way," I called after her, but I didn't know if she actually heard.

The guard parted the bush behind him, revealing a camp built off the side of a dirt road. Half a dozen huge tents made of red velvet and featuring square tops were set up in a random pattern. Thirty or so people milled around, doing various odd jobs. I spotted a couple other sheep maids in the mix—it was impossible to tell which was Shirley—but most of the workers were men.

My guide pointed to the largest tent of all, in the middle of the camp. "Red Queen is in there." With that, he turned and walked away without another word.

I watched him go, debating what to do. Manners won out, and I called after him, "Thanks."

He paused and glanced back. For the first time, he looked me in the eye. After a second, he nodded.

People glanced at me as I walked to Red Queen's tent. Most of them didn't even bother to look at my face but stared at my clothing with scandalized expressions. The slip was dry now, so it didn't cling. I could have removed Ace's shirt, but it smelled too good to take off.

Red Queen's tent flap was open, revealing the tiny queen standing in the middle of her quarters. Her red dress today was a little less exaggerated than the one she wore last night. It was still unbelievably poufy, but it didn't sparkle with stones at her every move. She was staring hard at something against the right wall. Before I could announce my presence, she stamped her foot on the decorative rug.

"I can't believe you did that, Lional!" Her voice wasn't a shout, but rose enough for me to hear the note of disappointment that would make anyone feel guilty. "To immediately do something like that, the instant I'm away."

Lional? My brows pulled together. Was she ranting to herself? Red Queen didn't seem like the type of person to do so, but I'd only known her for a short time. Confused, I shifted sideways until I could see more of the inside through the tent's opening. And froze.

It *was* Lional. He was standing inside, perfectly healthy though stubbornly trying not to look chastened. He stared at the ground with a miserable expression, his hands clasped behind his rigid back. His round lion ears, popping out of his wild hair, kept flicking back and then forward again as he tried to hide his shame.

I suddenly felt light headed. How ... how was it even *possible* that Lional was here? I watched him die. He turned into a pile of dust. Yet here he was, right in front of me.

Oblivious of my presence just outside the tent, Red Queen ranted on. "You are a Role Player, Lional. You can't just do something like throw your life away. Every day counts during the Alice Games, you know that. I wasn't there to help Ali. She was supposed to be your responsibility. I was *relying* on you."

Lional flinched.

She wasn't done yet. "We're lucky Ali survived. The Cheshire Cat's never gone after an Alice like that before. I was hoping that after his behavior in the last game, he would sit this one out, but no, you had to go and agitate him! How could you foolishly challenge someone you know you can't beat?"

Lional's face tightened, but he didn't look up or argue back.

I needed to sit down and put my head between my knees. I stepped away and half turned, resting the hand with my flower against my spinning head.

Just then, Hareson walked around a tent right next to me, fastening the cuffs of his sleeves. He spotted me. "Ah, Ali. They said you were over here. I'm so glad to see you unharmed. After we split up last night, I was quite worried. I am sorry. None of that was supposed to happen. I couldn't believe it when they said you were found just outside of

Cheshire Forest." He looked me over, frowning at the white and gray shirt. His eyes widened slightly and his ears twitched. "Aside from your odd clothes, you seem perfectly fine, thankfully." He peered more closely. His lips pulled down in concern. "Or are you perfectly fine, Ali?"

Before I could squeak out an answer, Red Queen piped up from inside the tent. "Hareson? Did you just say Ali was here? Send her in, please."

Hareson's ears swiveled toward the tent, then he relaxed. He double checked his cuffs were perfect, brushed at the sleeve of his brown suit, then motioned to the opening. "Well then, shall we?"

I didn't really want to, but I followed him anyway. It was hard not to stare at Lional. The huge man took up a considerable amount of space, and his golden head brushed the ceiling. Instead, I cast my eyes about the inside of the tent. I examined the dark wood folding table and chair. A polished metal mirror rimmed with silver flowers stood on the table. Golden knots patterned a red rug on the dirt floor, and there was an armoire on the far wall.

I jumped a little when I noticed Red Queen staring at me.

"My, Ali, are you alright?" she asked with obvious concern. "You look faint. Well, you did have a ... difficult night. What's wrong?" Her eyes wandered my form, lingering on my mismatched clothing. They landed on the flower in my hand and widened slightly.

"Um." I shifted, adjusting the bundle of clothing under my arm. I glanced at Lional, then away. "Look, I just wasn't expecting zombies to be in Oz, okay? Neither of the two stories we have in my world ever mention them. There wasn't anything about changing into animals either, but that's beside the point, I guess."

"What's a zombie?" Lional asked.

Hareson frowned, his ears twitching. "What are you talking about, Ali?"

I finally faced Lional, my hand tightening around my flower for reassurance. "I watched you die," I said. "That tiger, the Cheshire Cat, killed you and you turned into dust. It happened right in front of my eyes."

"Ah," Red Queen said. Her hands clapped together. "That's right. Ali wouldn't know yet."

"Know what?" I asked.

Red Queen smiled in reassurance. "You see, Ali. Every day, Oz resets."

CHAPTER SEVEN

"RESETS?" If she thought I understood, she was crazy.

She nodded, the small red gem on her crown flashing in the light. "Yes. It doesn't matter what happens during the day, if we get sick or hurt—or even die. The next morning everyone wakes up exactly in the same state they were the day before."

I stiffened in surprise. "So there's no death at all?"

Some people would say that was a good thing, but death was a part of a healthy life cycle. Without death, the population would grow out of control, and soon resources—like food and land—would run out. Ace's words surfaced in my mind. *Oz is alive.* He talked about the land like it was a person with a mind of its own. Did that mean the lives and lack of death of the people reflected the condition Oz was in?

Ace also said the reason everyone turned into animals at night was because that was how White Wizard thought of the people. Maybe the mental image of the ruler impacted the state Oz existed in. During the day, Red Queen was happy. She loved her people and loved the land, so during the day Oz was beautiful. During the night, White Wizard's feelings turned the land into winter and the people into animals.

Such polar existences would be confusing to anyone. Was it confusing Oz so much that it affected the life cycle? Was that why it summoned Alices, because Oz was so bewildered, it couldn't decide which ruler to follow?

"Well," Lional said, continuing the conversation. "There's no death for us."

But there was for me. That's what he was politely saying. I must be exempt from the no death rule because I wasn't a citizen of Oz. It also made me wonder how many Alices had died.

"How many Alices have made it to the Emerald Castle and gone home?" I asked, my fingers tightening on my flower.

Lional piped up again. "Twenty. Although only nineteen have come back out of the Emerald Castle to make the choice."

Confused, I frowned. "What do you mean? Don't I just stand in front of it and choose? Why do I have to go in?"

"You have to retrieve my wand." Red Queen clasped her hands tightly together. "Then I can be queen again."

I nodded, remembering how it exploded in sparkles right before I turned into a cat. But still. "So what if I didn't choose you—is there another object in there?" At their shocked looks, I threw up my hands in defense. "Look, I'm just curious. Are there other objects inside, to indicate other choices?"

"Death." Lional's low voice was as hard as his gaze. "The only other thing in there is death for anyone who touches it."

My eyes widened, and goosebumps covered my arms.

Red Queen looked down, her small hands gripping her skirt.

Lional cleared his throat, breaking the silence. "This conversation is over. There are more important things I need to attend to if we're to leave soon." He bowed to Red Queen then brushed past me in a wave of musky cologne.

Right, I thought, looking at the Yellow Path highlighted on the ground.

Hareson stared at me with a frown on his face, fingers tapping against his chin and ears flopped forward in thought. "Ali, where did you get that shirt? I think I recognize it."

"Ah." A blush instantly flamed my cheeks. It felt like I was caught with my hand in the cookie jar. Usually there's only one reason for a woman to walk around in a guy's shirt.

Red Queen covered her mouth with her hands. "Ali," she gasped. "I was so preoccupied, I didn't notice the state you're in. Poor girl! To walk around in such a revealing skirt and wearing a man's shirt. You must be so embarrassed!"

I frowned. I could have sworn Red Queen noticed earlier. Why was she acting so surprised now?

She rounded on the thin man. "Hareson, how rude of you to bring it into light like that." She started to usher me out of the tent. "Come, Ali. Let's go to my wardrobe tent. We'll find you something appropriate to wear."

"Ah, my Queen, about that shirt." Hareson jumped forward and reached out with his hand to get her attention. "I'm pretty sure it belongs to—"

"Hareson." Red Queen waved her hand. "It can wait until Ali is modest. Will you please have her breakfast sent to the changing tent?"

At the mention of food, my stomach roared to life, declaring its unhappy state of emptiness.

Hareson frowned in annoyance but nodded. "Yes, Your Highness." His arms were tight to his side as he bent in a bow.

I followed her out of the tent, confused. Why didn't Red Queen want Hareson to finish his point? It was clear they both knew who the shirt belonged to. Hareson's obvious concern and Red Queen's denial contradicted each other and confused me. I thought Ace liked them. Well, at least Red Queen. Now I could only assume the feelings weren't mutual.

After we entered the changing tent, the tiny queen looked up at me. "I have to say, Ali, I'm shocked at the condition you're in. I see you still have the original dress with you." She motioned to the material tucked under my arm.

I blinked and looked down at the forgotten dress. "Oh, yes. Here." I held it out and cringed inside at its dilapidated state. The water from the lilies had ruined the fine material, and there were dirt smudges on it too. *This is why I don't buy things that require dry cleaning.* I fingered the soft petals of my flower.

Red Queen took the bundle and turned it over in her hands. Her brows pulled together, perplexed. "Why are you walking around in those clothes and not in this?"

I bit my lips and looked to the side. "It's, ah, a long story." Honestly, wearing Ace's shirt was a lot more comfortable than any dress Red Queen could stuff me into. I felt safe. The idea of taking it off was disheartening. So silly, really. It was the shirt of a man I met this morning. But even as I thought that, my fingers fidgeted with the hem.

"Hm." Red Queen hummed, eyes still pondering me. Then she brightened. "Well, let's get you out of those awful clothes and into something more ladylike." She pointed to the corner of the tent where a changing divider stood.

I walked to the divider, paused, and turned to face her again. "About that. You see, I need to be able to move."

"Pardon me?"

"Well, the thing is, I can't move around in those dresses." I held my palms out in defense. "I mean, your dresses are lovely, really. But I have to be able to move. If there's one thing I learned last night, it's that I'm going to be on the go. I'm not the most athletic person, so I need all the help I can get. Dresses are nice to look at, but they aren't practical. And that's what I am. Practical."

Red Queen was completely baffled now. "Dresses are what ladies wear. What *women* wear." She examined the folded, ruined material in her hands. "You really are the oddest Alice I have ever met." Still frowning with uncertainty, she put it down on the red cushioned chair next to her. "Well, what would you like to wear?"

A sigh of relief escaped me. "Pants."

"Pants?" Her dark lashes fluttered in surprise.

"Yes. Ones that fit me. Plus a shirt I can move in. And boots or shoes, not high heels." I paused, thinking, tapping the flower stem with a nail. "You might have to use an adolescent's size to fit me."

Red Queen smiled a little. "Or just a skinny man." She motioned to a small, dark table on her right with a silver tray of heaven on it. "Why don't you eat breakfast while I talk to the seamstress? We'll have to ... re-evaluate the wardrobe we brought for you." She left through the door flap. I could hear her muffled voice from the other side, along with an unfamiliar one.

After making sure the water lily was safe on the table, I practically inhaled the food. There was a sandwich with egg and cheese, with an assortment of foreign berries arranged around it. A fruit drink of sorts finished it all off.

A couple minutes later, Red Queen came back in with some clothes in her arms. She handed them to me. "Try these. I think they might be close to what you want."

I took them and walked behind the changing divider. The pants were dark tan and a little tight around my hips but I could still move in them. I turned this way and that in the mirror to make sure they didn't make my butt look too big. Then I caught myself. Why should it matter if they made me look good or not? I didn't have anyone to impress here.

Laughing brown eyes flashed before my mind's eye. Annoyed at the blush that seared my cheeks, I pulled the white shirt on and buttoned it up the front. It fit the shoulders perfectly, but the billowing material fell straight down past my hip, hiding any shape I had. With a forlorn sign, I walked back over to Red Queen, rolling up the long sleeves to my elbows.

Red frowned. "Well, you can move in that fine enough. But I would be ashamed if I let you walk around looking like a man." She contemplated me for a minute, then brightened. "What if we tried this?" She hurried over to a wooden chest just off to the side, opened the lid, and leaned in. A moment later she straightened and walked back. "You have a nice figure, so all we have to do is emphasize it a little." She held out a black, leather cincher to me.

How steampunk-ish. My style was more t-shirts and jeans, but this would work. "Yeah, that might do." I slid the leather around my ribcage just under my bust and started to cinch up the tie that went down the middle. There were four sturdy bands that provided support for the shape but didn't restrict my movements. The cincher redefined my figure and made the white material on the bottom flare out like a miniskirt over my hips. *Not unpleasant*, I thought, admiring my figure in the mirror. It actually looked nice.

"Better." Red Queen still didn't look thrilled, but she nodded in approval. She pointed to some soft, black, leather boots on the ground next to her. "A maid brought these in while you were changing."

I pulled them on and wiggled my toes. They were slightly too big, but it would be fine. All done, I smiled at her. "Thank you."

Her face softened into a beautiful grin. "You're welcome."

I walked back to the changing divider and pulled Ace's shirt from where I'd draped it. I flapped it a couple times to straighten it, then contemplated the material. I should return it, but how?

Red Queen frowned at the shirt for a minute and cleared her throat. "You can just leave it there, Ali. We will return it for you," she said as if reading my thoughts.

I blinked. So she really did know who it belonged to? "Oh, okay." Reluctant, I draped it carefully across the chair next to the ruined dress and picked up my flower. I glanced back at the shirt one more time, feeling foolish, before following Red Queen out of the tent.

She stopped just outside, and I came up short, almost running into her. Her chin tipped up, and she stared at the trees, her tiny body still as stone.

I followed her gaze. There wasn't anything in the trees, just a bunch of pine needles and branches. What was she looking at?

"The wind changed," Red Queen muttered in shock. She turned her face to me. "Is that because of you?"

My brows snapped together and I looked down at her. "Why is it so odd that the wind changed directions?"

"Because, Ali, the wind hasn't changed directions since the first Alice Games began," Red Queen said. "Nothing has changed in Oz since then." She looked down. "Except for the Cheshire Forest. You were lucky to make it out. The hostile water lilies prevent access, but sometimes people make their way in. They don't come back. No one knows what happens to them. They shouldn't be able to die, but we never see them again." Her face wore the pained look of a mother who had lost her child.

Hostile? My eyes wandered in the direction of the water lilies, fingers fidgeting with the one in my hand. What's so bad about an aggressive splash pad? They might have seemed intimidating at first, but by the end they were funny. And fascinating. Was it because of who I was with?

"Have any other Alices made it out of the Cheshire Forest, Red Queen?"

She paused for a moment then shook her head. "Until you, none. Despite warnings, a previous Alice chose to go in and never came back out."

"And White Wizard won that round," I finished. So Ace wasn't there to help that Alice?

She seemed surprised I would know that. "Yes."

CHAPTER EIGHT

LIONAL WALKED UP TO US. “We’re ready to depart to the Emerald Castle, my Queen. We must make haste. We’re already several hours behind.” Apparently still smarting from the lecture earlier, he placed a fist over his heart and bowed meekly. It was almost comical to see the huge man humble himself before the tiny woman.

Red Queen bestowed a sweet smile on him. “Then we leave at once.” She motioned to me with a delicate hand. “Shall we, Ali? Lead the way, Lional.”

Lional nodded. He glanced at me, gaze falling to my pants. His golden head shook slightly in disbelief. “How odd,” he muttered under his breath as he turned and led us through the camp.

Torn between being annoyed with his chauvinist views and delighted at shaking his world slightly, I finally decided to take his reaction with humor. What would Ace think when he saw me in pants?

I stopped mid-stride. Why was he the first person I thought of? I wasn’t dressed this way for him. There was no saying if I would ever see him again, anyway. It was stupid of me to hope.

"Ali?" Red Queen called out.

"Coming." I hurried around the last tent and got a view of the first actual road I'd seen since I came to Oz. It was made of compacted dirt and just wide enough for the caravan of men and horses assembled on it.

Two horses stood in front of a large, open-topped carriage with a storage compartment in the back. Lined up behind the carriage, Lional, Hareson, and three men sat atop horses, with one glittering, riderless bay tied to a man's saddle horn. Red Queen ignored the horses and seated herself royally in the carriage.

She smiled at me. "We will ride in the carriage." Did she know that I didn't know how to ride a horse? I'd always wanted to learn, but growing up in the city didn't provide many opportunities.

As I passed Hareson and the short man standing by his horse, a snip of their conversation reached my ears.

"I can't, Lord Hareson. It's gone," the man whispered frantically.

"What do you mean, it's gone?" Hareson was just as urgent. "It's a shirt. It doesn't have legs." His hand rested on a rapier at his belt, and his face wrinkled with concern.

"What should we do?" The man looked around, peering into every shadow like it held a scary secret.

"Calm down," Hareson ordered and tugged at his cuffs. "Break camp immediately. Return to Ruby Castle. Even after last night, it's still the safest place." He paused. "And don't tell Red Queen." He emphasized every word with his hands. When he noticed me listening, Hareson focused on me. "Ah, Ali. Is there something I can get you?" he asked pleasantly.

"Uh, no." My hands waved in front of me. "No, I was just going to the carriage." I hurried away.

A man with a dog tail stood beside the step. He held out his hand and assisted me inside. Once I was seated across from Red Queen, he climbed up in the front and took the reins. With a quick snap, he sent the horses off at a trot, the caravan following behind us.

As we passed through the forest, I watched the scenery. I was dying to hop off the carriage and look at everything in detail, but I was just going to have to study from afar. Seeing all the strange plants reminded me of something Ace had said.

"I was told," I said, and glanced at Red Queen, "that Oz is alive. That it breathes and feels, just like you and me."

Red Queen smiled fondly, her eyes growing sad. "Yes, he would say that. He would know better than anyone. And he's right." Hareson chose that time to trot his horse up beside the carriage.

I wanted to ask more, but thought better of it. After all, it sounded like Hareson wasn't a huge fan of Ace, or at least didn't want to talk about him around Red Queen. Just looking at Hareson reminded me of a question Ace never answered. "You never told me what a Domain is," I reminded him. "Also, what's a Role Player?"

"You know about that?" Hareson puffed out his chest and spoke like a stuffy lecturer. "A Role Player is someone who has a part to play in the games. They also usually have a Domain, or a section of Oz, that they care for. Red Queen's Domain happens to be all of Oz, currently, but others tend a smaller portion."

I thought about it for a minute. "Do you and Lional have a Domain?"

He shook his head. "No, we are Role Players but don't

possess a Domain. We're too busy helping Red Queen at the Ruby Castle for that." He waved a casual hand.

Red Queen laughed. "So modest, Hareson. I'm sure Ruby Castle would fall apart without you. I don't think there's been a more efficient Retainer than you in all of Oz's history." She turned to me, her lips tight with concern. "You have so many questions. Ones far deeper than any other Alice." I couldn't tell if she was complimenting me or not. Her look reminded me of the one Ace gave me when we were talking. Like she didn't know what to think of me. "I have to say, I'm surprised about how much Ace has told you about Oz."

Hareson choked.

Well, that was a casual way to open a can of worms. "We've talked," I said evasively. "He seems like a nice person."

There was an immediate frown on her red lips, and her face tightened. "Listen, Ali." Her voice became serious. "Ace isn't someone you should be around."

Hareson snorted. "I'll say—"

Red Queen cut him off with a stern look. "Why don't you ride back with Lional?" she suggested in a steely tone.

He blinked rapidly, his ears erect. Then he nodded and turned his horse. "Of course, my Queen." His heels nudged the horse's flanks.

She watched him go. "He might have more to say, even if he knows I won't appreciate it," she explained quietly. "Ace is, after all, a sensitive subject for me." She turned back to me with a sad look on her perfect face. "You see, Ali, Ace used to be one of my personal knights. And during the Alice Games, he was in charge of all the Alices' safety."

Is that why he saved me from the Cheshire Cat and helped me get out of the Cheshire Forest? It also explained why he was so casual with me while the rest of the population treated me like the plague. "Used to be?" I pressed.

She nodded. "Yes," she said slowly. "Ali, there's something I want to explain to you. Ace's full name was Ace of Hearts. That's because his heart stands alone. Some even say that it's made of tin. While he can feel affection and amusement toward another person, he can't actually love anyone. Although many have tried to develop that emotion in him." She paused and stared at her hands clasped tightly in her lap. "I used to wonder if it was because of his Role. He lacks the ability to love, just like I feel love for everyone."

Her tiny hand reached out and grasped mine. "Either way, don't be deceived by him. He's capable of hurting someone without feeling a thing. Even if you thought he was a friend. Or more."

Her words hurt more than I expected. It's not that I felt betrayed or anything. I didn't know him that well. But I'd felt a connection to him during the brief time together. Now I wondered if it was one-sided.

He'd been so relaxed and made me feel comfortable with him. He even gave me a flower just to let me study it. He did throw a knife at me, but I was the one who wanted the knife, and he was on the other side of the room. It wasn't like he'd hurt me. He certainly had all the opportunities in the world, but he never did. He even saved me a couple of times. Was it an old habit from being Red Queen's knight?

My eyes dropped to the tiny hand grasping mine as I recalled the way he talked about Red Queen. The affection in his voice had been as honest as the concern she displayed now. A gaping pit formed in my stomach as I glanced at her. "You talk about him very personally."

Her solid brown eyes flared, and she looked away. "Of

course. He was my knight for a very long time, like I said. We grew up together. Ace, me, Hareson, and Lional. We knew each other well. Or at least, I thought I knew him. Recently, I've started thinking I never knew him at all." Her red lips pressed tightly together and she sat up, pulling her hand away. "With his catlike tendencies, Ace is affectionate by nature. It is easy to assume you're special and respond in kind. That's what I want to warn you about. There are many Alices who have fancied themselves special, but it's a farce. One you would be wise not to fall into."

It was like salt on a fresh wound. So what she was saying was that Ace was a playboy? Why did the idea hurt my heart so much? I wasn't looking for anything here. After all, I wanted to go home. I needed to go home. But even so, out of all the people I'd met in Oz, Ace was the one I felt most comfortable around. Out of everyone, he was the person who'd helped me the most.

I looked to the side, too agitated to find the beauty in the trees around me. My fingers tightened around my flower, needing the feel of it. For all her words, this flower was tangible evidence. Of what, I didn't know. But it made me feel better. A little.

"You just said yourself that you might not know him that well. What if you're wrong?" My tone was harder than I meant, the scratched emotion too close to the surface.

She flinched. Her hands clenched together and she glared at me, for once showing a backbone. "There are a lot of things I might not know about Ace. But there is something that everyone in Oz knows, that you should too, before you form any more delusions around him. He might have been my knight once, but now he's White Wizard's Cheshire Cat. Which means you're simply a toy he's playing with."

My insides froze. She just called Ace the Cheshire Cat. No, Ace wasn't the Cheshire Cat. Ace's hair was orange, not white. He was a tabby cat, not a white tiger.

Images of the Cheshire Cat raged in my head. Appearing at the top of the stairs and snarling. Standing triumphant over a pile of dust that had been Lional. Staring at me with dark, dead eyes. The pictures battled with my memories of Ace. His teasing smile and the light of mischief in his brown eyes. His warm hands holding mine as he laughed while running through water. How wonderful he looked, gazing out over the water lilies.

They were not the same creature.

My heart constricted painfully. I wanted to call Red Queen a liar. But why would she lie? She needed me to get to the Emerald Castle as badly as I did.

So that meant that the liar was Ace. But he never really lied to me. Everything he'd said had been true, including how to get back to Red Queen. He saved my life and offered information for just a small—albeit embarrassing, at the time—price in comparison. Why would he lie? It didn't make any sense.

Red Queen cleared her throat, distracting me.

"Now, I really must apologize to Hareson. Excuse me." She leaned forward and tapped the seat next to the coach.

Instantly, a guard trotted up with Red Queen's horse in tow. She placed a foot out and fit it into the footholds of the red saddle. With the carriage and horse still moving, she shifted her weight over and sat sidesaddle on the horse.

I watched her go, impressed despite my battered emotions. As much as I wanted answers to these new questions, I was also glad she left. I hated arguments. They always made my insides twist in barbed wire knots. Besides, I didn't want to fight with her.

With a moan, I rested my now-pounding forehead forward against the side of the carriage. Would anything in Oz make sense? My eyes dropped to the ground and the Yellow Path my ride straddled. Lional had called it the Alice Route, right? A lot of Alices must have gone this way. The dirt was compacted and the driver knew the way without being told.

As my eyes fazed out of focus, my hearing heightened. Red Queen's, Hareson's, and Lional's voices drifted over me.

"Are you all right, Red Queen?" Hareson asked. "Things were getting ... uncomfortable."

Red Queen sighed. "Yes. I shouldn't have done that. Said it like that. I just," she paused. "Ali is so different from the other Alices. I don't know what to do with her. Everything in this Game is different. I'm worried."

Lional snorted. "Why did that cat let her go? We all know where she was. She was wet with *water*. I'd almost forgotten those cursed flowers used to shoot something as innocent as water. Last time someone touched one, his face was melted off. And she's carrying one around like it's a harmless rose."

They lapsed into silence for a couple of seconds.

"You don't think this is about Blood, do you?" Hareson asked, his voice hesitant and worried. "Ali is the only one who can enter the Emerald Castle. Hasn't he tried to convince other Alices to get Blood for him?"

The trio fell silent again.

"Let's hope that isn't the case," Red Queen finally said. "Blood should stay where it is." She took a deep breath. "Oz is changing. Somehow. I can't help but wonder if it's because of Ali. If it is, let's hope that girl's common sense will prevent her from doing anything rash." She took a breath. "Either way, I do apologize, Hareson."

"Think nothing of it, your Highness. We both know it's a subject we'll always disagree on." Hareson's voice was very sensible. "If that's been settled, Red Queen, the town elders on the Alice Route have responded, and they ..." His voice faded until it was too quiet to hear.

I opened my eyes and focused on the dirt road under me, mulling over the conversation I overheard. So that was it. Ace was using me to get something out of the Emerald Castle. All the charming smiles, the warm hands. It was all another game.

What was Blood? It was obviously a name for something, but what? Sometimes it seemed they were talking about a person, but then they called Blood an "it." Lional had said the only thing in the Emerald Castle besides the wand was death. So, did he lie? I couldn't see Ace sending a girl to get something that would kill her. Even if he was the Cheshire Cat. Right?

My mind ran in circles, stewing over the situation for a while. Maybe the distracted look on my face discouraged anyone from approaching me. The men around me made casual conversation with each other but I was left alone as the morning ticked by.

Suddenly the Yellow Path veered off to the left, pointing into the short dense trees that lined the road.

I blinked out of my thoughts and stood up, wobbling a little, and patted the carriage driver on the back. "Wait, stop."

He jumped as if stabbed by a hot poker and pulled the horses to a fast stop. I sat down hard, wincing as the wooden seat paddled my butt. Red Queen rode up, Hareson, and

Lional on her heels. The rest of the men followed respectfully behind.

"What's wrong?" the huge man rumbled.

I pointed in the direction of the arrow. "What's over there?"

Lional and Hareson exchanged looks of surprise.

Red Queen's brow knitted in concern. "Is that where the Yellow Path is pointing you to go?"

I nodded. Apparently there was more to those innocent trees than first appearances.

"It's a Domain," Hareson answered stiffly as the rest of the men looked at the ground. The tension from the group was as thick as cement. "A rarely accessed one. Only three other Alices have ever entered it."

My brows went up. Out of twenty-seven, that wasn't a lot. So why was I supposed to go in there? "How many of those Alices went home?"

"Two of them," Lional said.

Then the odds were in my favor.

CHAPTER NINE

RED QUEEN LOOKED around the group. "We'll stop here to eat lunch."

The men dismounted and hurried to make up a small picnic area. Red Queen and I sat on folding chairs taken from the back of the carriage. The men sat on the ground, shifting their swords out of the way, as sandwiches and vegetables were passed out.

I ate in silence for a minute, but my nerves were still too fried to have much of an appetite. To distract myself, I asked a question I couldn't help but think of while they ate. "Why do you guys eat if you can't die? And do the farmers keep farming even though their lives aren't dependent on what they till? Do they do it just to keep up the practice or add variety to their days?"

The men glanced at me in surprise, as if this had never dawned on them before.

Red Queen laughed. "Well, eating is enjoyable. And even though we don't die, we can still grow weak and light-headed from not eating."

I nodded. "So your bodies still need to replace the calories they spend."

No one had anything to say about that. Maybe they didn't know what a calorie was.

"You know," I said, "in my world, there are two stories based off of this place. I'm starting to think that each one is a story passed down from an Alice who came back from here. Only they've been skewed by the different experiences. One story has a wizard who, though a good person, is not what he seems. The other story has two queens. The Red Queen is evil, and the White Queen is described a lot like you." I gazed at her, interested in her reaction.

Red Queen cocked her head curiously. "Hmm, that's odd. Why is that?" She took a bite of her sandwich. Even though she'd taken the least amount of food, she still had the most left on her plate.

The men around us exchanged confused looks.

Red Queen swallowed and clarified. "In the story, why is the Red Queen evil and the White Queen good?"

I nibbled on a red fruit that tasted a lot like a carrot and shrugged. "Well, probably because white is the color of purity and peace where I come from."

"How odd." She picked up a couple of pink berries and ate them. "I would never choose white as a color of peace."

I swallowed my bite. "Why?"

"It's a color of chaos," she said. Her red lips pursed as she collected her thoughts. "If you have a white bowl of paint and you add yellow to it, what color do you get?"

"Yellow," I answered, wondering what she was getting at. "Well, a pale shade of yellow."

"Exactly. But the paint wanted to be white, the color of absence. White is so brittle, it can't adapt. It's white or not white. The only way to make sure that it stays white is to erase everything that isn't white." She looked at the trees. "Just like what the snow tries to do every winter," she added softly.

I smiled. "How literal." Satisfied, I polished off my sandwich.

"What does red mean in your world?" Hareson asked.

I blinked in surprise. I didn't think Hareson was interested in my world. "It means a lot of things, depending on the culture you refer to. There are quite a few where I come from. But most of them associate red with the color of war." I took a drink of water and wondered how I could get this on Earth. I'd never tasted such fresh water. "It's the color of blood."

"The liquid of life," Red Queen added, and everyone lapsed into silence.

Something they lacked, I thought as I remembered watching Lional and the Cheshire Cat attack each other last night. It wasn't just the memory of fear that twisted my stomach, but the added knowledge that it was Ace who killed Lional. Why would he do that?

With the food finished, the men started to clear up.

I looked at Red Queen. Another question had been bothering me. "Everyone is scared of White Wizard, right?" I could see why. I'd seen his snow monsters, and those strange, hate-filled, ice footprints in the Cheshire Forest were White Wizard's, not the Cheshire Cat's. I'd seen Ace's footprints, and they didn't leave raised chunks of dry ice like that. "Why haven't you guys done something about him already?"

Everyone stopped moving and looked at me.

Red Queen's brows pulled together. "What do you mean, Ali?" Her voice was low and serious.

Under everyone's scrutiny, it was hard not to fidget. I

reached for my necklace but when my hands touched my bare skin, I tugged on my hair and tried not to look at the ground. "I mean, why haven't you guys gotten rid of him yet?"

She shook her head. "That's what the Alice Games are for. Whichever Queen Candidate the Alice doesn't pick is locked up."

Queen Candidate? Wasn't the White Wizard a man? I guess I had always assumed he would naturally be a king when he ruled Oz, and people kept using the word Queen just because it was a habit. Was that wrong? Was the ruler of Oz called Queen, regardless of gender?

I brushed it off and continued the conversation. "Until the next Games," I reminded her. "Which means that something's wrong. Why haven't you, as a people, tried to overthrow him? Get rid of him for good? Does he just keep coming back to life too?"

There was a murmur of surprise and unrest among the men.

Red Queen sucked in a breath. "A Queen Candidate has never died before. Are you—" She cut off, her face full of shock. "Are you proposing a *war*? Is that what you're trying to say?"

Realization dawned on the men's faces. Some seemed outraged, but others, like Lional, bobbed their heads in agreement.

I was just as shocked. "You mean, after all this time, you've never tried to fix it yourselves? You've always relied on outside help to put a bandage over the problem? Does White Wizard have that much power?"

Red Queen bit her lip. "Well, yes. He does." Her hands clutched together in her lap, and her eyes were luminescent with fear. It was the first time she'd ever looked like the child her size suggested.

Lional stood right behind her and folded his arms like an imposing giant.

"But don't you have magic?"

She cut me off. "What do you know? What do you know about Oz and how we handle things? Our government, our history?"

"You're right, what do I know?" I admitted, starting to feel defensive. "And I'm supposed to pick you to be the next Queen? All I know is that you're determined to stuff me into your mold every time we meet. You love dresses and parties and excel at pretending that everything is perfect. How does that make you the right Queen?"

Red Queen looked like I'd just slapped her, but I was on a roll, finally getting everything I wanted to say off my chest. "Are we even living in the same place? Experiencing the same Oz? I mean, you can't even die. Do you even know what it feels like to fear for your life? I do now. I learned it last night. When I was all alone and being chased by those ice monsters."

"Of course I know," she spat. The dull flush on her neck turned to a bright scarlet burn of anger that crept up to sear her cheeks. The rest of her face was pale as ash and tight with emotion. "I know exactly how it feels to have my death screamed in my face by the worst ice monster in Oz. To have him stare at me with those white eyes full of his twisted hate." Her hands fisted together and she leapt to her feet, not that it gave her that much height over me. Tears brimmed her dark, hard eyes. "Do you want to know why I do all this? The extravagant parties, dresses—useless things? To help my people forget about how dark and twisted their lives are now. To give them something to look forward to when they're reduced to livestock and left to freeze in the land that should be protecting them. To help them laugh, even though we know that *this* will never end." She flung her arms out, motioning around her.

I glared back, not appreciating how she included me in her 'this.' As if it was my fault somehow. "How do you know that it won't end? What have you done to actually help end it?"

"Everything!" Tears finally spilled over her cheeks. She shoved them away with a very unladylike hand. "I have done everything that I can figure out. But what has Oz done? It gave me a wand with the leftover magic that White Wizard didn't want and a title that's driven a mad man to hate me. Nothing else. Oz is supposed to help its Queen. We should be a pair, working together to make Oz wonderful, just like it did with the last Queen. Instead it's silent. And when it does help, it's impossible to understand. Like sending a girl from another world to do—what? The same thing over and over again? *For two hundred and sixty-eight years?*"

This cycle has been going on for that long? They've been repeating the same thing for that long? I shook my head. "Then why are you still relying on the Alices? Why aren't you—?"

"Oh, you're talking about war again?" she scoffed. "What good will it do? Sure we have some trained men, but we don't have the materials needed to make enough swords. It'll be farmers with pitchforks against White Wizard's monsters. Is that what you want?" She stomped her foot. "We might not be able to die, but we can still feel the pain of death. All that will happen is the next time White Wizard gets hold of an Alice, he'll be that much nastier to my people. Their lives are miserable enough. Do you know there are some people who wake up every morning and try a new method to kill themselves almost immediately? Sane, right?"

I grimaced. "I didn't mean you should go and do it, I was just trying to give a suggestion."

Her hand fisted at her side so hard, her arms shook. "You have no right to make suggestions. You Alices come, flounce around like you matter. And in the end, you make a little choice and go home. Then you get to live your life. Grow old, have children. Eventually you die. And my people will still be here in Oz, reliving the same day again. Forever."

As angry as I was, I could see where she was coming from. Finally. "You make it sound like that's my fault."

"I know," she wailed. She took a breath, pushing the air in and out. Her brows wrinkled and her tears grew as a new wave of emotion replaced her anger. Guilt. "I know. And I'm horrible for it." She choked and buried her face in her hands.

I stood there, staring at her tiny shaking shoulders as her sobs echoed in the small clearing. She looked so small and helpless. I didn't need Lional glaring at me to feel like a jerk.

Some of what she said was true. I showed up, immediately challenged everything and threw out suggestions like candy in a demented parade. She might have been unfair in her opinions of me, but I was equally unfair to her. To everyone. I'd only been looking at her like a doll in a china shop, not a real person who has been through Hell.

But what should I say now? Now that I'd ripped her apart and spilled her hidden guilts? In front of her own men. Was there anything that could resolve something like that?

Feeling horrible, I tapped my fist against my thigh, completely lost.

The men around us didn't look any more comfortable.

Hareson gasped. His long ears swiveled all around and twitched. He jerked about to face the trees on the opposite side of the road, ears stiff in attention. "Downwind!" He pulled a long rapier from its sheath and pointed it into the trees.

A low growl emitted from Lional's throat, and he brandished his heavy sword. He ran to the very front of the group, his tail swishing. "Protect the Queen and Alice," he ordered over his shoulder.

My stomach twisted in fear. Was it more ice monsters? Did they catch up because I slowed down? Or was it the Cheshire Cat? What would happen if Ace showed up now?

The rest of the men dropped whatever they were doing and ran into position. Some formed a ring around the queen and me, while the others stood with Lional and Hareson to create a shield. Despite the tears still in her eyes, Red Queen grabbed my arm and pulled me down to crouch. It didn't matter that I'd just made her cry, she was still thinking about my safety. It made me feel all the more guilty. The men were barely in position when a volley of arrows flung out of the trees at us. Two of the guards yelled and exploded into dust. Several others fell to the ground, groaning in pain.

I cringed and swallowed back bile.

Red Queen gasped, her hands covering her mouth.

The uninjured men stood at the ready, fixated on where the arrows came from. Then the sound of trees and bushes breaking and swaying echoed out through the forest. A group of twenty men rushed out of the bushes, yelling at the top of their lungs. They had shaggy hair and beards, and they wore dull, dark colored clothes that blended in with the trees. But they weren't actually touching the ground. They hovered an inch off it, the air pulsing and swirling under their feet.

Lional gave an impressive roar and ran forward to meet them, leading the line of guards. The small group of soldiers crashed into the men and weapons glinted in the sun as they hacked at each other.

The horses, caught in the middle of the men, panicked and jerked their restraints so hard that the pick in the ground pulled loose. They bolted down the road, tossing their heads and the carriage flailing behind them.

My hand jumped up on its own, reaching for the carriage that was already too far away. A heavy knot twisted in my chest with sudden loss. My flower was still in the carriage. My hand clenched and I jerked it back to my side. I shouldn't be so upset. That flower was a lie. Right?

I swallowed back more bile as another man screamed in pain and turned away. "Are these the White Wizard's men?" I peered between our guards. There wasn't a single man with orange hair and a cat tail. Despite the situation, a small bloom of relief budded.

Red Queen shook her head. "I don't know these men. There's something off about them." Her voice shook and there was a note of worried confusion. "It's like they aren't compatible with Oz anymore. Something like this has never happened before."

"Can't you do something? Do you really need the wand to use magic?" I winced when a guard was cut down and exploded into dust.

"I can't access Oz's magic without my wand. I couldn't do anything anyway. I can't hurt them. I only know healing and defensive spells."

That's useful. In a hospital.

Another guard exploded into dust, followed a second later by the two attackers in front of Lional. He fought as fiercely as his animal suggested, taking down man after man. Even so, there were just too many attackers. Hareson could barely hold his own, and the other guards weren't doing much better.

Red Queen looked like she was going to crumble. She took a breath and lifted her head high. "This is looking bad." She turned to me with set brows. "You need to leave."

"What?" I gaped at her.

Red Queen's face tightened more. "The Yellow Path is pointing to the Domain through the trees. During the Alice Games, no one can enter a Domain unless invited." She licked her lips. "And you have been invited. Just remember, Ali, there is more to Oz than logic." She took a breath and motioned with her hands. "Go, Ali. They can't follow you in."

Her sudden sharp words made me jump to my feet. "What about you and the rest of them?" My voice wobbled as another man turned to dust.

She almost smiled. "I believe they will leave as soon as you are gone." She turned urgent again. "Run!"

My gut sank. I didn't want to leave. I hadn't resolved things with Red Queen yet. But their safety was more important than my feelings. I turned and ran.

CHAPTER TEN

SHOUTS of alarm and shock echoed after me. "She's getting away! Stop her!"

Lional yelled over them, "Don't let them through! Attack while they're distracted!"

Adrenaline jolted my system, and my legs pumped faster. My arms came up to protect my face as I ran into the thick, short trees. The tiny branches tugged at my clothes. I tripped on bushes but didn't stop. Soon enough, the sounds of fighting disappeared. Were they still chasing me? I couldn't handle another chase like last night.

I glanced behind me and skidded to a stop. My breath puffed in and out as I stared at what should have been a forest behind me. It was gone. There was nothing but a barren field disappearing into stale smelling mist. The blue sky was gone too, covered with pale clouds.

"What?" I looked around, then stumbled back in surprise.

I don't know how it got there, but a huge stone wall stretched out to either side of me, my toes at the threshold of a door-like gap. Shouldn't I be in the middle of a forest?

Where did this wall come from? Seven feet tall, gray and imposing, the wall continued as far as I could see, until it faded into the mist. There were no breaks in it except for the gap before me. On the other side of the gap was another wall, about five feet away, creating a hall-like corridor.

I frowned, put off. It looked like the opening to a maze—a big one—and I didn't want any part of it. Shaking my head, I turned to walk the other way and jolted to another stop. My toes were at the opening of another maze. Where did this one come from? Alarmed, I looked over my shoulder, expecting to be sandwiched between two mazes, but there was only a barren field behind me. Brows knit, I shuffled my feet around until they were pointing the opposite direction. I know my feet moved—I was watching them—but so did the maze. No matter what direction my toes pointed, the gap in the wall stayed in front of them.

The Yellow Path, so merrily bright against the muted colors around me, led right in.

I stared at it moodily. I needed to get out of this Domain as fast as possible. It wasn't just the time crunch I was under—I needed to see if Red Queen and her people were okay, if running away actually helped. And I needed to tell Red Queen I was sorry.

I paused. I had only spent a morning, just a couple hours really, with them. Why was I so worried? I'd never cared about anyone so quickly before. We'd just been yelling at each other, but as much as I was attacking her, she was only attacking the situation. She might be completely opposite from me, but I finally felt like I could relate to her. No, not relate. But I had empathy for her. I would be frustrated if I was in her situation, too. It made all of her other actions understandable.

She was also willing to sacrifice herself and her people

for me to get into this Domain safely. Apparently it was safe here—if I took the right path. I looked around. As long as I didn't get lost forever, anyway. Well, not forever. If Ace was telling the truth, I would get sucked into the In-Between space between our worlds if I didn't make it to the Emerald Castle in time.

Maybe I didn't have to go through it. The smooth stone walls seemed endless, but to my back was an open field. Biting my lip, I took a careful step backwards. The wall stayed in place. With a sigh of relief, I took another step. Was it possible to back out of a Domain? Maybe by the time I did, Lional and Hareson would have the situation under control again.

"What are you doing?" The high-pitched male voice spoke from two different places, at my right and left elbows.

I jumped, not sure which way to turn. Unfortunately, I moved enough that my toes pointed in a different direction. In the blink of an eye, the maze appeared at my feet again. My shoulders slumped as the breath whooshed out of me.

"What are you doing?" the voice on my right asked.

Stomach still in a knot, I looked to each side and blinked in surprise. There were two short men standing beside me. Where did they come from? I'd looked behind me several times. With no obstacles in the field, I should have seen them. For that matter, I should have noticed a huge stone wall before it was at my toes too.

I'd seen twins before, lots of them, but these two were different. Even identical twins have slight differences, be it slightly different heights, weights, or the pitch of their voices. I'd even met a pair where one twin had moles on his nose and the other didn't. These two men had none of those differences.

They were both as tall as my elbow and had the same

amount of pudginess in the middle. Their scalps were showing through their brown hair in the same place, and their eyes were both too close together. They were even dressed the same, in yellow shirts, blue vests, and tan pants.

I took a breath and backed up a couple steps so they were between me and the maze. As I moved, the one on the right giggled with amusement.

"Ah, hi," I started. "I'm—"

"The Alice of Alice. We know," they said in perfect unison.

"Only an Alice can come in here once the game begins," the one on the left said.

My brows went up. Okay, I knew a lot of stuff, but I didn't sound that annoying about it.

"I'm Dean," said the one on the right

"My name is Winstum," the one on the left supplied.

Dean and Winstum. Dee and Dum. Oh, great.

"You're odd. Why were you walking backwards?" Dean asked.

Winstum rolled his eyes and looked at his twin. "Isn't that obvious? She was trying to get away from the maze."

"Oh." Dean giggled. "That's odd. It's impossible." He nodded his head in emphasis. "The only exits are on the other side. You could choose the right course."

"Or the wrong one," Winstum added.

I motioned to the maze. "You mean there's more than one exit?"

Dean laughed. "Of course there is. There are always choices."

"You could start on one path and end on another," Winstum said.

I shook my head, trying to understand what they were

saying. It sounded like they were implying it was more than a maze. "What is this place?"

"Bones of the past," Dean hummed.

"Secrets of the shamed," said Winstum.

Together they announced, "The path of decisions."

Past secrets were in there? Did that mean it was populated? I wanted to go in there less and less. "So, you're saying that I have to go through this thing?"

"Yes." They nodded in unison.

I swallowed a sigh and looked down, frowning. Well, there was one good thing about all this. I could just use the Yellow Path to guide me through. I might as well get this over with. "Okay." Determined, I stepped forward.

"Ah, where are you going?" Dean stuttered.

"Isn't it obvious?" I asked, marching ahead. "I have to go through there." I motioned before me. "I don't have time to wait forever."

"But we haven't told you—"

I skidded to a stop, but my momentum carried me across the line of the entrance. Instantly the open space behind me disappeared, replaced by a stone wall. My hand shot out and hit the wall. I didn't know if I was hoping the wall wouldn't be solid but it was. I winced and rubbed my aching palm against my pants. What had they been about to tell me? This was why it never paid to be too hasty. Mistakes happen more often.

I couldn't go back now. Taking a breath to calm myself, I followed the yellow line down the hall, which ended with a right turn. I rounded the corner and came to a two-way junction. I looked down.

My mouth dropped open. No. No, no, no, no, no, no. I turned in a full circle. The entire ground of the maze was yellow. All of it, in every direction.

"That's not fair," I groaned, shoving my hands through my hair. My words echoed back at me, the only noise in this eerily quiet place. So I had to figure this out on my own. What was new? My hands dropped, and I huffed out my breath.

The logical way would be to take every right turn. It wasn't the fastest way to go through a maze, but that way I wouldn't go in circles which could delay me forever. I took the right path, walked down that corridor, and took another right turn. Some of the corridors spilled into square rooms with multiple exits, and sometimes the halls were very wide, almost room-like themselves. The size of the corridors might be changing, but the dull gray stone walls all looked the same, blending in with the shadows. While I knew I wasn't going in circles, I was completely lost.

I came to a stop in a long wide corridor, wishing for the hundredth time for a map. That was when I noticed a brick path leading down the middle of the room—the first change in my surroundings since I entered the maze. "Why is there a brick path in a dirt-floored room?" Odd, but I stayed on the path anyway.

A sound stopped me cold. Somewhere to my right, people were whispering. I spun around. There was no one there.

The whispering kept up, but I couldn't understand what their excited voices were saying. I turned in a full circle, trying to pinpoint where the voices came from, then jumped back in surprise.

The wall in front of me shifted and rippled like a drop of water on a still pool. The bricks disappeared, revealing a bright, colored area, four feet wide by about three feet tall, like a picture frame. Confused, I tried to make out what the picture was. It was like someone had taken a photograph while standing in a crowd, looking up. The foreground was taken up with the backs of several people's heads, the sources of the whispers I heard earlier. The picture was aimed at a balcony where two people stood on display.

The woman was tall and thin, dressed in a rich, teal gown. She might have been in her seventies but she was still quite the beauty, with thick white hair piled in curls on her head. A crown nestled in those curls, with several different colored jewels sparkling in the sun. She had high cheekbones and deep pink, painted lips, and she smiled kindly at the people below.

Next to her stood a handsome adolescent around fifteen years old. He was almost as tall as her, with the growing, boney shoulders of a youth, his long limbs clothed in white and cream clothes. His hair was so pale blond it looked white, and his skin was only a few shades darker. He beamed down at the crowd, chest swelling in pride.

I was still contemplating it when the picture started to move.

CHAPTER ELEVEN

THE WOMAN LIFTED a hand and waved at the people below. "Good afternoon, my beloved people." Her voice was calm and soothing, but was still very easy to hear even though she was a ways away.

I gasped and stepped back, surprised.

The crowd in the front of the picture threw their hands in the air and cheered. Voices off screen exclaimed with adoration, "Jewel Queen!"

She smiled graciously and bobbed her head. "This is a momentous occasion. Your selection for the next queen has been accepted by Oz." Jewel Queen motioned to the boy beside her with a graceful hand. "It is my pleasure to introduce Queen Candidate White."

The people down below cheered.

Queen Candidate White grinned wide and raised a hand in acknowledgement.

My mouth dropped open. This was White Wizard when he was younger? He looked so bright and eager. So harmless and—from the way the people were yelling his name—so loved. How did he go from this young man to someone so feared today?

Whispers from the crowd off camera echoed from around the frame.

"So young."

"So highly recommended!"

"My son studies with him. I think we can expect great things from Queen Candidate White."

When the cheering began to quiet, Jewel Queen raised her hand, silencing them completely. "Now there are things that young Queen Candidate White and I need to discuss. There are also many things that need to be done for tonight. You are all welcome to come and rejoice with us in the castle gardens. Until then, have a pleasant day." She bobbed her head to the cheering crowd and motioned the young man off the balcony.

The camera suddenly zoomed in at a dizzying pace, up the wall, over the balcony, and through the door as White held it open for Jewel Queen. It was like trying to watch a shaking amateur's homemade film, shaking, spinning, and all. I put a hand to my forehead, trying to ward off the instant motion sickness, and squinted at the screen. I didn't know why I was seeing this, but I didn't want to miss anything either.

On the other side of the door was a lavish antechamber decorated in rich jewel tones. Jewel Queen walked over to a chair and took a seat. She folded her hands together and smiled softly at Queen Candidate White, kindness radiating from her thin face. The view was close enough that I could see the rich blue of her eyes. "I imagine you've had a busy day so far. We haven't had a chance to really talk since I called you to my throne room. How are you feeling?"

Queen Candidate White shut the door so that it barely

made a sound. "Wonderful." He smiled, so happy, so excited. "It almost doesn't seem real yet."

She laughed a little and nodded. "Yes. I remember feeling the same when I was first called."

The smile slid off his face a little, and his head cocked to the side as he contemplated her. For the first time, he didn't seem so innocent. Just curious. "Aren't you scared? I mean, me being called the Queen Candidate means that you ... won't be Queen anymore. I mean, uh..."

Still her expression was kind as she nodded wisely. "You mean, I'll die soon?"

He swallowed and nodded, looking away as if a little worried.

She reached up and took the crown from her head. She brought it down to eye level and stared at it, shifting it between her fingers so that the light caught on the precious gems and flashed rainbows across her pale face. "I've been Queen for a very long time. So long, I can't even feel the crown anymore. As much as I love Oz and my people, it will be a relief when I can rest." She placed the crown back on her head. "As light as this ornament is, sometimes, it's very heavy."

Queen Candidate White stared at the crown nestled in the folds of her white hair, desire burning in his eyes. He licked his lips. "What is it like to be the most important person in Oz?"

She tilted her head to the side, surprised by his question. "What do you mean?"

He winced and fumbled with his hands as he sought for words. "I mean, you're the Queen." He motioned to her.

"Ah, yes. You are Lord Larse's son, after all." She nodded slowly like that explained a lot. She stood up and walked over to him. "Listen, Queen Candidate White, because this is vital. I am not the most important person in Oz. I am no more important than a man in the field, pulling out beets."

His forehead scrunched up as in confusion under his white-blond hair.

My face must have mirrored his—I was just as surprised at her answer.

She put a hand on his shoulder and stared earnestly into his eyes, her rich blue against his pale grey ones. "As Queen, I am nothing more than a servant assisting the people. A mediator between them and Oz. A bringer of harmony. That is why it takes the people to elect a person and that person to be compatible with Oz before he or she is fully accepted as the new Queen. The Queens don't live longer than any other person in Oz. We are called, serve our purpose, then we die." She smiled softly, her hand moving from his shoulder to gently touch under his chin. "You see, while the job of Queen is the most important, it doesn't mean that I am."

He shook his head, still confused.

She nodded slowly, his hesitation troubling her a little. "In time, you'll understand." Her hand dropped and she stepped back to smooth out the skirt of her teal gown. She took a breath, her smile warming again.

He gave her a queer look. "How can you live with that ideal so simply? Isn't it hard, when people are bowing to you and giving you everything you want, to live with that mentality?"

She laughed a little then took his hands in a motherly way. Her face turned serious. "Above all else, it's important that you control your emotions by the time you are crowned. Dark and negative emotions, such as arrogance—and hate and resentment, for that matter—are like poison to your connection with Oz. Not only could it fog up your link, but the negativity may bleed over and those are emotions that Oz simply can't handle. Do you understand that?"

He nodded. "Yes, Your highness."

This was it—finally, a clue to what was happening to Oz. It seemed that White Wizard had once been good. I mean, he was elected and loved by the people. But now his very presence turned Oz into a frozen hell and the people into animals. What changed him?

Jewel Queen smiled as if all was well now. "Very good. Your link was forged only an hour ago, so you might not be able to feel it well yet, but give it time. Now why don't we have lunch together and we can get to know each other more? After all, we will be spending quite a bit of time together while you learn how to be the new Queen."

"That would be wonderful, Your Highness." He smiled eagerly.

She motioned to the side door, letting Queen Candidate White take the lead.

Just as he reached for the door handle, there was a knock.

The young man paused before opening the door.

A tall, broad man stood on the other side of the door. His hair would have been dark blond in his youth, but now the hair slicked back from his ears was white and silver. His chin was strong and square, eyes pale blue and cold. He was dressed in fine white and blue clothes. His perfect posture was controlled and stiff, his hands clasped behind his back.

"Father," Queen Candidate White said in surprise.

Jewel Queen gave a pleasant smile, but there was a cautious flicker in her eyes. "Why, Lord Larse. I didn't think we'd have the opportunity to see you at this hour."

Lord Larse's face split into a perfect courteous smile. He put a hand over his heart and gave a low bow to the queen. "Greetings, your highness. You are as radiant as ever." He stood up, still not acknowledging Queen Candidate White. "I was hoping I could have a word with my son. Congratulate him on his accomplishments."

The queen glanced between the two men then nodded her head to the side slowly. "Of course. I imagine you are quite proud of him."

Lord Larse nodded, looking at his son with the same polite perfectness he used with the Queen. "Yes, I am."

The young man smiled and looked at the ground, as if trying to hide his pride.

Jewel Queen put her hand on Queen Candidate White's shoulder then nodded to Lord Larse as a farewell. "I'll see you in a little while, Queen Candidate White. Until tonight, Lord Larse." She patted the young man's shoulder and walked out the door as the men bowed her out.

Lord Larse straightened and turned to his son. "Get your things. It's time we go."

"Where?" he asked in surprise.

"Why, to go see your supporters." Lord Larse motioned with a hand. "These lords spent a lot of time and money influencing the public and boosting you into this position. Now we have to make sure we properly thank them." He took a deep breath. "Just think, the fruit of my loins, the next Queen." It was like he was the one who got the position, not his son.

"Oh, yes." Queen Candidate White frowned and looked at the ground. "Could we do that a little later? Jewel Queen invited me to lunch and—"

"I have no use for a disobedient son!" Lord Larse

snapped, his voice echoing and amplifying in the small room. His eyes blazed with sudden anger and he leaned over his son. "You might be the Queen Candidate, but don't forget that it was me who put you there."

Queen Candidate White flinched and bowed his head even more.

With a small sigh, Lord Larse rolled his shoulders back into place. "Jewel Queen is a kind and forgiving woman," he reasoned. "I'm sure she wouldn't mind if you skip out this one time. After all, you'll be spending a lot of time with her from now on, learning how to run Oz. Of course, I'll be there as well, to make sure all goes well." He pushed at his cuffs, making sure they weren't wrinkled from his outburst.

Queen Candidate White's brows drew together, he was still torn. He glanced up, and his eyes widened in alarm when he met his father's angry gaze.

"Now," Lord Larse ordered.

Queen Candidate White nodded. All the emotions cleared from his face and he nodded. "Yes, father."

The image blurred and disappeared, leaving a blank brick wall in its wake.

"Poor White Wizard," the double voices whispered just behind me.

I jumped and whipped around, but there was no one there. Just when I thought I'd imagined it, they spoke again.

"Even as a Queen Candidate, he was still unable to escape the heavy hand of his father." Winstum and Dean said together. I could hear them, but they weren't physically there. I waited for them to talk more, but there was nothing but the sound of my breathing.

All the hair stood up on my arms. "Winstum, Dean? Was that–did I just see a memory from Oz?" I asked to the sky.

There was no response.

It was the only explanation that I could think of that made any sort of sense. It was a memory of Oz. No one had animal tails, and the feeling—aside from the young White Wizard and his father—was friendly and relaxed. It had to be before Oz broke.

I frowned. White Wizard was so young when he was chosen—and he'd been so eager to be important. Was Lord Larse the reason why Queen Candidate White turned into White Wizard? How different would he have turned out if his father hadn't been there?

My eyes roamed around one more time. When another scene didn't pop up and the twins didn't say anything, I started to walk again. The farther I moved into the maze, the less sense it made. I took every right turn, but the paths and rooms weren't square anymore. Corridors cut off with rounded stone walls, and rooms were shortened in ways that seemed against their design. Why did it start out so squared off and then change to this distorted pattern?

Where was the end? My legs were getting tired. I shouldn't be going in circles since I was taking all right turns, but I couldn't shake the feeling that I was.

I was just passing down a long winding hallway when the wall shimmered. I stilled as another picture appeared on the wall. This time it was taller than me and twice as long. It was made out of bright, vibrant colors, so different from the dim maze. The image rose up out of the wall, like a 3-D movie but without the annoying glasses.

In it, two men rode atop horses on a raised dirt path. On either side of the road were muddy farm paddies, freshly tilled and half full of water. In the background were tall trees, their multicolored leaves flashing bright against the blue sky.

One of the men was White Wizard. He was older, in his early thirties and handsome as he was in his youth. He wore white and rode a gorgeous white horse.

My eyes moved to the other man and I nearly fell over in shock. It was Ace! I couldn't stop staring at him, taking in the differences from this picture to now. He was younger, looking to be about my age. His cat ears and tail were gone. Human ears peeked out from under the orange hair he'd shoved to the side. His dark brown eyes held a naïve light that he didn't have today. He was laughing, carefree and comfortable in White's presence, and his blue and white clothes reminded me of a medieval squire.

Queen Candidate White was listening to Ace, a controlled smile on his face as he contemplated Ace's words.

Just like the last one I saw, the scene started to move.

White smiled wanly. "You like this Red girl a lot, don't you?"

"We grew up together. There weren't many playmates to choose from, you know?" He smiled softly, his dark brown eyes shining. "But she is very sweet. It's hard not to love her."

White frowned and glanced over his shoulder at Ace. A displeased expression flashed over his face before it settled to blank.

Ace missed the look, his attention on something ahead. White's horse tossed its head, pulling his attention forward. I turned my head and looked at what they were staring at.

In the middle of the road was a cart full of vegetables and an old man in worn clothes standing by it. One of the cart's wheels had fallen off, and the man was trying to get it back on. His old pony stood with its head down, blowing air at the dirt.

White frowned and moved his horse a little closer, Ace trailing behind. "Move, please." He might have used the word 'please' but the words came out like an order. "I have business at Jewel Castle that I must attend to." Gone was the young man that had cowered before his father. In fact, it was like Lord Larse was the one in the saddle, not White.

The aged man pushed up the brim of his hat with a weathered hand and squinted up at the horsed men. "Well, now. My cart can't move. The wheel's busted. You'll have to go around or wait till I'm done."

White's face flushed in anger. He glanced around, taking note of the obviously deep mud of the farm paddies. There was no way they could cross it and stay clean.

Ace shifted and swung a leg over his saddle to dismount.

White shot a hard look over his shoulder. "Stay."

Ace froze, mid-motion. He blinked, as if this was the first time he'd seen this side of White. "I'm going to help him fix—"

"I said stay." White turned back to the man. His horse shifted and tossed its head, trying to loosen the reins a little. "We can't wait. Push your cart aside so we can pass."

A black vapor formed around Queen Candidate White, like steam, only black. And wherever it touched the picture, the picture seemed to warp and bend around the smoke, like it wasn't compatible.

I frowned—why did that seem familiar? Oh! It was just like the men who'd attacked Red Queen's caravan before I entered the maze. Only, instead of just being where the men stepped, this angry black aura surrounded White and warped Oz wherever it touched.

Ace slowly sat back down and soothed his horse with an absentminded pat, his eyes wide with open shock. It didn't seem like he could see the black steam, it was what was happening in front of him that confused him.

The old man frowned at White. "That could tip my whole cart into the fields. I could lose my crop," he said, dumbfounded.

White dismissed him with a wave. "The matters of one farmer. The business that I have at Jewel Castle is far more important."

The man's weathered face turned mean and flushed purple. He pointed up at the man, dirty finger shaking. "Now, that ain't right. You, Queen Candidate White, are no more important than I am. You and your squire should be down here in the dirt, helping me."

White's face smoothed over into ice cold stone. The black aura around him grew. "You know who I am, but you won't move?"

"Why should I?" The man's arm folded across his chest.

"I said move!" White flung out his hand.

Instantly, the man and his wagon were encased in a huge block of ice. The old man's pony gave a scream of fright as the ice block slid off the road, following the movement of White's hand, and into the mud below. The whole thing landed with a slosh, mud splatting in the air.

I screamed and stumbled back from the picture, eyes wide and unable to look away.

Ace yelled in surprise, spooking his horse. He quickly shushed the beast, but couldn't erase the horror on his face.

The pony wiggled frantically, snorting and kicking its legs until it slipped from its mud-covered reigns. It struggled through the mud until it reached the trees and disappeared into the forest. The picture of Oz darkened and trembled, the color dimming from the sky and trees even though there were no clouds in the sky, as if Oz itself were affected by the murder.

White stared at the ice on the side of the road then down at his hands. "How ... easy." His face had a look of awe, his breathing wasn't even elevated at all. The bothered sounds of Ace's horse finally reached White and he turned around, as if remembering that Ace was there. His own horse's eyes were wide but it didn't have enough lead to move.

Ace stared at White. "You just—you—" He couldn't seem to say the words.

White turned his horse around and pulled up till he was face to face with Ace. "I just what?"

Ace turned to stare at the ice.

White reached out and grabbed Ace's chin. He turned Ace back to him. "Nothing happened." His words were heavy and cold as a glacier.

Ace's face contorted in horror. He took a breath and jerked his chin loose, his teenage face set in determined resolve. He drew the sword hanging on the saddle of his horse. "Queen Cand—I mean, Lord White, you are under arrest—"

"How dare you try and demote me!" White yelled in sudden rage, the black cloud around him growing larger. "I am the future Queen of Oz!" He shoved a hand towards Ace.

Ice circle blasted through the air and hit Ace square in the chest. It pushed him off his horse, and he landed on the ground with a painful grunt. His sword clattered to the ground feet from him. Ice formed around his chest and covered his arms, freezing them to the ground.

"Ace!" I gasped and reached out.

Ace's horse squealed in terror and bolted down the road, bucking as it went.

White Wizard moved his panicked prancing horse over to stare down at Ace, his eyes as cold as the ice in the field.

Gasping and shivering, Ace stared up at White as if he was looking at a monster wearing the Queen Candidate's skin. Or maybe as if Ace was truly seeing him for the first time.

"I have to say, Ace, for the first time since you've started serving me, I find myself disappointed. I have no need for a disobedient squire." White's rage had chilled, the black cloud around him shrinking down to vapor around his skin.

My hands crossed over my chest and rubbed at my prickled flesh. The air around me wasn't cold, but his voice sent chills up my arms.

Ace's eyes widened. He tried to glare defiantly, but his fear was all too obvious. It was as if he wanted to say something, but couldn't come up with anything.

"Or do you fancy yourself that you have some divine calling? Like those stories about the Knights of Oz you love so much?" White mocked. "Don't be ridiculous. You should be grateful to me. After all, you are nothing. Orphaned by your mother, abandoned by your father to your elderly, scholar grandfather. If you weren't one of the Children, you would have never been noticed. You would have been just a boy running wild around that Cheshire Forest for the rest of your life. But I noticed you, and made you something. Someone. So disappointing." He tsked.

The ice inched up Ace's neck. He thrashed his head, trying to prevent the ice from tightening on him.

White's horse blew a gust of air out his nose and chewed on the bit, its prancing hooves getting closer to Ace's face.

White took a calming breath. "But I'm a forgiving

person. And I might still have use for you." The ice stopped growing.

Ace's breath was short and shallow. "Do you honestly think nothing will happen to you?" he whispered, still resisting White Wizard.

"Of course not." White answered, as confident as the truth. "I will be Queen soon. That's why no one will know. Not Jewel Queen, not even your little Red friend. I haven't met her myself yet, but you make her sound like such a wonderful girl. It would be awful if something happened to her, wouldn't it?"

Ace's face went from white to ashy gray. "What does she have to do with this?" His hands fisted, red knuckles whitening.

"Nothing. Just like nothing happened here. As long as you do everything I say. *Everything*. Are we clear?" White smiled.

Ace swallowed hard, mind obviously running in circles. Slowly, the defiant glint in his dark eyes softened into defeat. His fist slacked and flopped on the ground.

White nodded smartly. "Good boy. Very wise." The ice melted off Ace, leaving his shirt wet and a muddy puddle under him. "You are about to learn about a whole new side of Oz that even Jewel Queen is too kind to understand," White said softly.

Ace's eyes widened, brows pulling together.

White turned his horse around, back down the road. "Now, we have taken too much time. Keep up." He kicked his horse into a trot, leaving Ace horseless.

Ace glanced at the ice block that was starting to melt in the sun. For a moment he looked ill, whether it was from the act he witnessed or his own decision, I didn't know. Then he took a breath, face tightening in resolution. He leapt lightly to his feet and ran after White.

The picture faded into the wall's dull gray bricks.

"And thus Queen Candidate White took his first step down a road no Queen should travel, taking his young squire with him," Dean and Winstum whispered around me. Then their voices were gone again.

Breathing hard, I stumbled away from the wall until my back bumped into the wall behind me.

Horrible. Everything about that scene was horrible. How had White changed so much? In the first scene he had been obsessed with his own importance but still content. So easily cowed by his father and desperate to please him. Now, anger and hatred radiated from his every action. Like murder.

Why was I even seeing these scenes? Did whatever showed this to me want me to know what type of person the White Wizard was, or did these random and horrible scenes have more importance than that? Whatever the reason, it was time to get out of here.

I turned and sped down the hall, took the next right, then another one.

"How big is this maze?" I asked as this hall opened up to another room.

And did a double take.

Red Queen sat in a chair on the right side of the room. She looked around, then stared down at her neatly folded hands, her face tight.

CHAPTER TWELVE

THE BREATH SWOOSHED out of me as words, apologies, and thoughts jumbling in my mind. "Red Queen, I—" My voice died when she didn't react to me. Confused, I glanced around.

Three walls of the room were made of the same stone wall I'd been staring at for hours. But the wall behind Red Queen was plastered white and decorated with hanging curtains and tapestries. Strong daylight flooded through large windows on her side, while my side was dim with cloud cover. A painted, white door was on the far left side of the wall. It was like two rooms had been combined into one down the middle.

I frowned and walked closer to Red Queen. She was slightly see-through. Her hologram image was younger. Barely. She appeared to be about fifteen, with youthfully rounded cheeks and innocence in her large dark eyes. Her turquoise dress was simple and devoid of any jewels. Her crown was missing as well. I don't know if it was just an odd angle for me, but there seemed to be a faint glow around her head.

The white door swung open, and White Wizard waltzed in, his steps large and his face set. "Okay, Bauer. What do we have scheduled today?" His projection stopped in the middle of the room, not far from me.

White Wizard had changed very little since the last scene, still in his early thirties and the aura around him still pitch black. Shoots emitted off him like solar flares. The image contorted when it touched the black, reacting like oil to water.

Bauer, presumably White Wizard's secretary, followed him into the room. He was a round man, with a plain face and plain brown hair. He seemed skittish, his hands clenching and unclenching on the corner of his blue coat. He shut the door quietly. "Well, Queen Candidate White," he said, his voice subdued, "in a few minutes you have an appointment with Lord Hatter."

White Wizard cut him off with a scoff. "That fool? How far do my father's friends think past favors can get them? If Hatter thinks he can trade bizarre hats for more land when I'm Queen, he's crazy. If that's what he wants, cancel the appointment." He turned and flung his hand in dismissal. "Cancel it anyway."

Bauer jolted. "But, but Hatter is the keeper of a large portion of land and one of your family's biggest supporters. Many people are under his guidance."

White Wizard sneered. "And soon they will be under mine." He turned and finally noticed Red Queen in the chair. "Who is this?"

Bauer looked, and his whole body pulsed like he was hit by lightning. "Ah, this is Miss Red." His voice was something close to a whimper now. He started to rock on his heels.

At her name, Red—who was not yet a Queen—stood up

and gave a lovely curtsy. "I was told you wanted to meet me. I apologize if I'm interrupting something." She looked at the men, smiling in spite of the mood. Her eyes shifted to the door as if hoping they would dismiss her.

"Ah, yes. You're the youngest of the Children, Squire Ace's friend." With a small, tight smile, White Wizard gave a quick bow, his movement perfect. "He often talks about you. I can see why. You're as pretty as a glowing rose." When he straightened, his eyes narrowed on her. His head tilted to the side as if he was seeing something strange about her. He stalked over and stopped right in front of her, staring at the light shimmering around her head.

Bauer's hand jumped up, but he didn't say anything. Instead his hand retracted until it tapped on his lips.

Red took a step back, taken by surprise at White Wizard's sudden nearness, and her eyes dropped to the ground. Then she peeked through her lashes to see what he was doing.

White Wizard stared her full in the face, towering several feet over her. I couldn't tell what he saw, but his brows pulled together and his jaw clenched. His finger thrust forward until he pointed at her chest. "This girl!"

She jumped and stepped back again. Her knees bumped into the chair. She sat down hard, blinking at the finger in her face with alarm.

White Wizard turned his head to stare at his attendant. "She has been marked as a future Queen Candidate." His hand dropped as he slowly prowled back to Bauer. "Is this the reason why you never set up the meeting before? I've been requesting to see her for almost a year now." His voice was low and cold.

Bauer started to tremble, his hands clasped together in front of him. "N-no. You are so busy learning everything to be Queen. I just didn't want to overwhelm you." His voice was thin. The color in his face paled.

White Wizard's head cocked to the side, his lips pulled down in cool interest. "And yet I requested to see her several times. How long has she been a potential Candidate? Years? Have you been hiding her to see who was better? Me or this child?"

"N-no!" gasped Bauer.

Red's hands clenched in her lap, alarm plain on her face. She didn't look surprised, so she must have already known she was a potential Candidate. But White Wizard's actions scared her.

"Liar," White Wizard hissed. "Despite all those sugar-coated words, I know what the people call me behind my back. Defective. White Wizard." The words grated through his teeth as his nose flared. He stopped walking and stood shoulder to shoulder with Bauer, facing the opposite direction.

"T-that's abs-surd," Bauer's hands fidgeted more than ever. "The people love you!" His words suddenly cut off. He jerked once, then his whole body went rigid as if he was made of ice. Because, suddenly, he was.

Red gasped.

White Wizard spun. As he did, ice grew down his right hand and formed a short blade over his arm. He struck Bauer's neck with the sword. With a deafening crack, Bauer's head broke off his body.

His head landed on the ground at my feet. His plain chubby face was frosted over, eyes wide with surprise and mouth open, still forming the syllables he never uttered. The stub where his neck should have been was jagged and bloodless. His whole head was frozen solid.

I gasped and staggered back, the blood pumping

through my body with fright and nausea boiling in my stomach. This was the second murder I'd witnessed from the hands of the same person. Yet I couldn't look away. My wide open eyes stared at White Wizard as the body crumbled on the ground.

Whatever I felt was amplified in Red, the actual person in the room. She screamed and leapt backwards, knocking over her chair. She tripped on it and fell back, catching herself on the wall. Her hands partially covered her face, muffling her screams. Tears streamed from her huge, terrified eyes as she half-gasped, half-sobbed.

White Wizard stared down at the body with open dislike. "Of course I'm the one those brainless beasts love." He turned his icy gaze to the girl on the wall. "I am the *only one*," he breathed and moved toward her with deadly intent. His pitch black aura pulsed and flared larger than ever.

Sobbing, she stared at the man, frozen with fear.

"Run!" I gasped, even though I knew she couldn't hear me.

She was too scared to move.

White Wizard's hand pulled back, getting ready to impale her.

She flinched, anticipating the attack.

Suddenly the aura around him turned yellow and his body jolted to a stop, held in place by the yellow aura. His eyes widened as he jerked his head this way and that, trying to get his body to move. His sword hand quivered, but that was all the movement he could manage. His teeth ground together and his head tipped back so he could scream to the ceiling in fury. "Oz! You betrayed me!" He howled like an enraged wolf. "I haven't even been crowned yet and you already plan my replacement!"

Red was gasping like a fish, her hands flattened on the wall. She started to slide across it, inching toward the door.

He jerked, trying to get her again, but the yellow shield held fast. His eyes were wide with murder. "You can't protect her forever, Oz!" he yelled. "The day she becomes a Queen Candidate, nothing will stop me from killing her! Nothing! *I'll kill her*!"

The picture started to shake and quiver as if his threat physically affected Oz.

Sobbing anew, Red broke from her spell and ran for the door.

White Wizard turned his head and yelled curses after her as the scene faded, leaving me in an empty room.

"And thus, the connection between Queen Candidate White and Oz was severed," Winstum's and Dean's voices whispered behind me. "Now he is the White Wizard."

I couldn't stay in that room. I was less careful than before, rushing through every right turn I came across.

The corridor opened up. I skidded to a halt in a large room. It was shaped like an octagon, but a circular balcony took up most of the space, the cracked concrete structure stopping just feet from the stone wall that surrounded it.

As soon as I entered, the scene started.

"Again?" I gasped.

The hologram filled the whole room around me until I was actually in the scene. All the cracks disappeared from the balcony, and an iron table and chair appeared on my right. Large, beautiful vases with tall flower arrangements decorated the granite railing, and ivy materialized around it. The walls were replaced by a lovely sunset backdrop framed in green trees.

When I turned around, my mouth dropped open. The

ceiling and wall had vanished, revealing the tall castle attached to the balcony that rose up into the blue sky.

Two people were in the scene with me. White stood next to the table, pouring a drink out of a crystal pitcher. He was in his normal white attire, looking elegant and pristine. Permanent frown lines marred his handsome face, and his movements were stiff. He kept shooting glances as dark as the aura surrounding him at the woman with him.

Jewel Queen was just as beautiful as before, but her age was catching up to her. Something about her seemed like she was being stretched longer than her limits should have been. Dressed in a shimmering blue gown, she stood by a flower vase in front of me, arranging the beautiful flowers with her thin, long fingers. Her silver hair was piled on top of her head, her jeweled, golden crown holding it in place. She cleared her throat. "Thank you for taking the time to see me, Queen Candidate White." She looked at him out of the corner of her blue eyes.

White bobbed his head elegantly. "Not at all. There is always time for you, Jewel Queen." His words were smooth and courteous, but his eyes were cold. He took a sip from his pink drink.

The Queen smiled, but it didn't show in her eyes, either. Despite their politeness, tension saturated the air. "My condolences on the sudden passing of your father. Many people regarded him with ... great respect."

White sipped his drink again. "Yes." That was the only reaction he had on the matter.

She watched him out of the corner of her eyes. Her smile disappeared, and she looked at the flowers again, concern on her face. "There is a reason why I called you here, Queen Candidate White. I chose this place so we can discuss the matter in privacy." She gazed at him long and hard. Could she see the black cloud around him?

White frowned and set his drink down. He knew what this conversation was about.

Jewel Queen focused on the flowers.

I wanted to tell her to not turn her back to him, but it would be useless.

"Serious rumors, too many to ignore, have reached my ears," she said into her flowers. "Ones that grieve me to no end. And when I ask Oz, I see only black haze. This is a serious problem, Queen Candidate White."

"Would you care to enlighten me about these rumors?" White said casually, shifting toward her. "I'm afraid I don't know what you are talking about."

The Queen's eyes narrowed. Lines appeared around her lips as she frowned. "There have been multiple accounts of you forcing knights—one young knight in particular—into servitude. It has been said that you hold the safety of loved ones over their heads to get them to do your bidding." She turned to see his reaction.

White didn't have one. If it was true, he thought there was nothing wrong with his actions. He didn't bother to deny or confirm her words.

Jewel Queen's expression didn't change, but there was a look of sad displeasure about her now. She looked back at her flowers. "There are other accusations against you, Queen Candidate White. Many of them. Threatening people, treating people and their property with contempt. Murder," she whispered. She glanced at him, but his expression still didn't change.

The breath came out of her in a silent sigh. "White, you are the Queen Candidate. One day, after I die, you will be Queen. Oz accepted you because the people loved you—

even though you were so young at the time. What has happened to you?

"You hold so much of Oz's power, yet your link with Oz is underdeveloped. Can't you see that it's getting sicker by the day? Forests are going wild and the children ..." she cut off and swallowed hard. "As the Queen of Oz, that is not something I can overlook. Oz and I have a pact together to maintain the peace of the people. I also have the responsibility to make sure the future of Oz is peaceful."

Her words were bouncing off him. He wandered over to the balcony next to her and placed his hands on it, looking out over Oz. From that view, his gaze became hungry. The black aura pulsed and enlarged.

The Queen's lips thinned and wrinkles formed around her eyes, as if she could see the smoke. She turned back to the flowers. "Is there anything you have to say?"

"Of course," White said in his silver voice. "How many years has it been since I was first picked as the Queen Candidate? Nineteen—twenty years?"

She nodded and waited.

"Do you remember the day I was chosen as the Queen Candidate? And you told me that Oz treats the Queens just like normal people. And that's why the Queens don't live any longer than other people. Yet, how old are you? One hundred? One hundred and five years old? It seems to me that Oz has extended your life." He gave her a hard look.

Her expression turned to pity. "It's waiting for you to finally learn the lesson I taught you that first day." She shook her head. "Oz won't wait forever for you to let go of your pride—"

"That's not what I wanted to ask," he cut her off. "My question was, why haven't you died yet?" He turned, an ice blade forming over his hand.

A yellow barrier appeared between them, and White's sword thrust into it. He gritted his teeth and pushed harder. Oz's protection wavered then suddenly cracked. Jewel Queen turned just in time for White to run her through the stomach.

She gasped, blood trickling from her mouth, eyes wide with surprise. Her body jerked once, then went limp. White Wizard pulled his sword out and dumped her body on the ground.

I screamed and covered my mouth with my hands.

The room's single scene broke into six different scenes surrounding me, cutting off the bloody balcony. The view looking out at Oz zoomed in all directions.

On either side of me, so close I could reach out and touch it, the hologram's ground splintered and cracked. I screamed again. This wasn't real, but it was so realistic. The room shook so badly with the ground's quaking that it disoriented me. It sounded like a movie theater's subwoofers were scattered around and turned up full blast.

I clamped my hands over my ears but it didn't do much good. The sounds vibrated through my chest and sent my ears ringing.

Out of the cracks, sharp steeples erupted. Two castles thrust out of the ground, flanking me. Tall, thin and beautiful, they grew until the mirror images towered above the land. The one on the right could have been made out of rubies. The one on the left was made out of polished white marble that gleamed like diamonds.

My knees gave out, and I collapsed to the ground. The image directly ahead of me displayed heavy mist, hanging just past a cliff. The mist began to swirl like a tornado, then suddenly the peaks of a green castle exploded through the clouds. It looked just like the other two castles, with multiple towers of different heights. But this castle wasn't on land. It floated on the clouds. A drawbridge extended out of the huge, wooden front door and attached to the edge of the cliff. Emerald Castle. Where I was meant to be going.

To my right in the small space between the Ruby Castle and Emerald Castle, a hologram of Red Queen appeared. She was seated in a plush chair, embroidering a piece of red cloth. Hareson sat at a desk next to her, a completely normal human and writing on a piece of parchment with a quill pen. As the ground started to shake, Red Queen and Hareson gasped and leapt to their feet, dropping what they were doing.

"What is going on?" demanded Hareson.

"The Queen!" Red Queen gasped in horror—she knew what had just happened.

Hareson yelled in pain and bent over, clutching his head. Between his fingers, hare ears thrust out of his skull and extended up.

"Hareson!" Red Queen screamed, and reached for him.

A long, slender, red wand appeared in front of her face. It hovered in the air, glowing and sparkling softly.

She gasped and stumbled back, staring at it. "What's going on?"

Face taut, Hareson gaped at the wand. "That—that's the power of a Queen Candidate."

Red Queen's eyes were wide as her right hand slowly reached out and grasped the wand. She started to glow red, her hair blowing back with the power. The glow faded, and she was left staring at the object in her hand.

Between the Diamond Castle and the Emerald Castle, a hologram of a completely human Ace appeared. He lounged in a grass field, alone and staring up at the sky. As the ground began to shake, he jolted up to a sitting position and looked around in alarm. He faced my direction without seeing me and gasped, "The Queen!"

His eyes widened in horror. "Red!" He jumped to his feet, then stumbled. Groaning, he bent over, clutching his head just like Hareson had.

"What's going on?" Ace gasped. Cat ears popped out of his orange hair and a long tail sprang out of the seat of his pants.

He didn't have time to investigate his new ears or appendage. The ground at his feet wrinkled, then cracked open, nearly knocking him from his feet. A long golden sword in a gold sheath rose out of the hole and floated in the air at eye level.

Ace's mouth dropped open. "A sword?" he whispered and glanced at the ground around him. "Why are you giving me a sword?" He wasn't talking to himself, he was talking to Oz. He reached out and grasped the hilt.

Gravity took hold of the blade, and it fell until Ace's strength took over. His right hand grabbed hold of the handle, and he pulled out the sword. He stared at the double blade in confusion.

The front door to the floating Emerald Castle slowly opened. A girl about twelve years old peeked her head out. "Hello? Is anyone there? Hello?" She walked out of the castle, blonde hair and blue dress swaying in the updraft from the cliff's edge. "What a curious place," she muttered. "Did I hit my head when I fell down that hole?"

The image's shaking and rumbling intensified. Holographic rocks fell from above, disappearing when they touched the ground. Mouth open, I looked up. Jewel Queen's castle was crumbling, falling apart like it was held together with wet glue. Screams and the sound of stone ripping from stone filled the air. All at once the castle collapsed on itself, sandwiching all its layers into one, forming the maze I hated so much.

It was enough. I was done with this place. Clawing at the ground, I scrambled to my feet and staggered to the door of the actual room. The ground wasn't shaking but the images moved so much that my balance was off. I grabbed the side of the door and pulled myself through. The images immediately disappeared, but my heart was still pounding.

"So the Alice Games began," whispered Winstum and Dean.

CHAPTER THIRTEEN

WHERE WAS THE EXIT? How could I get out of here? I didn't want to see anymore. I knew they were just visions, but they really happened. It was real. And I wanted to get out. Now.

I pelted down the corridors, taking every right turn as they came. It didn't matter how many times I turned; there was never an exit, only endless hallways and rooms.

Once I entered a room, and a scene appeared. A young woman—probably an Alice—stood in front of the Emerald Castle. She was beautiful in a blue dress, with her long blonde hair in curls down her back. She looked around at the people staring at her, then adoringly up at Ace by her side. He stood with his hand on his sword, body tense and a worried expression on his face.

No, no more scenes. None of this made sense anyway. Why was Oz showing me these things? I didn't even wait to hear what the Alice was going to say, just turned and ran out of the room and took the next right.

Finally I saw a difference from the dull gray of the stones. Light reflected off the wall ahead.

The opening. I had finally made it to the end of this horrible maze. I rounded the corner, relief nearly choked me, and promptly skidded to a stop.

It was an opening, an exit to the maze, but not one that I wanted.

Snow fell thick just on the other side of the maze's threshold, like there was a glass door keeping it out. Through the snow, blackened trees drooped under the weight of their burdens and past that, the outline of tall white castle peaks.

This wasn't a scene like everything else I'd seen, this was an actual opening. Snow. This was White Wizard's Domain.

Movement between the trees made me gasp and lunge back around the corner of the maze. Heart pounding a million miles per hour and all the hair on my body standing up, I peeked around the corner back at the opening.

An ice monster stood just outside the threshold of the maze, the vacant void of its eyes fixed on my location.

A lightning bolt of fear seared down my back. I slapped a hand over my mouth to stifle a small scream.

It lifted a clawed hand. It pressed against an invisible barrier between the Domains, gnashing its jaws together in frustration when it couldn't get through.

My hands shook as I slid around the corner and pressed my back against the cold wall. "It can't get in. It can't get in," I repeated over and over to reassure myself.

It was a small comfort. It was bad enough that I was stuck in this maze with these bloody scenes, adding ice monsters roaming the area would be worse.

My heart started to slow down some. I puffed out a breath and looked up at the cloudy sky. "Why did Oz bring me to the Diamond Castle?"

White Wizard wanted to kill me. That was a fact. He wanted to kill me and Red Queen. Everyone else was too lowly for him to care about, that much was apparent. But what about Ace? What made Ace so special that White Wizard still kept him around?

Ace was the Cheshire Cat. He wasn't always, but apparently he'd been doing White Wizard's bidding for a long time. I'd just witnessed that. It was one of the few things I understood.

It felt like there was a black hole in my chest, threatening to suck out all my air and leave me numb. I shouldn't be numb, I shouldn't be so upset about Ace betraying me. It had been just words so far—Red Queen's words. Nothing in Ace's actions had shown that he intended to hurt me.

It was all becoming too much. My emotions were in shambles, between thoughts of Ace and what I should do about Red Queen, and my nerves were strung about being lost in this stupid maze.

But it wasn't just any maze. I knew that now. It was the remnant of Jewel Queen's castle. Another testament of how White Wizard had hurt Oz. And for what? His father's pride, then finally his own? Because he couldn't understand the lesson Jewel Queen was trying to teach him?

Red Queen wasn't chosen until after Jewel Queen died. Did anyone ever give her the same lesson? Was she ever taught anything about her Role? What a heavy weight to have to try and figure it all out alone.

"Gah!" I clamped my hands over my ears. "Does anything in Oz make sense?"

I was seriously done with this maze. I pushed off the wall and hurried back the way I'd come. The hall divided into three ways. I stopped, frowning at the yellow path highlighting the whole floor. The reason why I came down this hall originally was because it was the next right turn in my constant right-only path. A logical path.

What was it that Red Queen said? There was more to Oz than logic. After all, the very emotions of the Queen affected Oz.

Frowning, I looked over my shoulder down the path to Diamond Castle. So the logical path took me to White Wizard. And Red Queen was anything but logical.

I should continue my right-only path, there was such a high chance of walking in circles if I didn't. Instead, I walked forward and went down the middle path. A part of me was hoping that a magic door would suddenly pop up and let me out now that I didn't choose the logical path. It didn't.

It was just a long, skinny corridor. Then a short, fat one. Sure that I was going in circles now, I took the next left.

"Shh!"

"Shh!"

I jumped and looked around wildly. Like before, Dean and Winstum weren't physically there. But the urgency in their voices made the hair on the back of my neck rise.

"He's here."

"Quiet. He's here."

Heart pounding like a jackhammer, I looked around. White Wizard? Was he mad that I wouldn't go into his Domain? I wanted to call out and ask who was here, but at the same time, that could give away my location to whoever it was.

Calm down, I ordered myself. Panicking wasn't going to do me any good, and I'd already done a lot of it lately. I took some big breaths, working on slowing my heart rate.

"Your fur's all ruffled," a lazy voice said from above me.

I jerked toward the sound. The air whooshed out of me in relief. "Ace." Then I paused. Should I be relieved?

He lounged along the top of the wall, dressed in the same clothes as this morning–shirt included. His chin rested in the palm of his hand, and his tail flicked lazily. Brown eyes stared down at me in curiosity, even if he didn't make any move to join me on the ground.

I leaned against the opposite wall and looked up at him, surprised how just his appearance slowed my blood pressure. He was the enemy, right? Careful not to lose my cool, I asked, "What are you doing up there?"

"Watching," he responded.

I shook my head. "How long have you been there?" And how had he gotten his shirt back? Not that I expected him to run around without one. But apparently he was able to sneak into Red Queen's tent and get it without anyone knowing, in the short time it took me to put it down and walk across the camp. Not an easy feat.

His shoulder jerked. "Not long. You're pretty lost, aren't you?" His head cocked to the side. "And shaken."

I let out a breath and looked away, my hand coming up to tug at my hair. Honestly, after what I've seen, who wouldn't be? Still, it was a policy of mine not to show that side of me to anyone. My lips thinned in annoyance. "Is it that obvious?" I glanced back up.

His ears twitched as he nodded. "Yes."

I sighed in defeat. Well, at least only one person saw me lose my head. "Sorry about that. I'm not used to seeing scenes and people appearing out of thin air."

"Scenes?" Ace eyes widened processing my words. "You mean, Oz is talking to you?" Shock laced his voice. He sat up and looked around, body poised and alert. "Here? In the Jewel Castle ruins?"

"Oz is talking to me? Is that what's going on?"

"What did you see?" His eyes were serious for once.

I stared up at him, trying to figure out what I should tell him. It would be nothing new to him, right? After all, a lot of what I saw involved him. It seemed like everyone knew when Jewel Queen died and how, so it wouldn't be interesting. And I'm sure everyone knew that White Wizard wasn't a fan of Red Queen. That left one scene. When White Wizard murdered someone for the first time and Ace failed to arrest him.

I played the scene over in my mind. Ace had tried to do the right thing in the beginning. It wasn't until Red Queen was threatened that he caved. To protect her.

I frowned. Ace was given a sword when Jewel Queen died, just like Red Queen was given a wand. That didn't seem like the type of sword to just leave lying around. Why hadn't I ever seen it on him? I'd only seen knives.

"Ali?" Ace prompted.

I blinked and focused on him. "Ah, sorry." My hand flapped casually. "I don't think I saw anything interesting to you. I don't even understand what I saw." It was only a half-lie.

His ear twitched, but he didn't contradict me.

Sighing, I turned in a circle and gazed at the walls. I needed to change the subject. "I just wish I knew how to get out of here. If I could at least see where I was going, it would make things so much better. I hate running around without a point of reference."

My feet stopped, facing Ace up on the wall. A thought came to me so strong that my palm slapped my forehead. How stupid. I could have seen where I was going this entire time. And maybe I would have been spared all the anxiety and might not have seen those awful things. Why hadn't I thought of climbing the walls? Only—Ace was up there now. If I went up there, that would be putting me in arm's length of him. And I didn't know if I could trust him—he was the Cheshire Cat. That said, I couldn't stay here forever. The clock was ticking for me, and I was who-knows-how-far from the way home.

Ace continued to watch me like I was an interesting movie.

Determined, I faced the wall under him and took a breath. I really wasn't athletic but I was going to attempt it anyway. The wall was seven feet tall. I only had a foot and a half to climb, as long as my spaghetti arms didn't give out. I didn't really want an audience right now, especially one that was trying not to smile over how serious I was being.

"What are you doing?" he asked.

"Something smart. Or something stupid. I'll tell you in a minute," I muttered.

With that, I ran at the wall. My right foot lifted, connected with the wall and boosted me up. Encouraged, my left foot tried to mimic the movement. I went another foot up before the turf under my boot slipped. Gasping, I lunged forward and clung to the top of the wall, my head leaning over the corridor next to me. The dirt was a long way down from here.

Ace leapt to his feet and reached for me. "What in Oz are you doing?" He grabbed my arm and started to pull me to my feet on top of the wall.

My breathing came in shallow little gasps. "If I can see where I'm going, I can find my way out of here. Why wander aimlessly in the maze when I can just walk on top of it and be done all the sooner?" My body shivered up to a standing position.

His daredevil smile opened wide over his handsome face. "That's clever. However ..." He didn't finish.

Suddenly the wall jerked. Or maybe the ground did. Whichever the case, the wall that was only seven feet tall rose to be twenty feet tall.

Ace bent his knees to adjust to the sudden change in height, the gleam of a challenge in his eyes.

I yelped and grabbed at Ace. One hand clutched the material over his heart while my other arm clamped around his neck. My teeth clenched as I buried my face into his chest—enemy or not.

He wrapped an arm around my waist and grabbed my elbow with his other hand. He wobbled us back into balance, then waited.

When the wall stopped shaking, I glanced down at the ground, suddenly so far away. "What just happened?" My voice was fainter than I wanted it to be.

He stared down at me, ears twitching mischievously. "What? Are you scared of heights?"

"No, not really," I muttered, trying to hammer the idea into my mind. "There isn't a logical reason to be. I mean, people go up and down every day. It's simply a change in elevation. I, ah, just wasn't expecting a sudden onset of it. Why did the wall, you know, rise?"

Ace nodded, amusement. "You broke the rules." He waited until I looked back at him. "It's not allowed for the Alice to go over the maze. Oz was trying to prevent that."

My eyes widened. "So it wants to kill me?" I was shocked. I thought this place was supposed to like the Alice.

"Not kill." Ace shrugged. "Actually, it seems to like you. I don't think it's ever talked to another Alice like this before. But Oz does punish those who break its laws." There was bitterness in his voice as his ears flattened back against his hair. He looked out over the ruins.

What rules did he break? I wanted to ask, but I couldn't. Was it things that White Wizard made him do, or ones he chose to do himself?

I stared up at him for a moment, then realized how close our faces and bodies were. "Ah." I stepped back. I was sure I imagined his hand flexing briefly in resistance against my back before he let go.

Ace came out of his thoughts. That playful smile spread over his face. "Is there a problem?"

Curse me, what was up with this constant heat on my face? "No, ah, there isn't." Except I really shouldn't be like that with him. You'd think I was smarter than this. I cleared my throat and looked around, not down, trying to find something to distract myself. From this height, it was easy to do.

At the same time Oz was punishing me for going over the walls, it was rewarding me too. The constant cloud coverage and perpetual mist that surrounded the maze lifted enough that I could see the whole layout of Oz around me. The three distant castles gleamed in the sun like jewels, putting buildings like the Neuschwanstein to shame. They were all structurally similar, but the air surrounding the buildings was very different.

Behind me, the Ruby Castle gleamed like a cozy fire, warm and inviting. Its glistening pale red walls and dark ruby roofs atop the turrets vibrated with life. The lush greenery around it thrived.

In front of me was the Emerald Castle. It was just as beautiful, but there was a feeling of mystery and separation about it. It wasn't just because the castle was literally resting on clouds, there was something off about it. As if, even though it was attached with a drawbridge, it wasn't fully connected to the land. While its pale green walls and deep emerald roofs gleamed, the light seemed to come from the inside, instead of the sun above it.

The last castle on my left was no less beautiful. It was the closest, looming overhead and jutting out of the ground like a frosted diamond, gleaming in the sun with assertiveness. It might be my preferred color scheme for a castle, but just like its owner, there was a feeling of coldness. The vegetation around the structure was few and far between. What plants were present looked shriveled and hampered under snow. I couldn't see them, but I knew there were monsters roaming around the snow, perfectly blending in. The Diamond Castle only had a few, small windows.

"It looks more like a prison than a castle," I muttered, not realizing the words were verbal until I heard them in my ears.

Ace followed my gaze. He nodded slowly. "That's because it is. The Diamond Castle is where White Wizard is locked up during Red Queen's rule."

"With the Cheshire Cat," I muttered softly. With Ace.

How was it possible the teasing man standing next me could be that scary tiger I met the first night I was here? He'd been so threatening, so vicious while fighting Lional and chasing me out of the Ruby Castle. Why was he so different now? Which one was he?

Ace's mouth thinned in distaste. "Yes. They are locked in there together—until the Alice Games begins." Contempt weighed heavily on his words. His own tone must have startled him because he blinked and looked down at me with a forced carefree air. "Well, what would you like to do?"

I stared at him a couple seconds longer before I frowned around at the endless walls. At least I was closer to the end than I thought. "I'm ready to get out of here." I pointed ahead, to the other side of Ace. "That looks like the other opening, right?"

It opened up to a shallow ring of forest. On the other side lay multicolored patches of farmland, surrounding small towns. Some distance beyond that was a forest that was slowly swallowed up by mist so thick, I couldn't see anything under it. Peeking out of the mist was the Emerald Castle.

"Shall we?" Since he was already in the front, Ace took the lead. He walked along the stone top with confidence.

I looked down at the narrow bridge I had to walk on. Just looking down made my palms sweat and my heart race. One wrong step, and I was in for a serious injury that I was sure wouldn't heal in the morning. Suddenly this didn't seem like such a good idea.

I swallowed and willed my heart to slow. I moved a couple of steps forward. My legs wobbled and my breath caught.

Ace walked back to me. Without asking, he reached out and took my hand.

The heat of his hand in mine seemed to travel up my arm and sit in my cheeks. It was embarrassing that I blushed like this every time I touched him, especially when there was no way to hide it. Even so, just holding his hand gave me a sense of balance that I didn't have before.

"So, Ali, tell me about yourself."

I breathed out a weak chuckle. His attempt to distract me was transparent—but still it was sweet. I drew a deep breath and moved one foot forward, clutching his hand. He raised his eyebrows, waiting. Oh, he was actually expecting an answer.

"Well, I'm, ah, just about to graduate high school and

start at Cornell. I was actually taking a tour of the campus when I," I paused, trying to come up with a good way to put getting shoved down two flights of stairs, "came here." I took another wobbling step forward, and Ace smiled, his eyes dancing.

"What's a Cornell?" he asked as he led me forward. He was careful to keep his tail tucked to the side so I wouldn't trip on it.

Holding his hand made things easier. It was hard to tell if it was because he improved my stability with the extra contact, or if his touch was that reassuring. I should let go, but a larger part of me didn't want to. Following him, my steps became sturdier.

"It's a university," I answered.

"What's that?"

"A university?" I asked in surprise. "It's a place of higher learning. People go there to learn more. You don't have them here?"

Ace's head bobbed in thought. "There's nothing like that here. Sounds like fun, actually. We do have a large library in Ruby Castle. Past Queens had people write down their skills and knowledge to be left in the library for those who could read." His voice grew wistful and maybe a little sad.

Right, he was the grandson of a scholar. "You don't look like the kind of guy who sits there and reads in a library." He looked like a Californian jock, ready to hang out on the beach and have fun with all the girls in bikinis. Definitely not the kind of guy who would hold my hand. A frown tugged at my mouth as pain stabbed in my chest.

He flashed a smile back over his shoulder, one ear flopped to the side. "Surprise you? I actually spent a long time in that library, reading about Oz and other things. The library in Jewel Castle was bigger, but after it was destroyed, we were only able to replace half of it." He faced forward as we skirted over a right turn. "It was a good place to hide when I wanted a break. There weren't many people who visited it, and fewer who could climb high enough to bother me. There was this thin, tall window at the top in the corner. It was the perfect place to read and look at Oz when I just wanted to relax." His voice was thick with nostalgia.

I smiled, just picturing it in my head. It sounded like a wonderful place. Briefly, I wondered if I was a person he would come down for. My eyes flared in surprise. No, I did not want to be special to him. He was the Cheshire Cat. Even if we lived in the same world, he wouldn't even see me in the crowd.

My toe caught on a rock jutting up, and I pitched forward. Before I could even gasp, Ace had me in his arms, wrapping his fingers around my shoulders and using his body to catch mine. Shocked at how fast he reacted, I stood with my cheek pressed against his pounding heart, hands spread on his chest.

He was so in tune with me, he knew I was tripping before my mind even registered it. That knowledge caused my heart to race as much as his closeness.

My cheeks went up in flames and I pushed back, an embarrassed smile on my lips. "Sorry, I'm a klutz sometimes."

"Really?" Ace's brows went up and his head cocked to the side. "I had the impression that you were overly observant and knowledgeable about your surroundings."

I looked to the side, blushing more. That was true, unless I was distracted by something—or someone—else.

Ace took my hand and started along the wall top. "What do you study at the university?"

"Botany. The study of plants." I relaxed, concentrating on the subject. It was safer to think about than the large warm hand enfolding mine.

Ace laughed. "Ah, I should have guessed." We walked around a left turn. "You were fascinated with the water lilies."

I sighed. I'd hoped we wouldn't talk about those flowers. "Yeah, they were interesting." I paused. "Red Queen and Hareson seemed to be afraid of them, but they didn't seem dangerous to me."

Ace shrugged. "It depends on who's around."

So if Ace was around, they were safe? Interesting. "I want to study them more. From the way you talked, no one else from my world has studied them. Think of the discovery I would make with all the information I could bring back to my world. Of course, I'm not even sure Earth's equipment would work on anything I bring back from here. Magic doesn't really exist on Earth." I paused, dreading what I was about to say. "Unfortunately, that can't happen anyway. I'm sorry, but I lost the water lily you gave me. It was in the wagon when I entered this Domain. I don't think I can get it back."

Ace glanced at me. "Hey, it's okay. It's just a flower."

"No, it wasn't," I mumbled.

His ears folded back against his hair but he didn't say anything. We walked in silence for a minute. Ace was the first to speak. "Why are you so interested in plants?"

Why did he have to ask that question? Did I really want to alienate him by telling him the honest truth? When I didn't answer at first, he glanced over his shoulder, expecting. I bit my lips together.

It wasn't until he looked forward—not at me—that I finally answered. "Plants don't like or hate you because of who you are. They're plants. They don't care if your IQ is higher than theirs or how low your EQ is. Or that you don't care about fads or fashion. They don't whisper behind your back because they don't understand you. I can go into a forest, be surrounded with hundreds of life forms, and be at peace."

I paused, a little shocked that I finally voiced the resentment I'd always buried. Usually I pretended not to care. Why should I bother with people who never tried to comprehend me? Despite how logical my mind was, my feelings weren't.

I looked to the side. "I'm sure you wouldn't understand."

Ace gave a mirthless laugh. I hadn't heard that tone from him before, so bitter and hard. It was chilling. "I understand all too well." He was quiet for a minute, tail twitching. When he spoke again, his voice was carefully light. "Did you have that lonely of a childhood?"

I shook my head, biting my lips. "No, not really. I have an older and a younger brother. I do have friends, but high school was tough. That's the learning place you finish before university. Everyone there was so hot blooded with hormones, it was stupid." My free hand jumped up and pulled at my hair. "I'm not very good with emotional people. I'd rather fix their problem and send them on their way than get tangled in it." I looked around the ruined castle. A lot of good that philosophy was doing me right now.

My eyes dropped to the ground, and I sucked in a breath.

He glanced back to ensure I was okay, then motioned with his chin. We came to a stop.

Grasping his steel-like arm to anchor myself, I leaned

around and saw what he gestured to. "Ah." I sighed, staring at the eight foot gap between the walls. "It's a dead end." We'd been getting close to the end, but now we'd have to backtrack a long way. How long would this place torture me?

"Here we go." That was the only warning Ace gave me before he scooped me up in his arms.

My heart dropped, and an extremely humiliating and girlish squeak escaped. We were twenty feet in the air!

"What are you doing?" I gasped and pushed against his chest, wiggling.

He grimaced and wobbled on the wall.

I froze, heart in my throat and ready to spew.

He set me down and held onto my forearms to help keep me balanced. "I'm taking you to the other side. That's where you want to go, right?"

I stared up at him, mouth parted. "How do you expect to do that?" I wildly motioned to the gap. "It's eight feet across. It's not like we can just jump."

He smiled and shrugged. "That's exactly what I'm going to do."

I gaped at him. Jump across? He could do that, while carrying someone? I'd already started to get the sense that he's not a normal human, but to be able to do that—I couldn't wrap my mind around it.

Ace was the Cheshire Cat. What if this was just a trick, and he dropped me on purpose? After all, wasn't he supposed to do what the White Wizard said? And the White Wizard didn't want me to get to the Emerald Castle. How could I trust him, and how crazy had I been to trust him this far?

I must have been quiet for too long because Ace gave a

little laugh and shook his head. "It's really not that hard. Trust me."

I blinked out of my thoughts and stared up into his rich, laughing, brown eyes. "Can I? Can I trust you?"

His eyes widened in shock when I turned his flippant words serious. His smile slid away, leaving his face blank. Then he nodded, his eyes piercing into mine. "Yes. You can."

I wanted to. Despite all the logic that said that I shouldn't, there was a part of me that wanted to trust him more than anything. Almost more than getting home. It was a part of me I normally didn't listen to, since it tended to get me in trouble. But for once, I didn't fight it.

I nodded slowly. "Okay."

His smile was instant and brighter than the sun. There was no tease twinkling in his eyes, just pure joy. It was breathtaking. But he only let me see it for a moment before he coughed and looked to the side. He swallowed hard, his Adam's apple bobbing, as he reigned in his emotions. "Here we go." He warned and scooped me up again.

Gasping anew, I wrapped my arms around his neck for dear life as I prepared to die.

We didn't fall. Holding me, he leapt across the gap and landed on the next wall as lithely as the cat he was. Maybe it was because I hadn't let go yet, but he didn't try to set me down.

"Are you sure you're not afraid of heights?" he asked in mild amusement, the skin of his throat moving against my forehead.

My fingers should have dug holes in his shirt by how tightly my shivering hands were clenched. "Of course not." My voice was barely audible, face pressed into his shoulder. I took a deep breath and forced my body to relax. My hands let go of his shirt and pressed against his chest. "But let's not do that again."

He set me back on my feet, taking hold of my hand again. His smile was quick and amused. "I'm afraid we'll have to unless you want to do a lot of backtracking."

I followed his gaze. There was at least one more gap before the end. Since he had the strength and athleticism, it would be easiest if he got me down too. My nostrils flared as I sucked in a breath and let it out. "Yes, we will."

His brow rose, ears coming forward with interest. "Do you always do things you hate?" He chose a direction and started to tow me across the wall.

I laughed. "I've done homework fourteen out of the eighteen years I've been alive. I might be good at studying, but it doesn't mean I enjoy math or English. I got A's in them, but still." I paused, realizing he might not understand all of what I just said. "Ah, an A is the highest score you can get in school." My hand tugged at my hair.

His head cocked to the side. "If you don't like it, why do you do it?"

"For a scholarship—ah, a free pass— to my university." We took a turn and continued to walk. "Universities are expensive."

"Your parents are poor or unwilling to help?" he asked. His ear cocked back to listen.

"Neither. They're both teachers and doing all right. If I asked, they would have been willing to help, but I wanted to do it on my own."

"You are an odd Alice." His head shook and tossed a smile back at me. "Do you ever ask for help?"

I jolted and glanced away. Color hit my cheeks as my brows furrowed. It wasn't a new realization. After all, my independence was the main conflict in the few relationships

I'd tried. "If it's my problem, I'm going to fix it." I looked back at him. "Haven't you ever done something you hated for a cause?" I asked, trying to change the subject back to him. Instantly I regretted asking the question. Because I already knew his answer.

Instead of laughing and brushing it off like a carefree cat, he broke my gaze and looked around the maze. "We should go. Red Queen will be waiting for you."

I bit my lips. What had he done that he hated so much? Was it things that White Wizard made him do? I'd seen and heard so many things in this maze that changed my initial image of him.

After our first meeting, he seemed like a laid-back guy who was too carefree to have loyalties. Now that wasn't the picture. Honestly, wasn't it the girl who was supposed to be complicated? This man-cat was the most interesting person I'd ever met. I was dying to study Ace and find out everything I could.

It made me think of something I've been wondering about for a while. "Ace, why did you stop being a knight?"

He stopped walking at a gap between the walls. "Whoever said I was a knight at all?" he asked, laughing like his usual self. "Here we go again." He scooped me into his arms.

This time I was ready for it. Sort of. I buried my face into his shoulder, and my breath stopped until he landed. The air whooshed out of me as he set me on my feet. "Red Queen did." And Oz. After all, it did give him a sword. First he was White Wizard's squire. Then he was Red Queen's knight, but now he's not? What happened?

His smile slipped. "Red Queen has countless knights. And Lional, the best Queen's Knight there ever was. Why would she bother with someone like me?" He shrugged it off, but the hurt undertone in his voice tugged at my heart.

Yet Red Queen said he was a sensitive subject. A confusing subject is more like it. I wanted to run my hands through my hair in frustration but was too afraid to let go of his hand.

A couple minutes later, we came to the edge of the maze. I stared hungrily down at the open ground. The stretch of bare dirt went only a short distance before it was swallowed up by small trees and bushes, like the ones I ran through to get to this Domain. The Yellow Path pointed in a narrow line straight to the trees.

"Last time," Ace said, and picked me up.

The leap down was worse than the leaps across. My stomach rolled as the air rushed by my ears. I'd have preferred a fifty-foot dive on a rollercoaster than that twenty-foot fall. At least a rollercoaster has harnesses and can't drop you. As it was, Ace didn't drop me, and we landed safely on the ground.

Still, my knees were like water, and I sank to the wonderful, flat ground when he set me down. I gulped in air and tried to settle my stomach. When I was sure I wouldn't humiliate myself in front of him, I gave a weak smile. "I should have said this earlier, but thanks."

Emotions played on his face, switching too fast for me to catch. His hand reached out, hesitated, and then brushed my hair with a feather-like touch. He crouched down in front of me and smiled, looking like he had somehow lost a game but was happy about it. "You're welcome."

Just like that first magical morning in front of the water lilies, I wanted time to stop. To stay like this forever, with his warm hand on my head and that sweet lost puppy look in his eyes.

Voices echoed out of the trees, and the moment was ruined. I turned toward them.

"I can feel her!" I recognized the deep voice rumbling through the foliage. Lional. "Can you hear her yet?"

"I think so. I heard two people. No—one? She's around here somewhere," Hareson answered. "Ali! Ali, come out!"

My muscles stiffened. Oh no. If they saw Ace, would it start another fight? The memory of the two large cats tearing at each other was bad enough. I didn't think I could handle seeing Ace, as a man, fighting with Lional again.

I turned around, then slumped forward to the ground, relieved yet slightly disappointed at the same time.

Ace was gone.

CHAPTER FOURTEEN

"ALI!"

Collecting myself and quickly categorizing all the information I had learned in this ruined castle, I stood up and started to push my way through the dense trees. "Hareson! Lional?" I called back to them. The patch trees of wasn't as wide as it seemed, and the words had barely left my mouth when I stepped out onto a bare road.

Hareson and Lional stood just feet from me. They both wore telltale signs of the fight that had been raging when I ran away, but they were both alive.

"Where's Red Queen?" I thought she'd be here with them.

Hareson motioned to the right. "She was needed at a Munchkin village a little farther down the road. We took her there before coming back for you."

I nodded slowly and tugged at my hair. "Is she okay?"

Lional snorted. "Of course she is."

I smiled. Of course she is. As if he would let anything happen to her. But I wasn't really asking about her physical wellness.

Lional and Hareson were still injured—Oz had not yet reset, so it was still the same day. I looked up at the sky. I wasn't an expert on time based on sun locations, but things didn't seem to add up. By the location of the sun, it was a lot later than when the raid started.

"How long was I in there?" I asked.

Hareson pulled out a watch from his breast pocket. He clicked it open. "Seven hours and twenty-three minutes. Why do you ask?" He snapped it shut and put it away.

I shook my head. "No, I couldn't have been gone that long." I was only lost for a couple of hours before Ace came. How much distance was between me and the Emerald Castle now? Was I going to make it by False Dawn?

Lional looked at the trees, face hard and almost regretful. "That Domain is separated from this world. It's time and ours are different."

I stared at him, a little surprised at how quickly he answered. After all, the last time I was with him, I'd been fighting with his beloved queen. My eyes skimmed over the torn patch on his white shirt and the gauze wrapped around his arm. His abrasive personality was off-putting, but I'd seen the way he fought to protect Red Queen and me. Even if he could permanently die, he would still lay down his life for her and, consequently, me. The perfect Queen's Knight.

What was it White Wizard had said to Ace? Something about the Knight of Oz. "Have you ever heard of the Knight of Oz?" I asked.

Lional jolted like he was struck with lightning. His lips pulled down in a surprised frown.

Hareson frowned too, but in a puzzled way. His head cocked to the side, ears twitching. "The Knight of Oz? Where did you hear that, Ali?"

"Ah, I don't remember where I heard it." I waved my

hands, trying to dismiss his question. “I just did, and I wanted to know if you knew who he was.”

Lional muttered something about “Odd Alice” under his breath and walked off. Not far away were three horses tied to a tree. He untied them and started back with them in tow.

Hareson motioned with his hand, and we started to walk to Lional. “The Knight of Oz is a legendary person. There have been five known Knights of Oz throughout Oz’s history.”

“Six,” Lional corrected. He handed the reins of a horse to Hareson.

Hareson’s ears flopped as he nodded his head to the side, apparently as surprised as I was that Lional would know. “Ah, six. So sorry, Ali.”

So they did know about it. I didn’t know if the Knight of Oz was an important element to fixing Oz, but it was best to know all the facts when trying to solve a problem.

Hareson mounted a brown horse and waited.

Lional faced me. “Have you ever ridden a horse before? Some of the more recent Alices hadn’t.”

That was probably because our technology had changed. As curious as I was to ask when the last Alice Games was held, it wouldn’t reflect on the time on Earth, since the two worlds were on different times. “Ah, no. I’ve always wanted to.”

Lional nodded. Then he reached down, grasped my waist, and set me sidesaddle on a bay horse. The horse snorted and looked back at me, obviously sensing I was a newbie.

Without further ado, Lional hopped on his palomino, took my reins, and started us off down the road. They might not be able to see the Yellow Path, but they obviously knew the direction to go. The yellow line stayed dead center on the dirt that our horses clopped on.

"Thanks," I muttered. "Next time, I can get on by myself." I grabbed the saddle horn as the horse started to shift under me. I'd never been on one before and could only base my judgment on books and movies, but next time I wanted to ride normally. It felt too easy to slip off on side saddle, and I wasn't even wearing a skirt.

"Maybe, but I bow down to only one person," Lional grumbled.

I can step in the stirrup by myself, I thought, but I let it go. Instead I went back to the more interesting subject. "What does the Knight of Oz do?"

Hareson glanced at Lional to see if he would respond. When the large man didn't, the hare-man spoke up. "Well, legend says the Knight of Oz is a helper to the Queen. You see, the Queen is the go-between of Oz and the people. When the Queen needs help for various reasons, Oz will choose a Knight of Oz. There haven't been very many, though, because the Knight is allotted special privileges. While the rest of the people are under the Queen's rule, the Knight of Oz only answers to Oz."

"Is the Knight always male?" I asked, intrigued. After all, 'queen' to them was gender-neutral.

"There has been one female Knight of Oz," Lional said, his voice a low rumble as if he really wanted to answer.

I nodded. I guessed Oz really didn't care much about gender. And if the Knight was given special powers like the Queen, physical strength didn't matter anyway. "Who is the Knight of Oz?" I asked. "Is it you, Lional?"

His head tilted to the side and he looked at me like I was crazy. His tale flicked twice.

I shrugged. "Well, you have the perfect physique for it,

and you are very loyal to Red Queen. You seem like the perfect candidate."

He shook his head. "No. I only want to be a Queen's Knight."

Hareson tugged at his ear then smoothed his hair back into place. "There is no Knight of Oz right now, Ali. As I said, there aren't very many people with that title. It's not like a constant position that one holds, and it's hard to acquire. It takes a very special type of person to be a Knight of Oz, and no one even knows what skills that position requires. Apparently that type of person doesn't exist in Oz right now."

I wasn't giving up yet. "Maybe, but would you recognize the Knight like you would the Queen or the Alice? Is it possible that the Knight does exist, but you just don't know it?"

My questioned surprised them.

"It's possible," Hareson admitted slowly. "The only one who knows who the Knight of Oz is would be the Queen. If the identity weren't disclosed, the people would never find out."

Lional scowled. "If that is true, then damn that Knight. To hide all this time and make us wait all these years." His voice turned into a snarl by the end of his words.

"What if they didn't know?" I said. My voice dropped in volume. "If Oz can only talk in pictures, how can it give clear instructions of what needs to be done? Everything that you know so far about the Alice Games is from trial and error and random guessing, right? What if the Knight of Oz has never figured out what he or she was supposed to do?"

Lional shook his head. "Oz, talking? Oz hasn't spoken since the Alice Games began."

Hareson's ears jolted straight and twitched. "Ali, where

did you learn all this?" He looked perplexed and more than a little alarmed.

They were that shocked to hear about Oz talking? Maybe I shouldn't tell them about it. "Is it so weird for me to know something about Oz?"

Hareson's hands moved while he tried to figure out how to explain. "There's never been an Alice who learned about the Knight of Oz. I can only think of a few people in Oz who might even know about it. As well as knowing about Oz speaking. The only one who is in the position to hear it is Red Queen."

But she even admitted that she couldn't hear Oz very well. So why could I? Did it have to do with where I had been at the time, in the ruins of Jewel Queen's Castle? Was I compatible with Oz somehow? Or did it just want to talk to me that badly, it forced the connection?

Connections ... What did Jewel Queen tell White Wizard when he was first elected? That some feelings clogged up the connection a queen could have with Oz. She specifically mentioned anger and resentment. Both of those, White Wizard had.

Red Queen had at least one of them too, I realized. I personally listened to her vent her frustration of her situation, when my own frustration hit the top. While I completely understood her feelings, what if those feelings were damaging her connection to Oz? Did Oz show me that scene because it wanted something from me?

"Enough of this chatter." Lional snorted. "We know the role of the Alices and what they need to do. It's not necessary for them to learn more."

My gaze dropped to the ground.

Hareson shot a glare at his companion. "Lional, that's not kind."

"It's true." His golden tail swishing in annoyance.

"I don't think so." I met Lional's golden eyes head on. "Knowledge is never unnecessary. Even if I'm just a visitor. I understand why you feel uncomfortable around me. I'm different from what you're used to, but everything about this world is different from what I'm used to. It might feel like I'm prying into your lives, but I don't want to make a mistake by overlooking a small detail. If I'm supposed to fix a problem, I'll fix it. Simply getting a wand out of a castle isn't good enough for me to risk my life for."

It was his turn to drop his gaze. His tail stilled.

Hareson watched the exchange with some surprise. "Come, let's hurry. Red Queen is not far away, and we need to get to Munchkin Town before night falls."

The forest gave way to farmland surrounding a cluster of brick buildings. It looked like a toy set from far away, with the bright red bricks and white trim. That impression didn't change as we got closer. The buildings were short, just like I expected from a Munchkin town. Munchkins milled around the fields, bringing in whatever they needed before sunset. The tallest person I saw—aside from Hareson and Lional—was about five feet tall. Finally seeing these people, it clicked why Red Queen was so short. She probably had Munchkin blood in her.

"Red Queen is this way." Hareson pointed to a building to the outside of the cluster. "She's in a meeting with several of the town elders in the region. They have come together to discuss how things are changing in Oz." His nose twitched. "Since this town is on the Alice Route, it was decided to meet here."

We rode over. When Lional helped me dismount, his hands were not as stiff as when he threw me on the horse earlier. Just as we got to the short door, it opened.

Red Queen stepped out and smiled at us. "Ah, Ali, Hareson, and Lional. Perfect timing." She walked over to us and turned to watch the seven or so people coming out. She smiled and waved to all of them as they gave farewell bows to Red Queen and walked away.

"What did they say?" Lional asked as soon as the last person was gone.

Red Queen's face fell in sorrow. "We have decided to go to war. They are on their way to collect their people. We'll meet at the Game Board tomorrow morning." She didn't look comfortable with the decision.

Guilt pounded through my veins, and I shifted uncomfortably. It was my casual comment that had started all this. I took a breath. "Red Queen?" I waited until she looked at me. "I'm sorry. I said a lot of things that I regret now. I wasn't trying to hurt your feelings. And ..." What else should I say? "I get that we are very different from each other. But I think we want the same thing. Not just for me to go home, but to fix Oz. Can we start working together?"

Slowly her shocked expression melted into an apologetic smile. Her eyes softened and shone like a chocolate diamond. "I am also sorry. I shouldn't have yelled at you like that. It was unfair of me." She took my hands and squeezed them. "And I would be so happy to work with you."

It was impossible not to smile back, even though I was surprised how fast she forgave me. Was that how it was for her? So simple, so quick to find the best? I nodded slowly. "I'm also sorry about the whole war suggestion. I just threw it out there, trying to come up with something new. I guess it was very Earth-like of me."

Red Queen gave a big sigh. "It was a suggestion that a lot of people liked. Maybe it's something we should have tried long ago. I still don't see the point of it, but the people want to try. They want to fight White Wizard's ice monsters and lock White Wizard up themselves. Make him stay in Diamond Castle with our own power. Maybe it's what Oz has been waiting for this whole time." Her hands trembled under mine.

"If it doesn't work, the people will just wake up tomorrow," Lional said casually.

And if it does, people could die forever, I thought.

Red Queen nodded and let go of my hands. "The plan for now is for you three to stay here for the night. The town elder himself is letting you stay in his house. With so many people around, it should be safer for you, Ali. The rest of the citizens will arrive here throughout the night. Then in the morning, we'll all travel to the Game Board together. Hopefully if Oz sees how serious we are, when you bring my wand out and White Wizard is bound, he will stay locked in the Diamond Castle forever."

I nodded, liking how decisive her voice was. Still I couldn't help but wonder what would happen to Ace then? "And the Game Board is?" That was the second time she mentioned it.

"The Domain around the Emerald Castle," Hareson supplied. "Not only is it where you need to go, but it's the best place to battle White Wizard and his monsters."

"Why is that?"

"Because it's the only location in Oz where White Wizard and I can be in the same place," Red Queen said, her face grave. And pale.

Hareson's nose quivered when he blew out a burst of air. He straightened, tucked an arm around his back and motioned to the door with an open hand. "Shall we fill our stomachs? There are people waiting to finally greet their Queen before the sun falls."

I looked around the buildings. Was there really one big enough for all three of us to stay in comfortably? I'd been in a Munchkin building before, when I first met Ace, and it barely fit two people sleeping. How would it fit a full grown lion and then some?

The thought made me pause. I guessed I wasn't going to be able to meet Ace again. He didn't like to be seen by other people—with obvious reasons that finally made sense to me. I'd never get to say goodbye. I sucked in a breath through the sharp pain in my chest and let it out slowly. *It's okay,* I told myself. *It's probably better this way. No closing for no beginning.*

Lional insisted on accompanying Red Queen to meet the people, which meant that Hareson and I had to come, too. It was intimidating to step out of the elder's tiny house, where we'd just had a peaceful dinner, to a sudden onslaught of people rushing at us.

Red Queen gave me an encouraging smile, then turned her radiant face to the citizens around her, touching hands and accepting flowers.

I shifted under all the curious stares. The people were as lost about what to think of me as I was of them. The Munchkins were all dressed in Old Dutch-like clothes, colorful skirts and pants with white shirts that matched the decor around them. The random tall people mingled in the crowd were dressed with a Renaissance flare, indicating they were from a different town.

But there was something strange about the crowd. The munchkins might be short, but there were no young people around us. I glanced up at the setting sun, just hovering above the tree lines. I was no expert on children, but it seemed a little too early for bed, right?

"Where are all the children?" I asked Red Queen.

Red Queen frowned at me. "No one's told you yet? There are no children. I was the last person born in Oz."

"What?" My wide eyes roamed the cluster of people squeezed between the red brick buildings. "How is that possible?"

Her brows pulled together. "It's common for the birth rate in Oz to slow when a new Queen Candidate is chosen, until the Candidate can build a connection with Oz. But babies stopped being born altogether about five years after White Wizard was chosen. Since the Alice Games started, birth, aging, and death do not happen here in Oz. Everyone has stayed the same age they were that day." Her features relaxed, and she moved over to someone beckoning to her, Lional and Hareson following in her wake.

I was more bothered about the idea than she was. She must be too used to it to care anymore. How many years had this cycle continued? If she was the last one born, then Oz must have already been sick at that point. Was that about the time when White Wizard started to change? I shouldn't be so surprised, I guess. Now some things I'd seen in the Jewel Castle ruins made sense. According to the scenes I saw in the maze, he used to be a likable person, but I could only conclude his personality changed when he became a Queen Candidate.

But Oz had brought in the Alices then, presumably to fix things. So why hadn't their choices been finalized? Why was Oz still going in a big circle? I only had one more night and a morning left to figure it out.

A flash of orange out of the corner of my eye caught my attention, and I turned my head to the right. Was that a person with bright orange hair sliding behind the red brick corner? Ace? My heart flipped with a sudden shot of adrenaline at the thought of seeing him again.

I glanced at my escorts. All three of them were in discussions with people. No one would notice if I slipped away and said goodbye to Ace. I had to be fast; the sky was starting to turn yellow.

Casually, I shifted over to the narrow alley. When I was sure no one was watching, I slid around the corner. The alley was empty. I flushed with embarrassment. I'd expected him to be there, waiting for me. Maybe I was being presumptuous. It wasn't like Ace has done anything expected since I met him.

A flash of color caught my eye, then ducked around the end of the alley.

"Ah, wait!" I called. "Ace!" I hurried after him. I rounded the corner at a run and staggered to a halt, barely stopping short of running into someone.

A tall man grinned down at me. Not a nice grin, either. It was more like he flashed his teeth at me. He was scruffy and unkempt. The orange that I'd mistaken as hair was an orange bandana around his black hair and, now that I was closer, easily the wrong shade.

Something else was wrong with him. His feet didn't fully touch the ground, just like the bandits that had attacked us earlier.

I stepped back, bells ringing in my head and my gut twisting in knots.

"If you were smart, you wouldn't go looking for him,

you know." He laughed, making my stomach sink farther. "But then again, if you were smart, you wouldn't leave the safety of Red Queen." He grabbed me.

I fought back, clawing, kicking, and biting. He yowled and cuffed the side of my head with his fist. I staggered backwards against the wall, seeing stars. By the time my vision cleared, my hands were bound, and he'd stuffed a gag into my mouth.

"Lord Hatter wants to talk to you, Alice," the man snarled in my face. "He hates to be kept waiting." He grabbed my bound wrists and hauled me to my feet.

Shock vibrated through my mind. No matter how much I tried, my screams never made it past the gag. How stupid. I should have screamed right away. The real stupidity was leaving Red Queen's side to chase after a possibility to begin with.

The sun was almost set, the air around us a dark shade of red. In minutes, Red Queen would be gone, and I doubted Hareson and Lional would find me in time. Desperate, I called out for someone who might actually care, but Ace's name never made it out of the gag, either.

"Quiet, girly," the man ordered. He started to drag me through the back streets toward the farm fields and the forest on the other side.

I wasn't going along without a fight. In minutes, I'd be a cat. If this man was an animal bigger than me, I would be in trouble. Well, more trouble. No matter how hard I wrenched at the coarse ropes around my wrists or kicked at him, nothing worked. He was so much stronger than me. I was like a doll. The only person hurting was me, as the ropes burned into my wrists.

"Stop it, girly." Irritated, he shook me until my brain rattled. "You stupid Alice."

Stupid for trying to save myself? It was obvious this man and the Hatter meant no good. It wasn't like they were kindly inviting me to have a tea party with them. This was a mafia.

By now it was harder to see in the street. As we passed by the last alley, I could see lamps around the square being lit. Suddenly there was a loud commotion behind us. Maybe Red Queen had finally noticed I was gone.

The man swore. He grabbed me and slung me over his shoulder.

I struggled harder than ever.

A second later, an unpleasant but familiar sensation hit my stomach. It hurt more because of the man's shoulder in my gut. I groaned with pain even though I was looking forward to changing. As a cat, I could slip out of the ropes and get away.

The man tossed me to the ground.

I yelped when my head hit the ground. *Don't pass out*, I prayed. The ropes started to slide off my thinning wrists. My body shrank more, and brown cat fur sprang from my every pore. It was like being forced into a tight rubber suit, and more painful than an ulcer, but maybe I could escape now. As a cat, I struggled to my feet. My front paws were shaking and my back legs could barely support my weight. My head was still spinning but I had to move.

I barely took a step when something grabbed the scruff of my neck. A hand? How was there a hand? Wiggling and clawing uselessly, I was wrenched into the air, a yowl escaping me. Helpless, I was swung around until I was nose to nose with the creature holding me. A new fear twisted my gut.

A baboon. He turned into a baboon! People think monkeys in general are nice since they assume they are closely related to humans. What people don't know is that primates, baboons in particular, are responsible for hundreds of human maulings every year.

The skin of his rainbow muzzle pulled back in a horrible grin. "Stupid girly." His other hand came up, revealing a cloth sack. Before I could protest, he stuffed me in it.

CHAPTER FIFTEEN

I WAS BOUNCED and tossed around in that suffocating bag for what felt like hours. The only saving grace was a small hole at the bottom of the seam. It wasn't large enough to get my paw through and didn't have loose strings I could pull at, but it provided fresh air.

Forever later, the bag I was in swung through the air and I landed on something flat and hard. When it didn't move, I assumed it was the ground. I curled into a ball, ears flat against my skull as muffled but obviously loud animal sounds penetrated the bag's material. The knot at the top of the bag started to jerk around, and the material loosened.

All the hair on my body stood up as the excited animal sounds coming from outside the bag got louder.

A baboon hand shoved its way through the opening and grabbed me.

I clawed and bit at him but was powerless as he dragged me out.

"Stop that," the baboon snapped, and shook me.

When my eyes stopped rattling, I got a good look

around the very noisy room. We were in a tall, gothic-style building. The marble might have been white once but now it was gray and stained, turning the potentially beautiful architecture dreary and threatening. Abused tables and benches were scattered around the cracked floor and pressed against the beaten walls and pillars. Even the beams overhead were marred with claw marks and feces.

A large group of predatory animals circled around me, mostly baboons and hyenas. They were unlike the host of animals I'd first encountered in the Ruby Castle. This group seemed to revel in their animal shape, showing their savagery by snapping and shoving at each other, barking and chattering in hot-blooded excitement. They stared at me, vicious intent seeping from their wild eyes. They were all tarnished and dilapidated. The dirty ground vibrated under their feet, as if Oz didn't want them to soil it.

I instantly wanted to be back in the bag.

"My, my. Boon, you've done well." A delightfully delirious, high-pitched male voice spoke up.

The animals shifted to reveal a raised platform at the top of the room. A battered, purple velvet throne was perched on top. Seated there was a hyena with a bulbous stomach and a top hat tied to his head with thin, black strings. Around the brim of the hat was a dingy, gold crown.

To the side of the throne a large copper bird cage was suspended a foot off the ground by a thick chain. The baboon walked over, opened the door and tossed me in roughly. He flicked a switch and locked it.

My claws squeaked against the copper bottom to steady myself as the cage shifted. I growled at the primate, then glared at the psycho on the throne. Apparently no one told him the hyena population was a matriarchy.

His upper lip pulled back in a toothy smile. "Welcome, Alice, to my Domain. I am Hatter."

I didn't bother to correct him since I didn't want him to call me by name anyway. "I gathered that already." My voice was flat, the best I could do in my bluff that I wasn't as scared as I actually was. "Why did you kidnap me and bring me here?"

He giggled. "Simple. I want something from you."

My tail swished, the copper bars messing with my fur. Who would have thought that a few hairs out of sync would be so annoying? Instinct demanded that I lick the offending fur back into place, but there was no way I was going to lick cat fur. "Why do you want something from me?" As if I would give him anything.

Air puffed out of his nose. "Because only an Alice, or someone possessing an Artifact from the other world, can go into the Emerald Castle." He gloated with excitement.

I paused, processing this new information. Ace had something from my world. He'd insisted on it the first time I met him. And I'd innocently given it to him—the Cheshire Cat.

Hatter's words crashed through my thoughts. "And now I can—" He paused and peered at me closely before jumping off the throne and running over.

He loomed over me with narrow eyes, and his lip pulled back as he sniffed desperately. This close, the crazy glint in his dark eyes was all the more apparent. He pushed at the cage, sliding me around in it, as he tried to get a better smell. "Where is it?" he yelled, his voice a clipped bark.

I flinched from the loud sound in my sensitive ears. "What? Where is what?"

"The Artifact! Where is it? Do you know how much

effort I had to go through?" He threw his head back and howled into the crowd. "Shirley!"

Movement in the crowd drew my attention from the crazy carnivore.

A sheep, the only one in the building of predators, waltzed to the front of the crowd. She was tall and skinny, her legs looking almost too long for her body. Her white hair was dirty in places, and her steps were bold but uneven. Every other step she took, her foot didn't touch the ground, as if she wasn't entirely rejected from Oz yet. She stopped, her body posed in a way that she must have thought was appealing.

Hatter glared down at her. "You dropped that necklace, right?" Hatter demanded. "You said you dropped the necklace." He stamped his foot like a child throwing a tantrum.

Dropped the necklace? I'd found it half hidden under my skirt after I was changed. My mind quickly played over that event again. The maids who'd dressed me in Ruby Castle all had sheep ears? Was this sheep one of those maids? Why was she here?

Just then her name clicked to me. Shirley. Wasn't that the name of the maid who'd found me right after the water lilies? She said she was helping look for me. Had she actually been looking for the necklace? But by the time she got there, Ace had already gone.

Shirley the sheep nodded eagerly to Hatter. "Yes, my Lord. I made sure she got it. I watched her pick it up." She was trying to act strong, but her voice wobbled.

At the sign of weakness, the hyenas in the crowd turned their heads to her, ears erect with interest. The hunters' eyes narrowed and their nostrils flared.

Pity swelled in me as I watched the maid. She looked

like some of the kids I've seen in school. Someone trying so hard to fit into a crowd that would just as soon eat you as call you a friend. I'd lost friends that way and never understood why someone would do that to themselves. Walk into such danger just because they wanted to change or feel accepted—even though it would never happen. It wasn't logical.

Hatter stared at her for a full minute before his disposition calmed. "Come here." He beckoned her.

She hurried to him, her moves dainty and poised to show off. She tip-toed up the stairs, knees jerking high in the process.

"You may touch the hat." Hatter tilted his head toward her.

A shiver went through her body. Her nose rose up and carefully adjusted the hat until it was dead center on his head. She shivered again, elated.

My tail twitched as I shook my head. This was crazy. "Why couldn't Shirley have just brought it to you?" I asked Hatter. "It would have been easier and spared us both the hassle."

Hatter looked at me like he'd actually forgotten I was there. "They would have known she had it, of course. It never would have made it out of Ruby Castle. And she would have been punished. And Shirley is just too precious for that." He leaned forward and *almost* touched her cheek with his nose.

She looked ready to swoon.

Animals in the crowd shifted and made noises of annoyance and jealousy. They were mostly female, I was willing to bet.

I couldn't figure out his appeal. Didn't the shmuck

know she was being played? I guess the promise of power was too seductive.

But Hatter's words made me think. Ace said any Role Player could tell where I was because I smelled different. And Hareson and Lional had been able to find me on the other side of the Domain boundary while I was in the maze. It must apply to my things, too. If Shirley had it, they would have been able to smell it on her and take it away. My smell must have masked the necklace so they couldn't tell it was still on me. It wasn't a bad plan. No one noticed I still had it except for one person.

I frowned. Ace had insisted that I give him something of mine. He knew it was there. Why did he want it so badly? He must know it could get him into the Emerald Castle. My mind drifted back to the conversation I overheard of Red Queen and Hareson. They said he wanted to get Blood out. What was Blood? Whatever it was, given the name, I can't see how it could be good in the hands of the Cheshire Cat.

It felt like my heart was in a blender and being pulsed to nothing. Was that the reason why he saved me the first night? The necklace disappeared with all my clothes when I became a cat and he needed to wait till I was human to get it? Was that why he'd been so kind to me? And after he got the Artifact, it was because I was nothing but a plaything?

I shouldn't be so hurt. I already knew from when Red Queen warned me. But I had thought that he was different with me, that maybe he even thought of me as different. I had thought he was someone I could trust. That everyone was wrong about him. I guess I'm as much a fool as Shirley is.

"You're handling this calmly." Hatter walked over and nosed the cage so it would swing.

My paws splayed out, claws protracting and scratching

against the metal cage in an attempt to stay steady. What was it with these people and swinging my cage? It wasn't bad enough I was in here, now they wanted to make me seasick too?

I shook my head, the pain in my heart strong enough to lessen the fear of my situation. "Why do you want to get in the Emerald Castle so badly?"

His ears perked. "Why? Why? Look at me." He posed, apparently ignorant to the fact that hyenas and top hats didn't mix well. "I am Hatter. The savior of Oz." He turned to the animals below. "The savior of Oz!" he shouted slowly and tossed his head up.

Cheers, growls, and shrieks exploded from the animals, causing me to flinch from the sudden ringing in my ears.

I stared at him, shocked at this new level of madness. How on earth could he believe something like that? Didn't he know anything about Oz? Even I knew that it reflected the feelings of the ruler, even in the Domains. That Oz was beautiful when Red Queen was in charge and a winter for White Wizard. Even the Cheshire Forest reflected Ace's vibrant, wild, and seemingly random attitude.

But this Domain was horrible. So dirty and distorted that even Oz didn't like it, as was apparent from the fact that the people here couldn't even touch the ground.

Couldn't Hatter see this?

I shook my head. When the cheering quieted, I asked, "I thought the only two Queen Candidates were Red Queen and White Wizard?" Although Shirley had said that there were other options. She was obviously wrong.

"Why should that little girl and that icicle be the only Queen Candidates?" Hatter sneered. "They've played long enough. I have just as much right as they do. It's time they bowed to me. And they will after I *save* Oz from their petty squabble."

My tail twitched. "I thought the Alice chose the next Queen."

The hyena snorted. "That's stupid. You don't live here. Why should you have a say? The people should choose, and they chose me." He motioned to the animals below and beamed when they started to cheer again. "Besides, it doesn't matter how the Queen Candidate is chosen if I have that red brat's wand and the sword. Then I'll show them what real power is."

What sword? I knew that Ace wanted to get Blood out of the Emerald Castle. Did Blood have a sword?

I was jolted out of my thoughts when Hatter swung my cage again.

"You're supposed to be more interesting," he whined. "You're taking this too calmly. Be like all the other Alices, and cry."

My ears perked up as a shock went through me. "Other Alices?"

He nodded. "I tried to befriend some of them, but it became a hassle. I only got my hands on two of them, though. It's taken me a couple tries to figure out how to get in the Emerald Castle." He hummed to himself. "You might have lived if I had gotten the Artifact. After all, I reward those who serve me."

My stomach knotted. I'd been so distracted with my thoughts of self-pity, that I spaced the situation for a minute. But hearing those words brought it all back. "I doubt that."

"But now I have to find a new way into the Emerald Castle. Only something from the other world can enter that place." His head cocked to the side, all pretense disappearing. "And the only thing I have from the other world is you."

He wasn't looking in my eyes anymore; he was looking at my body.

"What are you saying?" My voice was steadier than I felt. Luckily the cage had stopped moving, even if my stomach was still rolling.

Hatter didn't clarify immediately. He actually disregarded me entirely and started to talk to himself. "Carrying her body around would be annoying. Even carrying an arm or leg would take up too much room."

He is really contemplating this earnestly, I thought with disgust with how seriously he was dismembering me in his head and trying to figure out how my body would be convenient to him.

"I could just take her blood," he concluded brightly. "If I wear it on myself—that should be enough. With it smeared on my skin, I won't need to hold onto her." He nodded.

My mouth almost dropped in shock. "You're kidding." How could he think of something so twisted so quickly? Like walking around in someone else's blood was fine. This took the term "mad" to a new level. No wonder Oz was rejecting him and his people.

He jumped, remembering I was still right in front of his nose, and giggled. "Oh, I mean it." His head cocked to the side. "But she doesn't have enough blood in that cat shape. And what if it's tainted right now?" he mumbled to himself. He nodded slowly and raised his voice, like he meant to be heard now. "You're lucky, Alice. You get to live until dawn." Hatter turned and promptly ran into Shirley the sheep.

She stumbled and fell down.

Hatter staggered back. He shook his head furiously, the movement displacing his hat, and glared. "What are you doing here?" he demanded. "Get back down where you belong!"

She scrambled to her feet with a small bleat of fear and ran down the stairs. Animals bumped and snapped at her as she merged with the crowd.

Hatter sneezed after her. He gasped when he realized his hat was stuck to his cheek. "Hat!" he howled. "Hat!"

A female baboon and a hyena jumped out of the crowd and hurried over to him. They looked at each other and immediately started to snap at the competition while their prize continued to holler about his hat. The crowd burst into cheers and encouragement. The baboon finally landed a hard bite on the hyena's scruff and shoved her off the platform, causing the crowd to cheer louder.

The baboon proudly adjusted the hat back onto the center of Hatter's head.

He immediately calmed down. "Silence!" he yelled and turned to the baboon. "Get down."

She hurried down the stairs.

A growl rumbled from my throat.

"You're boring," Hatter whined. "Why aren't you funner?"

"More fun," I corrected.

He didn't hear me. He brightened. "Or do you think someone's going to save you? That brainless lion or the stuffy hare?" He giggled. "Which is it?"

The crowd erupted into laughter, high and manic.

The hair on my body rose and I glared. I wanted more than anything to say a name, any name, but honestly, I didn't have enough faith that anyone would come. I was left with nothing but being the butt end of a joke. One of my own making. After all, I was the one who wandered away from Lional and got captured—all because I thought I was special to Ace, that he'd come to see me one last time. And Lional can't come into Hatter's Domain during the Alice

Games unless he's invited to. I highly doubt Hatter's going to let him in.

Honestly, I deserved to be laughed at.

"Oh, that was good." Hatter stopped laughing, and the crowd slowly followed suit. "Stop laughing," he yelled to the few still going. He sniffed and looked at the people. "Go away. I want to sleep."

The crowd immediately began to disperse.

Hatter paused. "Shirley! You stay here!"

Angry chatter erupted in the crowd. From the center of it, Shirley pushed her way out of the agitated animals. Her prideful strut was marred by a newly acquired limp.

"Stay with the Alice." Hatter nodded towards my cage. "If anything happens to my property, it will be on your head." He turned and walked off the platform with Boon, my abductor baboon, following behind.

Shirley bent her knees and bowed her head low. The last person shut the door, and we were the only ones left in the room.

Feeling too stupid to be pitiful, I lay down, curling my paws up under my chest. It was oddly comfortable and relaxing, as if I curled up tight enough to protect myself from everything. Of course, that was all in my head, but I was content to lie to myself for a little while longer. My tail curled around me and flicked. Needing a distraction, I gazed at the daft sheep below.

If she was gone, I could figure out how to open the lock. It wasn't even padlocked—it had to be simple enough a baboon could operate it. And it was at nose level, right in front. Perfectly accessible to a cat's nimble paws. No one would know until dawn when I would be safe with Lional and Hareson. But if I opened it now, Shirley could hold it closed or call for help. Even if I ran, I was sure I would be caught. The idea of going through the physical pain they would be sure to inflict wasn't very appealing.

Shirley looked around the deserted room. I wasn't the best at reading sheep thoughts, but her human-like body language implied she found the now empty and messy room slightly distasteful. She brushed at the ground in vain for a second before she gave up and lay down on the dirty ground. She glanced at me, then jumped when she noticed I was staring at her.

"Why are you here?" I asked.

She jolted at my voice, then recovered and scoffed. "Lord Hatter told me to. Remember?"

"No. Why are you here, in this Domain and not at the Ruby Castle? You must be one of the maids who changed me when I first came to Oz. And you led me back to Red Queen after I came out of the Cheshire Forest."

She gave a mean laugh. "The Ruby Castle? You mean back where I'm just one of the many faces? There are thirty-one other maids who look just like me. Same face, same clothes. Here, I'm one of a kind. There's *no one* else like me here."

My eyes rolled. "That's because they've already eaten all the others, I'm sure." I shook my head. "Is this what you meant when you told me there were other choices? You can tell that it's not safe here. These people want to hurt you."

"That's not true." Her voice wobbled because she knew I was right. I'm sure her leg was still smarting.

"And you weren't limping a minute ago, either."

She leapt to her feet. "I'm special. Lord Hatter says so!"

One of my ears flopped back. "Of course he does. You're his mole in the Ruby Castle."

She cut me off. "I'm a sheep, not a mole."

"I meant you're his spy. He'll say anything to get what

he wants, and what he wants is your blind obedience. But as soon as he doesn't need you, he'll toss you to the carnivores."

"I'm special," she said, voice almost desperate. "When he becomes the Queen, he'll make me his wife. Then what will they say? No one can call me one of the crowd or useless. I'll be the only Queen's wife. The most important woman in Oz."

"Wife? That's rich. No, he wants a slave. If he does pick a wife, it'll be someone flashy or with big assets. Not a little maid."

She looked away, like I'd hit a soft spot. "Why does it matter to you, anyway? You'll be dead in the morning."

It wasn't so scary when she said it. How interesting. "Maybe. But then the Game will end and White Wizard will automatically win. Hatter won't have time to make it to the Emerald Castle, and you'll be stuck as a sheep in a swarm of predators waiting to eat you over and over again. Every day until the next Alice Games begins."

Her breath sucked in sharply. "No. That's wrong. Lord Hatter's plan is flawless." Her breath was faint, like she just realized what I'd said was actually a possibility. It would be a fate worse than death.

Her doubt was encouraging. It was just the reaction I was waiting for. "His plan is crazy and made of wishful thinking, not fact. And you're going to take the fall when it doesn't work. He's playing you."

I'd gone too far, too fast. Her defenses came back up. She bleated a laugh. "That's impossible. Everything you've said is a lie."

I shifted and focused on the problem at hand. "No, it's not. You should get out of here now. Before it's too late."

Shirley shook her head. "So that's what this is all about. You're just trying to escape."

I'd lost her. Like a balloon with a small hole, I let the air out of my body as a sinking pit formed in my stomach. I should have kept going with the failed plan and her taking the blame bit. Well, next time I'd know better. If there was a next time. This was why I hated dealing with emotional people. It was too hard to pound logic through their thick, easily bruised skulls.

"No, I'm trying to get you to escape."

She laughed. "Don't lie. There's no reason for me to escape. I'm not the one in bars."

"At least I can see my cage," I said and put my head down, shifting until my back was to her so I didn't show her my disappointment.

Now to figure out a new plan. This one might still work, but only time would tell. She might bolt in the middle of the night, but I didn't have high hopes for that. Red Queen had already explained that no one could enter a Domain without permission during the Alice Games, so the odds of Hareson and Lional charging through those doors were slim to nil.

The only person I'd ever seen in a Domain outside of the designated Role Player was Ace. Depression filled me. Ace wasn't going to come and rescue me, he already had what he wanted from me. I was on my own.

After a couple hours, I still hadn't come up with a good plan. Everything I started to think of fell apart because of some obvious reason or another.

The only thing that would maybe work was trying to talk Hatter out of killing me in the morning. I could point out that if he did, the Alice Games would end and White Wizard would win. I had to convince the Hatter that he needed to kill me in front of the Emerald Castle so the Games wouldn't end. That way, he'd have to take me outside of his Domain alive, where hopefully Red Queen and the army she'd collected could stop him.

I took a breath, committing to the idea. I'd have to try to convince another emotionally crazy person. The score was zero to one, not very encouraging, but it was worth a shot. Right now, it was my only shot.

The night was too long. I didn't sleep well because my mind was going wild with horrible thoughts of what might happen in the morning. After I finally got those under control, the cage started to swing as I shifted, jolting me awake again.

It was comforting, at least, to know that Shirley got as little sleep as I did. Every time I looked at her, she was shifting or pacing the ground. But she still didn't leave the room.

I'd just gotten to sleep when a huge bell went off somewhere at the top of the building. I jumped up, hair on end and hissing on reflex. Then I covered my ears with my paws, trying to block out the sound that echoed horribly through the building and my body. After the bell finished ringing, I sat up and looked around, finally able to see the thin windows on the stone wall.

The sky was in a pre-dawn navy blue state. It wouldn't be long before the sun breached the horizon. Since I slept through yesterday morning, I could only assume that sunrise was the time when people turned back to their human state.

Just looking at the lightening sky made my heart race. Not just because of Hatter's gross plan, but because today was the day. In four or five hours was False Dawn. I needed to be at the Emerald Castle if I wanted to go home. If I wasn't, then I'd—what did Ace say?—wink out of existence and get stuck between Oz and Earth. And I was currently locked in a cage, who knew how far away.

Shirley was on her feet, hurrying to brush off the ground's dirt the best she could.

A door opened with a loud squeak and shut with a thud behind me. I turned to see Hatter and Boon walk onto the platform. My pulse started to hammer faster, but I wasn't going to let him see how worried I was. Instead, I tried to give an imperial look that cats are normally so good at.

Today the hyena wore a black velvet top hat. Around the brim was a tarnished golden crown. Hatter first checked the cage to make sure I was still there, then looked at the sheep below. "Well done, Shirley. Go open the doors."

She trembled with excitement at the compliment and ran to push open the door.

It took some time because they were a lot bigger than her, but eventually the huge, wooden doors cracked open. The instant they were cracked, baboon hands reached in and pulled the doors all the way open. She had to jump out of the way or be trampled by the animals rushing in. Alarmed, Shirley scrambled up to make sure she was in the front of the loud crowd.

When all the animals were in, Hatter lifted his head. "Shut up!" he yelled. The room went quiet. "Well, my wonderful subjects." Hatter beamed around. "Welcome to the event of the century. With the blood of this Alice, your beloved ruler is about to become the most powerful Queen ever!" He tossed his head in the air.

The crowd cheered.

"It's not going to work," I said, glad that my voice was even. It wasn't hard to figure out that Hatter loved panic and chaos.

Hatter flinched at the sound of my voice and turned to

me. "What did you say?" He walked over and pushed my cage with his nose. "What are you talking about?"

"Stop that." I hissed at him and clawed at the bottom of the cage as it swung. "I said, your plan is not going to work."

He let out a high hyena yip. "Of course it's going to work. My plan is flawless."

"No, it's not. Whenever an Alice dies, White Wizard automatically wins. If you kill me right now, the game will end, and the Emerald Castle will close. You won't get in that way, even if you have all my blood."

"Impossible!" he roared. "You're just trying to keep me from killing you." He calmed down. "I already know how I'll do it. You'll be strung up, and Boon will chop off your feet. Then all your blood will drain into a bowl under you."

I stared at him, barely able to breathe. That would ensure that he'd collect all my blood. It would only take me a couple of minutes to bleed to death. A couple of very painful minutes. Stay calm, I ordered myself. "So you'd have my blood and no throne. You're in the wrong location. The choice has to be made in front of the Emerald Castle, right? The only way you can kill me and not have the Game end immediately is if you do it in front of the Emerald Castle."

I never thought I'd see the day when I would explain to someone where to kill me. This was bizarre.

Hatter hesitated.

Hope started to build inside me.

"Lord Hatter!" someone yelled from the back of the room. "Lord Hatter!" A male hyena pushed through the crowd to the front. "There's an army!" He let out a peal of terrified laughter.

Hatter's ears flattened against his skull and he looked over his shoulder. "What are you talking about?"

"There's an army out front. It's led by Sir Lional and Sir Hareson! They want the Alice back!" the hyena panted, wide eyes rolling.

My ears perked up, impressed with how awesome that made Lional and Hareson sound. They really brought an army with them to come and get me? Unfortunately, they still couldn't enter yet, but it was definitely enough to scare the people holed up in this mad Domain. Then again, Red Queen was in charge of all Oz. I bet once morning came, and she returned from the moon, she could come in and bring whoever she wanted.

Hatter sucked in a breath. "Hurry!" he yelled. "Boon! Hurry! We must finish before they get through the barrier around my Domain! Get the chains! The bucket! Now!"

The hair stood up as my back arched. Any control I had on my emotions broke. My breathing came so fast, my chest hurt. A fine tremble shook my body as panic set in. How was I going to get out of this now?

People started to run in every direction, grabbing things. Vultures I hadn't seen before appeared and started to string up chains from the rafters. Shirley pulled a bucket from a baboon's hands and ran with it up to the platform. She positioned it under the chains, checking it twice.

Boon walked over to the cage. He opened it and grabbed me out.

I curled around his hand, trying to inflict enough damage to make him let me go. All it did was make the baboon shake me so hard I got dizzy and had to stop.

"Hurry," Hatter snapped. "We need to have her ready to be chained as soon as the sun peaks." He started to shuffle his feet in excitement.

His mood reflected on the rest of the animals. They shifted and made excited noises. A fight broke out somewhere in the back, animals snapping and snarling at each other.

The hair on my body rose, and I hissed for all I was worth. Terror took hold good and strong. I was actually going to die now.

A lazy tiger yowl echoed through the building.

CHAPTER SIXTEEN

I FROZE, recognizing the sound that had tortured me so much two nights ago.

Instantly the crowd's mood changed. Their excited noises changed to fright, and they shifted around, trying to pinpoint where the sound came from. Dirty raptors and vultures dropped from their perches, mingling with the animals on the ground for security.

"The Cheshire Cat!"

"He's inside!"

"How did he get here?"

Hatter yelped and started to fidget. He moved so much that his hat slid sideways on his head. He didn't seem to notice. "Where is he?" His voice shook.

Again I was shocked at how scared the people were of the Cheshire Cat. What did Ace do to merit this fear? I knew why I was scared of this huge white tiger. Just the sound of that yowl brought up the memories of watching Lional turn into dust and being chased through the frozen trees. My pulse hammered just thinking about it.

And yet, there was some tiny hope in me that everyone

else was wrong. That Ace wasn't the Cheshire Cat. That I wasn't the fool.

Another yowl echoed. The acoustics of the rafters picked it up and made the sound louder, and a white tiger appeared on a middle rafter next to a gargoyle. He was just as big and beautiful as the first time I saw him, white fur almost glowing against the dark ceiling. His rich brown eyes, the same color as Ace's except they weren't full of laughter, stared down in anger. His black-tipped tail twitched quickly, and his ears were half back.

Hatter jumped and looked up. "What are you doing here?" he demanded in his high voice.

The Cheshire Cat looked at me dangling in Boon's hand and then at Hatter. "You have someone that belongs to me," he drawled.

The sound of his voice made my heart sink into chaos. Flat and harsh as it was, there was no mistaking Ace's voice. Hatter had been right. Red Queen had been right. Shame on me for thinking I knew better.

Hatter mumbled, "Boon."

Boon opened the cage and flung me back in, slamming the door shut after.

My nose hit the bars on the far side, and I hissed and clawed at the floor as the cage swung. Nose throbbing, I looked over as Boon walked off the platform.

He stopped just under Ace's location on the beams and pushed out his chest, as the rest of the animals whispered and squeaked assurance to him. "Eh, finders, keepers." He sneered in contempt, flashing his three inch long canines. I couldn't tell if he was bluffing or not, but the crowd loved it.

The tiger looked down at the baboon, completely ignoring the crowd. His ears pulled back all the way, and his lips lifted to reveal his own teeth. "You are the one who got in my way last night." His voice was deadly. "You cost me a lot of trouble and time." His eyes flicked to me. "And you damaged her." That was the only warning he gave.

He vanished. Before anyone could make more than a peep, Ace appeared on top of the baboon. In a lightning fast move, he clawed the primate's shoulder and flipped him over. The tiger's head darted in and crushed the baboon's exposed neck in his jaws. Boon exploded into dust.

The animals around the tiger scrambled away, some even running out of the room with sounds of panic.

Hatter howled in shock and despair.

I cringed and looked away. I'd seen something like that many times on TV, but it was still horrible to watch in real life. Maybe because the baboon that died wasn't just a baboon and the tiger that killed him wasn't just any tiger. Or just any man. Stomach still rolling, I peeked out at the scene in front of me, but my gaze never got past the door on my cage.

It was slightly open.

I'd had enough of this Domain, with its crazy people and a scary Ace that I didn't know. I shoved the door open with my nose and jumped down, the muscles of my forearms absorbing the force of my fall. Without waiting, I turned tail and ran towards the open door in the back of the platform, my paws silent on the hard surface. Hatter had come out of there. There had to be a way out, whether it be door or window.

I'd only made it a couple steps when the morning sun burst through the thin windows. The golden light hit me and I stumbled to a stop, collapsing on the ground as I started to change back into a human along with everyone else in the room.

In a dizzying whirl, I felt my body stretch. My arms

grew and the fur disappeared as my clothes magically appeared back on my body. As much as it hurt to turn into a cat, there was a feeling of liberation that came from becoming human again, like sliding out of too-tight pants. I was left on my hands and knees as a human. Unable to resist, I glanced over my shoulder at the bottom of the platform.

Under the sunlight, any vain denial I could have clung to faded.

At the bottom of the stairs, human Ace stood where the tiger had been. But it wasn't the Ace I knew. Somehow he still seemed to be more of a tiger than a man. There was a bloodthirsty gleam in his eyes as he gazed at Hatter. The only indication that he was the same man whose company I enjoyed so much was the necklace—my necklace—around his neck.

Hatter hissed in a breath, drawing my attention to him. I wished I hadn't looked. He wasn't some cool, red-haired clown with mismatched clothes and tennis ball eyes. He looked like a greasy, used car salesman. His eyes were too small for his flabby face, lips too big. The round gut stretching his purple shirt gave his chest a concave appearance, and the purple cape around his neck made his shoulders look rounded and diminished. His only selling point was his thick black hair.

He stared at Ace, fear and bluffing courage shifting around him. He seemed to have completely forgotten about me. His eyes narrowed even more. "You have an Artifact. How did you get that? The Alice never made it out of the Ruby Castle with it. Or else I would have it."

Confusion lashed painfully at my heart. Was it any better that Ace had it over Hatter? I needed to tell Red Queen about what I did.

Ace didn't reply. He took a step forward.

I scrambled to my feet and ran, still aiming for the door.

People gasped behind me and Hatter howled, but I kept running. I was almost to the door when Ace suddenly appeared in front of me. No smoke, no wrinkling in the air. He simply wasn't there one second and standing in front of me the next.

I skidded to a stop, falling to my butt in the process.

Ace looked me over, taking in my obviously rumpled appearance. It was probably the worst state I'd ever been in front of him, which was saying something. His lips thinned more, making him down right intimidating.

After shooting a glare at Hatter over my head, he reached for me.

The malice coming from Ace was so intimidating that I shrank away from him. His eyes narrowed, but his hands compensated for my movements. I gasped when he grabbed me and flipped me over his shoulder like a sack of potatoes.

I squawked as my stomach hit his shoulder. The air whooshed out of me and I gasped. My hands fisted in Ace's shirt so I could hold my head up. He let me shift enough to look over my shoulder, but that was as far as his restricting hands let me move.

No princess hold for me anymore. After all, why should he care? The joke was up, it was impossible to play pretend now. Tears pricked my eyes. Why was he here? What did he really want from me? It was his job to kill me. Was he just taking me somewhere to do the job himself?

"Wait, wait." Hatter shifted and put up his hands. "Wait, just a second. Why don't we talk for just a minute?"

Ace smirked. "What do you and I have to talk about?"

Hatter licked his lips and reached up to touch his hat. He paused when his hand encountered only hair. "Hat!" he suddenly yelled. "Hat! Now!" He swung side to side in furious panic.

Shirley, still dressed in her Ruby Castle maid uniform, and another woman came running up the stairs, tugging a full-sized top hat with a crown around the brim between them. Neither would let go, and they finally had to work together to daintily place it on Hatter's head.

Ace glared at Shirley, open in his displeasure at her treason. It wasn't hard to tell he'd just figured out how the necklace got out of the Ruby Castle.

Shirley flinched under his gaze and hurried off the platform with the other woman.

Hatter settled down with a sigh.

Ace scoffed. "I don't have time to talk about hats, Hatter. Especially ones made with such bad taste." His brows flicked to the dented crown around the top hat.

Hatter took a breath. "No, no. That's not what I wanted to talk about. It's about the Alice." He paused then motioned to me dangling over Ace's shoulder like he still had a bargaining chip.

I started to wiggle, trying to slide off Ace's shoulder, but he shifted and tightened his hands on my legs and back.

Hatter's hand twitched up to his hat and tapped a finger on the rim. "You see," Hatter went on and puffed out his chest. "I need an Artifact. You could say it's for personal interests." His eyes were bright with excitement. He was obviously not upset at all about his right hand man's death anymore.

"Why do you need an Artifact?" Ace frowned at him.

Hatter laughed and flapped his hand. "Why, someone with as much power as I do should have a chance to be Queen too."

Ace gave a dry laugh, nonplussed. "What power?"

"What power?" Hatter gaped like a fish. His arms flung open and motioned to the people cowering around the walls, trying to stay as far as they could from Ace even though he was on the other side of the room.

"Look at my power!" Hatter yelled, high on his thoughts. "I am a Queen here. A Savior. I should be Queen of all Oz!"

Ace snorted. "Apparently you don't understand what power is." He looked around the room, daring anyone to challenge him.

The mangy-looking people just shifted around, staring at the ground.

Hatter stamped his foot, insulted. Then he adjusted his hat and smiled. "But think of all the more power I would have if I could get into the Emerald Castle," he continued. "I need access to it. All you need is the Alice dead. Why don't we help each other out? I'll even do your work for you. You can go off, have a pleasant day, and tell that icicle that the job is done while I clean up."

Ace's eyes narrowed for a split second.

"Or, if you want to do the work yourself, we could trade. Your Artifact for the Alice," Hatter proposed quickly instead.

Ace's smile was easy but chilling. "See, this is why they call you mad, Hatter. Why should I make a bargain with you when they both already belong to me?" He walked forward, towards the double front doors.

Even though his demeanor was threatening, enough to make people back away, his hands on my legs were gentle and his strong steps were careful so his shoulder didn't jar my stomach. My fist came up to my eyes to press away the moisture in frustration. How was I supposed to understand anything with all these mixed messages?

"Stop him!" Hatter yelled. He hopped up and down on his toes, wrung his hands, and pulled on his hat but didn't take a step closer. "Stop him!"

Ace smirked at him and faced the front door. The crowd parted even more as he stalked through the room. A couple men fidgeted, but fear kept them in place as Ace left, Hatter's frantic voice fading behind.

CHAPTER SEVENTEEN

ACE MOVED through the battered Gothic buildings, providing me with a short glimpse of the closed front gate and the Yellow Path pointing to it. The loud sounds of thousands of voices echoed in the air, coming from the other side of the huge wood gate. Lional's voice was loudest of all, demanding my release. A few of Hatter's people ran back and forth in confusion in front of it.

Ace turned the opposite direction and headed to the far side of the town. He opened a small cast-iron gate on the high stone wall and walked through. A coniferous forest with thick, tall pine trees immediately loomed on the other side. He wove around the trees, obviously familiar with the area. Soon enough, the sounds of Red Queen's army and Hatter's domain disappeared.

I couldn't take it anymore. "Put me down, Ace." I was proud that my voice didn't wobble. It was stronger than my quivering heart.

He didn't say anything, and his step didn't falter.

Was he going to ignore me? "Put me down," I repeated a little louder.

He was silent still.

"Put me down now!" I yelled.

He flipped me over his shoulder and set my feet on the ground.

It happened so fast I didn't have time to catch my balance. I staggered until my knees buckled, and I sat down hard on the ground. My mouth screwed to the side as I scowled up at him. So much for my knight in shining armor. My annoyance helped me focus.

Ace stood over me, hands on his hips and an irritated expression on his face. "You didn't say please."

I still didn't know if I should thank him or not. "Why are you here?" I'd had enough with the games and the blind trust. "You're the Cheshire Cat. Aren't you supposed to kill me?" Maybe I should be more scared of him, but I was too angry.

Ace blew a breath out his nose and looked up at the sky through the treetops. "Of course you'd start with that question. Always quick to the point. The answer is yes."

I swallowed. "Why haven't you, then? You've had plenty of opportunities."

He vanished. A second later, he reappeared crouched over me, his face inches from mine and his sharp knife resting against my neck. I didn't have time to flinch. But even with his threatening position, there was no threat in his eyes.

Ace sighed, his brows tipping up. He gave a bitter half laugh. "Why did it have to be you? I finally decided I was going to be the person all of Oz thinks I am. *The Cheshire Cat.*" He spat the words. "After two hundred years of that White bastard's abuse, I finally couldn't take it anymore. He'd already turned me into a walking weapon, why not actually be one? But I can't kill you any more now than I could at the river."

The knife at my throat disappeared, but he kept talking. His deep brown eyes searched mine, as if looking for an answer to a question he couldn't ask. The harsh lines smoothed out, leaving an Ace that I knew.

"You intrigued me. You hung on to that log for dear life, struggling against the water, yet you didn't call for help. I've never seen an Alice do that before. Normally they scream and cry. I figured that anyone with that much drive should live a little longer. So I put it off until the morning. Then you looked at me like—like you had no idea I was the Cheshire Cat, no idea I planned to hurt you. And you talked to me. Asked my opinions. You actually listened to me as if I were a person to you. Do you know how long it's been since someone did that?"

He shook his head. "I was so angry with Red Queen for letting Hatter get a hold of you. And at myself for luring you away from her. All because I got you another stupid water lily. I'm just frustrated. I'm sorry for taking it out on you."

So it really was him that slid around the corner of the alley.

He looked so troubled. My hand came up and hesitantly stroked the hair at the base of his ears before diving into his kitten-soft hair.

His eyes widened a second, then closed with pleasure. He leaned into my hand until I was massaging his scalp. With a sigh, he collapsed onto my lap and snuggled his head into my stomach.

This wasn't the reaction I was looking for. I don't know what I was expecting, but this was sweet. I ran my fingers through his orange hair, my mind racing. Would he continue to avoid my questions now that he'd opened up?

"Ace?"

"Hmm?" He sounded like a purring cat.

I smiled despite myself. "Why are you so feared?"

He peeked at me, then closed his eyes again. "You're awfully good at asking all the wrong questions. I think of it as bad luck. When I was younger, I had a natural affinity to swordsmanship that drew White's attention. So I became his squire." His mouth twisted in dry humor. "Lional was so jealous. Even I thought he should have been the Queen Candidate's squire. He's the one who worked so hard at everything. And I was just the lucky one." He paused. "You know, if Lional had been White's squire, I don't think any of this would have happened. When White went crazy, I don't think Lional would have choked. He'd have known what to do and done it. But I ... I failed." His face wrinkled in self-loathing.

He was talking about when White killed that farmer, I realized. "But weren't you just trying to protect someone?"

He didn't look any more relieved. "That's what I told myself. He promised everyone's safety in exchange for my obedience. He made sure that I was martially skilled enough to back up anything he wanted. Ruthlessly so. Even I don't know why it had to be me. White was so much stronger than I was, so much ... And I started to believe him when he told me I was nothing but his knave, his slave.

"Even after the Alice Games started and I was around Red Queen all the time, I still was never truly happy. I could smile all she needed, but there was always that voice in the back of my mind that whispered I didn't deserve to be happy. But it was fine, because I wasn't meant to be happy. I just had to be and do whatever was necessary to make sure everyone else was. But even the people thought I was different from them. After all, it was common knowledge of who I was before the Games."

My heart tightened just listening to him talk like that.

Ace shook his head, cheek rubbing my tummy. "It didn't help that I was given Blood, the Vorpal Blade."

My mouth parted with surprise. I did witness him being given a sword, but I didn't know it was the Vorpal Blade. In one of the stories on earth, wasn't it used to slay a dragon or something? But I'd never heard it called Blood before. If he owned it, why was it locked in the Emerald Castle? "Why does that matter?"

He made a dismissive sound. "Well, I'm the only one it allows to touch it. Although, maybe Red could, but I'll never test that idea. It's also the only thing that can permanently kill someone. They don't come back in the morning."

"Oz gave Red Queen a wand that channels her power," I thought out loud. "Why would it give you a sword?"

He shook his head again. "I don't know."

I sobered. "Did you really kill the Alices?" Slowly I pulled the length of his hair through my fingers, completely comfortable despite laying on the ground with Ace's head on my stomach.

He sighed. "Just the first one that died in Oz," he said. "It was an accident, but that doesn't matter, I guess. It had never been done before. I broke the rules and marked Oz with the blood of an outside world. So I became a contradiction."

"How did it happen?" I asked softly.

A bitter smile touched his face. He opened his eyes and stared off to the side. His hands tightened around my waist. "Alice number eleven. She was the most beautiful Alice I'd ever seen, had this long blond hair and perfect smile. But she was crazy. She treated Red like a brainless child and acted like I was some show pet. Had this delusion that she should be Queen, and I should be something else. She said it was a male Queen. It had a weird name."

"King." My mind whirled as something he said clicked. A beautiful, blonde Alice? My eyes widened with shock. I'd seen the beginning of this scene in the Jewel Castle ruins. I'd been too disturbed to stay and watch what happened, though.

He nodded. "That's right. Weird, huh? Why have two names for the same thing?"

I smiled. "I guess in my world, we have lots of words for the same thing."

"What an odd world."

Like he was one to talk.

"Anyway, we were in front of the Emerald Castle, and White Wizard was almost locked up when it happened. She was holding Red Queen's wand and making this long speech about being Queen. That's when I realized she was going to make her joke real. I couldn't let it happen. I would make a horrible Queen, and she would be even worse. And since there was already an Alice here, we'd never have another Alice Games to replace her." His lips twisted. "I tried to make her stop talking by covering her mouth. I must have been too intense—she'd never seen me upset before—and it startled her. She started to struggle. I don't even know how it happened, honestly. One second she was pulling at my clothes and the next, the Vorpal Blade was sticking out of her stomach."

He took a shaky breath and swallowed before going on. "There was so much screaming. I can still hear it when I close my eyes. When Alice's blood touched the Vorpal Blade, it reacted. The blade turned from polished steel to blood red, screaming the whole time. The taint of another world's blood on it was horrible. It *hated* it," he whispered.

He talked about the sword like it had a consciousness. Was that because Oz made it? Did that mean Red Queen's wand had a consciousness too?

"Red Queen was yelling. It was the most horrible 'no' I'd ever heard. Her wand was pulled out of the dead Alice's hands by an invisible force and sucked into the Emerald Castle. Red Queen couldn't resist as she was forced into a glowing red ball. Then the ball whisked away and locked her in the Ruby Castle. The people turned into animals as snow fell from the sky."

Ace licked his lips and his hands tightened on my waist like I was a life line that he desperately needed. "The worst was Oz's screaming. I haven't heard it scream like that since Jewel Queen died, the last time I'd heard Oz's voice. It was in pain as it was forced to adjust the rules of the game to accommodate the death of Alices. They weren't supposed to die. Their blood is like poison to Oz. It rips it apart and makes holes to the other world."

My heart ached just hearing him talk about it.

"I was punished with equal severity." His eyes narrowed. "I was ripped from Oz to In-Between. It's the place between our worlds, remember? When you came to Oz, you passed through the Emerald Castle, which is a portal between our worlds. It protects you from the darkness between the places. When I go to the In-Between, there is no comfortable Castle. There is nothing. No light, no sound. Just me and my guilty thoughts in an endless void."

The In-Between. Ace mentioned that the first time we met, in that Munchkin shack. It sounded like a horrible place then, but to think that he was stranded there for years. I shook my head. "That sounds awful," I whispered.

"It was. Is. I've gotten used to it. I spend a lot of time in In-Between between Alice Games. It's better than being in the Diamond Castle with that bastard and his opinionated lashings." He was quiet for a minute.

When he spoke again, his voice was less haunted. "I digress. Eventually I learned how to use In-Between. There wasn't a whole lot else I could do. I couldn't die. I figured out how to use it as a portal to wherever I wanted in Oz. By the time I got out, several Alice Games had passed and I was marked as White Wizard's slave. Not like it was a new title." He snorted. "They called me the Cheshire Cat. They knew I was still alive since my Domain, the Cheshire Forest, was still alive. But they also knew it was warped. My poor forest. It used to be the most beautiful land in Oz."

So that's how he was able to disappear and reappear wherever he wanted. He was using In-Between to teleport. Because he could go anywhere he wanted in Oz during the Alice Games, the Domain boundary rule must not apply to him. He could simply appear on the other side of it, instead of being stopped by it. I paused, thinking. "Red Queen said you used to be Ace of Hearts?"

He laughed, this time with fondness. "I haven't heard that name in a long time. She gave me that title when she first became Queen, since she couldn't make me a Queen's Knight."

I looked down at him, still sifting my hands through his hair. "There's another title you preferred," I whispered, wondering if it was too mean to bring it up.

He glanced up into my face. His hand reached up and brushed my hair. "Oz talked about me a lot. But I'm not that surprised—it likes you. I'm sure it's just grateful to finally have someone to communicate with again. You're right. There was another title. *The Knight of Oz*," he mocked then sobered. "It was a childhood fantasy, thinking that I could actually help people." Ace's hand dropped and he frowned to the side. "It doesn't matter anymore. When I became a contradiction to the rules, I lost that title." He smiled painfully. "Contradictions can't coexist with peace."

Yet, he still loved Oz so much. And it seemed that Oz couldn't cancel a position once given. White Wizard was an example of that. I decided to drop the idea for now. "What happened to all the other Alices that died? The people have credited you with their deaths."

He shook his head. "White Wizard ordered me to kill them, but I couldn't. He'd punish me over and over again. I can't even count all the times he's almost frozen me to death, only to keep me just enough alive to know what was going on. So I simply stopped saving them. It doesn't take just me to kill an Alice, as you know. Even hiding in In-Between didn't always work, he just punished me all the more when I came out. Eventually Red's face started to fade away. Her sweet smile and gentle words became as cold as that prison castle."

He swallowed hard. "I just wanted out. There was nothing left for me to hold onto, just White's twisted words filling my mind until I couldn't think. Couldn't feel. I was so desperate to get away, I was willing to do anything. Even if it hurt Red. Even kill an Alice. You." His voice cracked and he closed his eyes. He covered his face with his hands, hiding the grief that plagued him. "I'm so sorry, Ali."

His emotions, broken and raw, seeped from his quivering body into mine. This was the man they said had a tin heart? Why couldn't they see what he was hiding behind that teasing smile? Tears pooled in my eyes, but I didn't let them fall. I needed to be strong for him, since he couldn't be right now. Instead, I hugged him tight to me and waited for his trembling to stop. "I don't blame you, Ace. No matter what happens, I won't blame you."

His hand slid from his face and snaked around my waist. He hid his red eyes in my stomach. "You should," he whispered but held onto me like I was a lifeline.

"How can I save you?" I asked. "How can I help you get away from White Wizard?"

He took a sharp hiss of breath. Then he gave a small laugh and shook his head, his usual shield of a smile back. "You can't. I made my bed—and I'll lie in it until the end."

I grabbed his face and made him look at me. "I can't accept that."

When did I get this forward? This strong? I was the girl who didn't want to get involved with anything or anyone. But I couldn't leave him like this. It was different than my drive to help Red Queen, which originally stemmed from pity. With Ace, it was a gut wrenching need to help him. There had to be something, somehow.

My mind raced and I grabbed at the straws, thinking about the information I'd learned so far. "I heard that you wanted to get the Vorpal Blade out of the Emerald Castle. Will that help you?"

"No!" Horror and shock cracked his mask away.

I jumped and blinked in surprise.

Ace clenched his jaw and looked away until he could control his face again. "No. I did—do—want it out. It's a part of Oz, but it's almost a part of me, too. But it's too dangerous. Ali, you must *never* try to touch it. The Vorpal Blade is nothing but danger. For you and Red. It," he swallowed hard, "needs to stay in the Emerald Castle. Where White can't get it."

"Hatter wants it, too," I remembered. But how could I help Ace now?

Ace's lips pursed as the new thought preoccupied him, brows pulling low over his eyes. "I knew he was interested in becoming Queen. I just didn't know he'd figured out the way into the Emerald Castle. That information is usually kept secret. That's why I took your necklace, to make sure White didn't get it. It stays in In-Between when I'm around him. I'm sure Red Queen doesn't know about Hatter yet, either. She's usually pretty lenient on Role Players and how they rule their Domains as long as there's peace." He paused, thinking. "It's a problem now that Hatter's decided to act this way. Red Queen and White Wizard share all the power given to the Queen right now. Granted, White Wizard has most of it since he was the original Queen Candidate. If it came down to a fight with the Hatter, Hatter would lose, hands down. White Wizard wouldn't hesitate to act. Red Queen would never use her power like that. This is going to bring more chaos to Oz. It's ready to collapse as it is."

My mouth pulled to the side, trying to understand him. "Listening to you talk, it sounds like you're still on Red Queen's side."

He frowned and laughed bitterly. "They've already rejected me. I'm no longer welcome on their side. I stopped trying to fight against it long ago." One cat ear twitched away from my fingers. "I never wanted to tell you any of this. I wanted you to go back to your world, still thinking I was one of the good guys. But it seems I never had a chance."

I let my head fall back against the ground. "Why is everything so complicated here? People keep telling me I should fear you. You included. But you don't feel like a bad person. You were trying to protect your world and your Queen. It wasn't for self-gain. Just like any soldier in a war. And how many decades—centuries—have you been paying for it?"

He peeked at me again but didn't say anything.

I stared at the blue sky above us, wondering how much longer we had before someone came. Ace's hearing was probably ten times better than mine and he hadn't moved, so we had a little longer. "I wish ..." I cut myself off.

He waited. When I didn't say anything, he pressed, "Wish what?"

"It's stupid, really," I muttered. "I wish we had met in my world. We'd run into each other at Cornell and exchange a couple of words. Then you'd ask me to dinner. I'd hesitate because I'm shy but can't say no. There's this botanical garden that I've been dying to see and they have this amazing library. We'd walk and hold hands, talking about whatever came to our minds. There would be no queens or wizards or Oz. Just you and me."

He smiled. "That sounds wonderful."

I was quiet for a minute, lost in my thoughts. Then something Red Queen said crashed through. "You've played with a lot of girls, haven't you?"

He shrugged. "I'm a cat by nature. I'm prone to pick things up and play with them."

Then dump them. Was I any different to him? Or was I a plaything too? It was so easy to fall back into the trap the more time I spent with him. My hand stilled in his hair as that thought sank in.

He looked up at me. "You are an Ali, not an Alice. The only Ali. There's a difference."

The sincerity in his deep eyes made it hard not to smile.

His comment touched my heart. My hand started to move again.

"You know," he said slowly. "Cats like to take pleasure. We also like giving it back." He looked at me through heavily lidded eyes. He planted his hands on either side of me and rose up, slowly and deliberately. His lips brushed mine softly.

My lashes fluttered closed as I leaned into the kiss. I'd been waiting for this. It was, after all, something I'd thought about since I'd met him. His lips were tender and sweet. My pulse went wild, and I wanted more. His hand cradled my cheek as the kiss deepened, and he tangled his tongue with mine. Under my hand, his heart hammered.

"Ali! Where are you?" a familiar male voice called.

Ace pulled back, the same regret I felt was mirrored on his face.

"Ali!" This time it was Red Queen. She was closer than Hareson.

Ace leaned forward and brushed his lips against mine, soft as a butterfly. Like sand in a storm, he faded away until his kiss was all that was left. Then it, too, was gone.

Groaning, I flopped back onto the ground and buried my face in my hands, trying to get a handle on my breath and wild emotions. Some denizen of chaos he was. He kept sending me back to Red Queen. If he really was bad, he'd keep me for himself. Heaven knew, I would readily follow.

Then again, his habit of doing good despite his reputation was throwing me off balance. I didn't know whether he did it intentionally or if that was simply his true nature.

What I did know was that after only twenty-four hours, I was falling in love with Ace.

CHAPTER EIGHTEEN

FOOTPRINTS CRUNCHED on the ground nearby, prompting me to move my hands from my face.

"Ali!" Red Queen walked around a tree and almost stepped on me. Tears of joy brimmed in her eyes. "Ali! Oh, I'm so glad you're okay!" She covered her heart with her hands. "I was so worried when they said Hatter kidnapped you!" She dabbed at the tears with a finger. "Ali, why are you lying on the ground like that?"

I smiled. "I'm sleep deprived and going crazy." Although I was oddly okay with this kind of crazy. Even if it was over a man who I would never see again after six hours.

Red Queen was immediately alarmed. "Hareson! Lional!" she called out.

I laughed. "No, I can stand." To prove my point, I did so.

The men came running through the trees. Both had hands on their swords.

Lional skidded to stop at the sight of me. "You look awful."

For once, his comment made me snort a laugh. "Do you

honestly expect me to look like a bunch of roses after spending the night in a mad person's Domain?"

"What happened?" Hareson asked, walking up to me. He started to brush leaves and pine needles off my shoulders and out of my hair. "Why did Hatter kidnap you?"

I brushed at the dirt on my pants. "Hatter was going to try and use my blood to get into the Emerald Castle." I looked at Red Queen and paused, holding in the breath I took to tell her about Ace having my necklace.

If he was hiding it in In-Between, it seemed unlikely that White Wizard was going to find it. I didn't doubt that if Red Queen asked for it, Ace would give it to her. At the same time, I kind of didn't want her to have it. I wanted it to stay with Ace. Let him have something to hang onto when I am gone.

Hareson's eyes widened in alarm. "That's insane!"

Lional hissed something vulgar. "I told you we should have done something about that flea house long ago."

Red Queen frowned. Her arms crossed in front of her. "I worried he was going to try something drastic the moment they told me you were gone. I just didn't think it was like this. Unfortunately, we don't have time to remedy the problem." She met all of our gazes. "False Dawn is in three hours. We don't have time to stand here and babble. Hatter will have to be dealt with at a later time."

We took her cue and started to walk.

Hareson glanced at me. "How did you get out of there?"

I waved a hand, coming up with a quick lie. "When they heard about your army, they panicked. While they were running around, I snuck out the back." Or I was marched out the front door on the shoulder of the Cheshire Cat. But I wasn't about to tell them that. I wasn't in the mood and didn't have the energy to fight with Lional's opinion. It was clear he wasn't a fan of Ace on any level. It was best not to mention him at all.

Red Queen glanced at me, clearly reading between the lines. Her red, heart-shaped lips thinned and she looked away, her beautiful face strained. Hareson looked between us, and his brows shot up. Lional was oblivious.

I broke the silence. "So, you have an army now?"

Hareson nodded. "Yes, the first army ever assembled in Oz. We have Knights that settle small disputes, but there's never been a need for an army before."

I nodded. Maybe that was what happened when the whole world was one country and people loved the Queen. Maybe it was smart of Oz to lay out the ruling like this.

Red Queen clenched her hands at her sides. "This time, we're going to try and defeat White Wizard ourselves. Win or lose, we're going to try."

Three riders pulling four extra horses trotted up to us.

"Your Highness." One man bowed at the waist from the horse. "Congratulations on finding the Alice." He straightened and turned to the lion-man. "We are ready to move out, Sir Lional." He handed him the reins for all the horses.

Lional nodded. "Right. Ride back and give the word. We need to move out as soon as possible. We have a lot of people to move in only a couple hours." As the men rode away, Lional distributed the horses. He walked my horse over and pointed to the stirrup. "Step right there with your right foot." He pointed to the saddle horn. "Then grab here and pull yourself up."

I paused in surprise. "Thank you." I looked at the saddle. "If I step with my right foot, that puts me sidesaddle, right? And if I use my left foot, then I'd straddle the horse, like you do, right?"

Lional scratched his golden, spiky hair. "You are an odd Alice. But yes."

I smiled. "Thanks." I stepped up with my left foot. It took me two tries, but I pulled myself up and got my leg over.

Lional took the time to adjust the stirrups for me, but he didn't hand over the reins. He mounted his horse, wrapped my reins around his saddle horn and took the lead. Still, it was better than before.

Some time later we joined up with the army. It wasn't a large army compared to the ones formed on Earth, but there were easily more than two thousand men and some women moving together in loose lines. The downfall was that most of the people held farming tools, and half of them were under five feet tall.

Red Queen and I were transferred to an open-topped carriage and the party moved out, leaving the people of Hatter still locked in their town.

Hatter stood atop the wall above the large front gate. His hand fiddled with the brim of his hat as he stared at the commotion just outside his Domain. Even from this distance, and safe with Red Queen, I could feel his eyes on me as I moved. It made my skin crawl. Unfortunately, I had a feeling this was not the last I'd see of him.

My eyes cracked open and blinked around the empty carriage. I didn't remember falling asleep, but it wasn't like I'd slept last night.

My mind cleared as I blinked up through the open top of the carriage. All I could see was thick mist, swirling between the leaves of deciduous trees. Where was I? And where was Red Queen?

I bolted up to my feet and looked wildly around.

Two guards standing next to the carriage jumped when I stood up so suddenly. One almost fell over completely and the other put a hand on the sword at his hip. They stared at me open-mouthed, apparently as lost as I was.

I gaped back then looked around, able to see slightly more from up here, although the mist still distorted most of the scenery around me. The horses were gone from the front of the carriage, presumably taken care of elsewhere. The colorful fabrics of tents mixed with random foliage tinted the air until they were swallowed up by the whiteness. The air held a muted feel, the sounds of the army that I knew must surround me were hushed, as if no one dared to fully talk. I recognized the huge, red, velvet, square-topped tent closest to me and guessed that Red Queen was in it.

"How much time do I have left?" I asked.

The guard that didn't almost fall over recovered first and cleared his throat. "A little less than two hours. Red Queen is there, when you are ready, Alice of Alice." He pointed to the tent, confirming my suspicions.

"Ah, thank you." So I had some time to think, I hope. The guards continued to stare at me. I tugged at my hair and shifted under their scrutiny. Were they going to just stare at me the whole time? I motioned vaguely with my hands. "If you need to do something, you can go. I'm sure I can find her tent on my own." I wasn't ready to go in yet, I still needed a moment to think and this still, foggy air was a lot better than what I'd breathed in lately.

The men exchanged looks, then walked slowly away.

But they didn't completely leave. They stopped near a tent around twenty feet away and turned back to stare at me.

I guess that was as good as I was going to get. I climbed out of the carriage and sat down on the step.

I was here at the threshold of the Game Board, the Domain around the Emerald Castle, and I still didn't have all the answers. I felt like I'd been given most of them, but hadn't connected them all together.

Everyone expected me to choose, and I had made my decision. It was easy, especially after everything I'd learned about Oz. But if it was that easy, why did Oz go through all this trouble? Everything Hatter said had sounded crazy. But what if something he said was right? Or almost right? If the people chose the Queen Candidate, why should an outsider choose the Queen? Unless I wasn't actually supposed to choose, but instead help someone else make the choice?

"Is that it, Oz?" I asked out loud and looked up into the misty sky. The guards were far enough away; I wasn't worried about being overheard. "Is that the problem? It was never the Alice's choice? Then whose is it?"

The land was as still as the mist around me. What was I expecting? A voice in the sky?

"Ah, they're beautiful," Red Queen's familiar voice gushed from my feet. "I love them."

I jumped. How did she get so close without me noticing her? I frowned. Her voice was different, younger, and coming from my feet. I looked down and did a double take.

In a puddle, just ten or so inches from my feet, was a moving scene. In it, Red Queen and Ace sat on a grassy slope. The picture was bright with rich colors and crisp lines. It was like watching a TV embedded in the ground. Given the foliage and cattail reeds that rimmed the picture,

I could only assume the point of view was from a pond or lake.

Red Queen looked the same age she did now, but without the adult authoritative air she possessed now. She wore a red dress that was as frilly as her current style and sat with her feet tucked under her. In her arms was a bouquet of red roses.

"I'm glad you like them," Ace said. A happy, carefree smile played over his handsome face.

A flattered flush colored her alabaster cheeks as she daintily sniffed the flowers. "You always bring the best roses. Are they your favorite flower?" Her dark eyes held a coy gleam.

This had to be before the Alice Games started because Ace was completely human. No cat ears. Was this before or after White Wizard went crazy? Ace looked to be about my age. He sat with one leg stretched out, the other knee bent high so he could rest his elbow on it. If he noticed the flirty way she looked at him, he didn't show it. He flashed a smile at her and chuckled. "No. But I think they suit you best, Red."

Frustration and pleasure mingled on her pretty face, then she grinned. "You've been so busy lately. I've missed you."

Ace nodded, gazing out at the nature around them. "Being the Queen Candidate's squire is busy work. There've been a lot of training sessions. I've learned so much about Oz, it's been amazing." He shrugged. "But you can't be that lonely. Lional visits you at least every other day." He leaned his head back, basking in the sun. "With all the roses he brings you, you have a constant garden room in your house. As soon as one starts to wilt, he replaces it."

Red gazed at him for a minute. Her eyes drank in his

sun-kissed features just like mine did. Then her eyes fluttered down, and she brushed her fingers over the blossoms. “But they aren’t always red roses,” she said softly.

Ace shrugged. “So paint them.” His mouth quirked up at his own joke. “Cut him some slack. He’s doing the best he knows. He’s just a little rough around the edges. I’m sure by the time you’re elected he’ll be the best knight, a Queen’s Knight.”

I shook my head, wondering if Ace was insulting or complimenting Lional.

Red blushed and looked down. “You shouldn’t say things like that. You don’t know for sure it will happen.”

Ace brushed off her concern. “Maybe, but that doesn’t change the fact that you are compatible with Oz.”

Red smiled, pleased despite herself. Then she gave him a puzzled look. “Don’t you want to be a Queen’s Knight? You are Queen Candidate White’s squire.”

“Nah.” Ace flashed a smile at her. “I’m going to be a Knight of Oz.” He tipped his head back to the sun.

Red buried her face in the roses to hide her pout. “A Knight of Oz, huh?” Could she tell he was preordained, just like her? “Like a shield for everyone?”

He laughed. “A shield? Nah, I’d rather be a sword. Shields are nice, but you can’t act with one. They aren’t decisive enough. A sword can change things.”

The scene disappeared from the puddle, leaving me to rock back in shock.

CHAPTER NINETEEN

I ROCKED BACK to sit straight on the carriage step, hands fisting in my lap, processing what I just saw.

Oz showed me this scene because of Ace. He was important to everything. I knew he was, even if everyone had already disregarded him. Oz chose him as the Knight of Oz. Ace had already admitted that. Apparently no one other than White Wizard realized it. No, Red Queen knew too. That's why she gave him the title of Ace of Hearts and put him in charge of the Alices. Didn't he say it was so she could keep him around? She couldn't make him a Queen's Knight because he was already the Knight of Oz.

How confused he must have been, caught between two potential Queens demanding his attention. White Wizard used fear and manipulation to control him. Ace loved Red Queen too much to say no, even if it wasn't the type of love she wanted. He was so perplexed by it all, he couldn't make a decision.

I took a calming breath, my mind clear for the first time since I'd come to Oz. "So that's it," I whispered. This was what it was all about. It was the Knight of Oz's decision. My fingers came up and tapped on my lips. *A sword can change things.* That's why he was given the Vorpal Blade, to make it so there was only one Queen Candidate.

Who should I tell? They were all so convinced Ace was a bad guy, who would believe me?

"Ali?" Hareson walked out of the mist toward me. He was dressed in light armor over brown material. He smiled kindly at me. "The guards said you were awake and just sitting here. It's almost time. Is everything okay?" His right ear flopped back. "You're not—not confused about the decision, are you?" For the first time, he didn't seem like a stuck up butler. He was looking at me like a friend.

I smiled and waved a hand. "No, Red Queen is supposed to be Queen. She has her flaws, I've discovered, but it's clear what Oz and the sane people of Oz want." If her conflicted emotions about Ace and resentment of her situation were her only mistakes, then that was a good thing. But it still should be addressed. I couldn't help but think of the warnings Jewel Queen gave White Wizard that he never heeded. About how a less than tranquil heart can damage a Queen's connection to Oz. And in Red's case, it had. If it hadn't, Oz wouldn't have had to wait for an Alice to connect with it and answer all the questions.

I tugged on my hair. "I'm just trying to figure out *how* to make the decision."

Hareson nodded. "It's easy, actually. By bringing Red Queen's wand out of the Emerald Castle, your decision is made, and the White Wizard is locked up."

Until the next Alice Games, if I didn't do this right. "And if I bring out the Vorpal Blade? Will Red Queen's wand stay locked in the Emerald Castle?" Ace might have told me to leave this idea alone, but I wanted—needed—to help him somehow. Free him from his curse.

Hareson sucked in a quick breath, eyes widening with shock. "Where did you hear about that cursed blade?"

They were quite the pair, the Cheshire Cat and Blood, weren't they? People regarded them with the same amount of fear. "Does it matter?"

His ears twitched. "No, I suppose not. But we've never had an Alice learn as much as you have about Oz before. None of them seemed to really care." He paused, his head cocking to the side. "But I'm glad you came. Oz has changed for the first time since the Alice Games started. Even Lional has changed, a little." He smiled.

His head straightened. "To answer your question, I don't know what will happen if you bring out Blood. It's never been done before. We know that the Cheshire Cat is bent on getting it out. He has a connection with it, like Red Queen has with her wand and White Wizard with his ice power." Hareson took a breath. "I know you've had contact with the Cheshire Cat. A lot more than we thought, apparently. But don't let him deceive you. Nothing good will come from the Vorpal Blade coming out of the Emerald Castle. Oz locked it in there for a reason."

For a reason, yes, but why? Oz couldn't take away Ace's position, so why did it remove the sword from his side? Ace was still the only one who could make the decision. Why did Oz take away the sword and make it that much harder? I knew it was obligated to punish Ace for killing an Alice, but there must be more to this.

Hareson meant well, like Ace, but I couldn't help but believe the Vorpal Blade had to come out. After all, Oz has specifically shown it to me twice. With how few times Oz could talk to me, why would it waste time showing me something that wasn't important? But I couldn't leave the wand in the Emerald Castle, too. Ah, this just got a lot harder.

Hareson checked a pocket watch. "It's almost time for you to go. Red Queen would like to talk to you briefly before you set off."

I nodded. I wanted to talk to her, too. I followed Hareson to the tent.

He opened the flap and motioned me in ahead of him.

Lional sat in the corner with a bronze cup in his hand. He was in full armor, the hard steel highlighted with gold accents on the chest, shoulder, and thighs. Right then, he looked like a king.

Red Queen was clothed in a mellow dress compared to her normal look. Her red gown was still poufy but not drastically so, and sparkle-free for once. Her hair was pulled into a bun with her gold crown circling it. A gold breast plate covered her torso, emphasizing her feminine figure. Apparently, this was her war outfit.

She smiled at me. "I hope you rested well." She opened the tent flap and motioned out to the mist. "Ahead is the end of the Yellow Path, the Game Board."

I looked out but couldn't see anything. It was probably Oz's protection of the Emerald Castle. Sure enough, the Yellow Path pointed straight through the mist.

"Once you get into the Emerald Castle, you'll be safe," Red Queen said.

My head tilted to the side. "So I'm going in alone? You aren't coming with me?"

"The Game Board is a neutral zone, where harm can't be done." The wobble in her voice and worried expression implied there was danger somewhere, though. "Only three people can enter the Game Board until you go into the Emerald Castle. Then the rest of Oz can enter the Domain, but no one can set foot on the board until you come out again. Then, well, anything is fair."

"And you would be left alone with White Wizard the whole time. Then completely defenseless when I come out," I finished saying everything she didn't.

Red Queen bit her lips, looking guilty. "But it is a neutral zone." She stressed the words as if trying to make herself feel better.

But it was still too dangerous to leave her there alone. It really was best that she stayed here with Lional and Hareson. After all, this whole game was to help Red Queen become the only Queen of Oz.

One word she said caught my attention and I frowned. "Only three?" I asked. "Are you sure it's not four? The Queen Candidates, the Alice ... and the Knight of Oz?"

Hareson and Lional looked at me sharply.

Red Queen physically jumped and gaped at me with huge eyes. "Where did you hear that?" Her words were faint.

I took a breath, my mouth twisting in a mirthful smile. "Oz told me."

Red Queen's eyes widened with hurt. "Oz talked to you ... but not me?" She bit her lips and looked away. "I'm sorry, Ali. But there is no Knight of Oz," she whispered.

"Yes, there is. We both know it. Just because you call him by a different name doesn't change what he is." I didn't want to hurt her. I didn't want to rub it in her face that she couldn't talk to Oz, however, this situation has gone on long enough. Someone needed to address it, because I couldn't stand to see him being treated like this anymore, knowing how much it hurt him.

Lional looked at the silent Hareson. "What are they talking about?"

Red Queen shook her head, looking childlike with her lost expression. "No, that's not true. He's not the Knight of Oz anymore."

"Why do you deny it?" I challenged. "One of the lessons that Jewel Queen taught White Wizard was that dark emotions like hate, resentment, and fear can affect a Queen's connection with Oz. You wouldn't even let Hareson talk to me about Ace. You said it was a delicate situation and brushed him away. Why?"

She closed her eyes, trying to block me out.

"Why?" I yelled.

"Because he never chose me!" Red Queen gasped and slapped a hand over her mouth, shocked that she had raised her voice. But she couldn't take it back, so her hand dropped. She faced me head on. "He betrayed me. He never once chose me. He was always too busy with the White Wizard. He followed that evil man around like a puppy, doing whatever he said. Then when the Alice Games started, he was too busy with the Alices. I had to make up a silly title just to keep him coming around. He stayed with those women all the time, flattering and wooing them. Making them think they were special. They all fell in love with him." Tears brimmed in her eyes. "Then he killed that Alice. And trapped me in the Ruby Castle. It took two Alice Games to get out!"

Understanding hit Lional. He looked away, a bitter, hurt expression on his face. He set the cup on the table.

Hareson's hands clasped together, and he stared down at them. His ears flopped forward.

I couldn't leave it like this. "Why did he do all that?" I asked, even though I already knew. She might have been alive for several hundreds of years, but she was still a teenager. She was blatantly ignoring the reasons, stubbornly clinging to her wounded emotions and not looking at the whole picture. She was stuck in the same cycle as the rest of Oz, unable to progress. What if she let this scar fester like White Wizard had? "Why was Ace with White Wizard and the Alices all the time? Why did he kill that Alice?"

She shook her head, biting her lips. Her face wrinkled in pain, and her hands fisted in her dress.

Lional stood up, his demeanor suddenly threatening.

I ignored him. It wasn't hard to understand that that type of behavior might be why Red Queen's never had someone to help her heal. As soon as she cried, Lional stepped in and spoiled her so she could keep living in a delusion.

"Why?" I asked the tiny woman.

"It was because of me," she cried, tears spilling over. Her fists jumped up and pressed against her wet cheeks. "It was all for me. To protect me." She sobbed.

"He was White Wizard's slave to protect you. When Ace first witnessed White Wizard turn evil, White Wizard used your safety to force Ace's obedience. But you kind of already knew that, didn't you? And when Ace became the Knight of Oz, White Wizard became more obsessed with Ace."

She nodded. Lional slowly sank back into his chair, looking stricken. Apparently he never knew.

"You said Ace was in charge of the Alices' safety. Weren't you the one who asked him to do that?" As much as I found talking about him with other women distasteful, it was a subject we needed to discuss.

"I was always with the Alices. I just wanted him to be near me. I didn't ask him to play with them so much. I didn't ask him to make them love him." Her voice hardened.

"You know him well," I said softly. "Why do you think he did it?"

"For me." She moaned, emotions calming down. "It was so he had sway over what they decided. It started when White Wizard first tried to charm them. Ace wooed them instead so they would choose me. Then it became a habit for Ace to treat them like that." She shook her head and brushed daintily at the tears on her cheeks. "But I never asked him to do that. I didn't need him to." Her brow pulled together. "I wanted him to love me. Just me." Her voice broke again, but she didn't sob.

Lional's hands clenched on the table, and he glared at them.

I looked at the floor. "He always has." I lifted my eyes, a bitter smile on my face. "Couldn't you tell? Just because it wasn't the love you wanted, doesn't mean he didn't. Do you think he would have done all that for you if he didn't love you?"

She took a sharp breath. "Then why did he betray me? Why did he kill that Alice and lock me up? Why did he become the Cheshire Cat?"

"Because she was going to make herself Queen." I let that sink in as they all stared at me in surprise. "What would have happened to you, to Oz, if that happened? He didn't mean to kill her, just stop her. You would have known that if you actually asked him. At the same time, he'd do—and has done—anything for his country. In my world, we would call him a hero."

She looked away.

Lional scowled. "What does it matter? This is the past. He still abandoned us."

"We'll see." I looked at him, finally understanding Lional's jealousy of Ace. Ace had gotten everything that Lional ever wanted without even trying. And Ace didn't even want it.

Red Queen was quiet, standing still with her hands folded together in front. There was a slight frown on her red lips as she stared at the decorative rug on the floor, thinking and wrestling with the emotions I just forced her to face. Slowly, the lines on her brows smoothed out. I don't know what conclusions she came to, but the tranquility that set in was a good sign in my book.

Finally, she took a deep breath and turned to me. "You said yesterday that you didn't believe falling in love could happen so quickly. You feel differently now. But you're just like me now. Neither of us can have him." There was no venom in her words, just sorrow.

I smiled at her through the sting in my heart. "I guess the difference is, I've always known I couldn't keep him." My eyes dropped to the ground. It hurt, it really did. But it didn't change the fact that I might have already seen Ace for the last time.

Still, there was something else I wanted to say. Someone else needed credit, too. I looked up at Red Queen. "You said you felt love for everyone by nature. But it seems like you are blind to the love other people give. There are other good men here in Oz. One has been professing love to you over and over again his whole life. Maybe you'd be surprised at how happy you could be with him."

Lional glanced at me in shock.

Red Queen's eyes widened in confusion.

I sighed. Enough mushy stuff. It was time to end this. One more test and I could graduate from this place. As much as I was looking forward to going home, the sad sting I felt at the thought of never seeing these three people or Oz again was unexpected. I'd been hunted, soaked, and forced into princess dresses. I'd been turned into a cat, kidnapped by a baboon, and had my murder planned in detail by a mad hyena.

And yet, when I thought of Oz, I thought of a magical place. Where glistening mist hangs in the air and watery rainbows leapt from the center of white flowers. And a handsome man smiles down at me, so relaxed and full of laughter.

I'd go through all this again just to relive that one minute.

But time only stood still in Oz, it didn't go backwards. I blinked out of my thoughts and smiled at them. "Well, I'll see you when I come out of the Emerald Castle." I walked to the door and opened it. "Let's see if I can be the last Alice." I waved at their shocked faces and walked out.

The mist wasn't white anymore, but a golden pinkish color, like the clouds during the sunset, even though it was just before noon. False Dawn. I'd better hurry. Like a trusty bloodhound, the Yellow Path was bright against the dull ground, pointing right through the mist.

People of the army stopped what they were doing to watch me leave the encampment. I didn't know what they were thinking, but I had their full attention. Within seconds, the entire camp was swallowed by mist and disappeared.

CHAPTER TWENTY

THE EMERALD CASTLE LOOMED OVERHEAD, peaking through the mist and casting a faint green color that tainted the rosy pink mist, even from a distance. It was so beautiful with its slender spires and whimsically arched windows, yet striking and almost puzzling because of the overpowering variations of green.

The sky behind it was a rainbow of warm colors that complimented the hue of the castle all the more, as they slowly faded into night with each step I took in the direction of the castle. With my objective so obviously ahead, there was little reason for me to use Yellow Path, even if the stale mist that surrounded me was so thick it rippled when I waved my hands.

The trees had long since thinned out until they were gone, leaving a ground that was hard and flat, with bushes that were few and far between. Then all at once, the Yellow Path ended.

I glanced down and paused. The ground had changed. It wasn't just brown dirt anymore. It looked like someone had painted a giant checker board on it. I crouched down and scratched at it. It wasn't painted or imprinted onto the surface; the dirt was naturally white or black, depending on the spot. I dropped black dirt on a white square, and the dirt immediately turned white. Shaking my head, I looked around and jolted when I saw a plant sitting on a white square.

Brows knitted, I walked over to it. I touched the green, spidery leaves. This was a silver brake fern, a very common plant in America, both in pots and in the wild.

Glancing around, I spotted other plants that belonged on Earth. Not Oz. There weren't many, but history has proved it didn't take long for a foreign species to snuff out a native one. To a closed ecosystem like Oz, it could destroy everything. How did it get here? Ace said that the blood of Alices was ripping holes in Oz. Was this what Ace meant when he said Oz was on the verge of collapsing? Was being connected with my world for so long contaminating Oz?

I stood up and brushed my hands clean. I had to get into the castle before time was up. If the deep orange bleeding into the sky was any indication, I needed to hurry.

The pink haze thinned above me, revealing stars that twinkled in the noonday sky. All at once, the mist flooded across the ground like water and rushed over the side of a cliff, finally exposing a giant void between the castle and Oz, gapped by a hanging wooden bridge.

It wasn't that far, I realized with relief. Just a simple walk across this stretch of checkered ground, and I was safe. I took a couple hurried steps, then stopped.

All the hairs on my body stood up as goosebumps prickled my arms. Frowning, I looked around. Someone was out there, watching me. "Who's there?"

It wasn't Ace. He liked to announce his presence immediately by making me jump. Besides, I'd never experienced this tense feeling in my gut with him. I was about to call out his name as a scare tactic to whoever it was, when someone walked out of the mist.

It was the only person in Oz who wouldn't be scared of Ace. He was dressed in a white tunic, off-white pants, white boots, and short white cape over his right shoulder. His chin was high, and pale blond hair swept back from his face. Every step he took left an ice print in his wake. He stopped in front of me and stared down with pale gray eyes.

I froze. My gut screamed to run as fast as I could, but I couldn't go back. There wasn't enough time. I couldn't reach the Emerald Castle with him in the way, either. Was this where he would try to kill me? Red Queen said this was a neutral zone, but would that include White Wizard dragging me off the Game Board to kill me?

My chin tipped back and I met his gaze levelly. "I assume you're the White Wizard? I've heard a lot about you."

A cold smile cracked his lips. "My, an Alice who's actually charming. Quite different from the earlier versions. Yes, I am Queen Candidate White. The rightful Queen of Oz."

I leaned on a hip, trying to act like I wasn't as scared as I was. "I've heard a couple of people claiming that title. How are you any different?"

His hands thrust out wide. Suddenly, the ground around us was frozen and under six inches of snow. "As you can see, I don't need people to tell me I am the right Queen. Oz itself submits to me."

My arms clamped around my body to fend off the sudden freezing air, but there was nothing to do about my feet. "Some people would call that oppression." Sarcasm laced my voice.

His hands fisted and fell to his side. "Charming and

cheeky. Very different indeed. I might have a use for you, after all." His hand came up and rubbed his smooth jaw in thought.

"Why would I help you? You want me dead."

A cruel smile touched his lips. "It's because I want you dead. You see, I don't need you to pick me as Queen. I could have killed you a number of times since you got here and achieved that."

I gasped when ice wrapped around my legs, effectively locking me into place.

"However," he went on, "there is something I want out of the Emerald Castle that only an Alice can get."

My brows drew together, and another foot of ice rose over my legs. Shivering in earnest, I glared at him. "And what is that?"

"The Vorpal Blade."

My eyes widened. Ignorantly, I thought he wanted the wand. Then he'd possess all of Oz's magic. But why would he? It contains magic that he's already rejected. But Vorpal Blade can do something that he can't.

White Wizard smiled wide. "If there is only one Queen Candidate, there won't be a need for another Alice Games. After that little Red girl is dead, Oz will be mine."

So that's what his play was. No wonder I hadn't seen him yet. He was after a bigger target than me. He must not know that Ace had my necklace. I hid my fear with disdain. "Maybe. Now tell me why I should help you when you're freezing my butt off?" I motioned to the ice.

"That?" He smiled. "It's a promise. If you don't agree to help me ..." He left the sentence hanging. The ice grew another foot up to my waist.

"What do I get out of the deal?"

"To live. Simple, isn't it? Once the Queen has been

selected, the Alice is sent home. You won't even have to die." His logic was chilling, even to me.

"Ever thought I'd say 'yes' to get out of here, then betray you?" I stammered through chattering teeth.

He laughed. "That would be foolish. After all, I will be waiting for you right here. That Red child doesn't have the persistence to come here and help you. Depending on what you carry out of the Emerald Castle, you'll either live or die. Understand?" He turned and walked back into the mist.

When he completely disappeared, the ice around me vanished. My freezing legs collapsed onto the frozen ground. Muttering curses at him, I clawed my way off the snow patch and flopped onto the warm white and black dirt. I lay there for a while until my feet stopped tingling, thinking about what he had just said.

So he'd come to the same conclusion I had. The only way to stop the Alice Games was to make sure there was only one Queen. And it sounded like he knew how to do it.

Of course he wanted Red Queen dead. I'd witnessed him yelling it at the top of his lungs to her face. I frowned, thinking of that scene. He'd threatened to kill her if she ever became a real Queen Candidate. It was the combined effort of Ace's obedience during Jewel Queen's rule and Oz postponing Red Queen's election until the moment the last Queen was murdered that kept Red Queen alive until the Alice Games began. Then the two Queen Candidates were physically separated.

Ace was given Blood at the start of the Alice Games, and he lived in peace with Red Queen—until he broke the rules and became the Cheshire Cat. Then Blood was taken away, and he was forced to live with White Wizard.

That couldn't be a coincidence, could it? The Vorpal Blade was the only thing that could permanently kill someone. But why couldn't people die, anyway? I'd thought it was because the land was sick. Maybe that explained the lack of births, but not the deaths. After all, Bauer and Jewel Queen died, and that was when Red Queen, the last born child, was about sixteen. Again White Wizard's face came to mind as he furiously screamed, *The day she becomes a Queen Candidate, nothing will stop me from killing her!"*

Was that it?

In order to protect Red Queen, Oz stopped the death cycle for all of Oz. Then to get around the problem that no one could die, not even the Queen Candidate it wanted to replace, Oz created the Vorpal Blade and gave it to the Knight of Oz.

I paused, remembering the scene I saw with Ace and Red Queen sitting happily together. That event happened before the Games started, but it was still an example of how things were supposed to be. While Ace was with the correct Queen, he could keep the sword while Oz waited for him to understand and do his job. But as soon as he was banished to chaos, Oz took away the sword so it wouldn't fall into White Wizard's hands.

I bit my lips, staring at the stars that were getting brighter in the dark red sky. Why am I here? What was I supposed to do? But even as I thought that, I already knew. Oz couldn't talk to anyone here in Oz, so it looked for outside help, someone it could talk to. To help those figure out what they should do.

"It makes sense now," I said out loud. "I'm just the delivery girl. And here everyone thought I was so important." I laughed, realizing the joke was on me. It was a relief, yet at the same time, it didn't make things easier. I looked over at the large green castle, frowning.

"Well, it sounds like I'll have to make sure both packages get to their rightful owners."

The faintly glowing Emerald Castle was pretty no matter how I looked at it, but it didn't change the fact that only pale clouds supported it. Not very comforting. And the only way into said floating castle was on a wooden drawbridge with no railings, also dangling in the almost black air. At least the door was open, even if it looked dark inside.

Scowling, I shoved a hand through my hair and pulled tight, trying to make the pain distract me from the nausea churning in my stomach. This sucked. A lot. Well, standing here wasn't going to get it over with and I was almost out of time. "Here goes," I whispered, and took a big breath. Man, I really didn't want to do this.

I ran for the door as fast as I could. The first step onto the bridge, where I could see the beams of blue sky between the cracks of the planks almost turned me back. But the wood stayed steady, and my momentum carried me to the next step. The updraft coming from the cliff blew my hair in my face. I flinched but kept running. It took me a couple steps to realize that with each time my foot hit the wood, the green castle in front of me glowed brighter and brighter as if taking the place of the sun.

I squinted and lifted a hand to block out the light as I tried to keep my eyes focused on the open door, but my gaze slipped to the side. Below, there was nothing but clouds highlighted in green, floating in the black pitch. It really did look like the end of the world. I tripped on a plank and staggered, arms flailing wildly, before gaining my balance. My stomach twisted, and it took everything I had not to hurl.

I would have given anything to have Ace's hand to steady me now, but that wasn't an option. It was my turn to help him. I clenched my teeth together so tight they hurt and ran faster than ever to the door. When I passed through the threshold of Emerald Castle, I bent over, sucking in air and trying not to melt into jelly. I did not want to do that again. Unfortunately, I still had to give Red Queen her wand and that drawbridge was the only way out.

I looked up, and my mouth dropped open. "Oh, wow."

I didn't see any furniture, but the castle didn't need it to be amazing. The glowing, green walls were covered in moving pictures. To my right was the Shibuya Crossing in Japan. I watched as the cars stopped moving and people swarmed the intersection, walking whatever direction they wanted to go. To my left was Times Square, with all the people bustling around the taxis. The ceiling resembled a green sky, complete with clouds and birds flying in the direction opposite of the entrance. On the green marble floor was a mural of a rainforest floor somewhere with insects and small animals scurried around in the same direction as the birds.

I took my cue and started walking.

The pictures around me changed with every wall I passed. A car raced by a sign that said Highway 66, horses running across a meadow, airplanes passed overhead, and whales breached the water's surface before diving again. No matter what the moving picture was, it always had the same theme. Everything moved in the same direction, telling me which way to turn. Each picture was a transition or migration, getting from one place to another. Just like the Emerald Castle was the transition from Earth to Oz.

I trailed my finger along a scene of ants walking along a tree branch and stopped when the endless hall opened up to a room. I'd walked the whole castle, and this was the first room I'd seen. Not that this castle needed any rooms. No one lived here, and only two objects were kept here.

In the middle of the circular room were two rectangular stands. The wand floated above the stand on the left and the sword floated above the stand on the right. My eyes wandered over the red sparkly wand. It was a foot long, slender and seemed almost ... feminine? For a smooth, red stick, anyway.

The scabbard was gold with silver swirls around it. I guessed the intricately designed handle should have been gold, too, but it was stained red. Blood red. The color wasn't uniform but a tie-dye of light and dark. Though beautiful, the weapon seemed to pulse angrily. Like it hated being here and the state it was in. Given the aura that it gave off, I could see why people feared it so much.

And I was going to touch it.

I swallowed and walked closer.

The images of twenty women, ranging from early teens to late twenties, appeared and moved on the round wall. Most of them were beautiful and blonde. *They must be the Alices that made it to the Emerald Castle.*

I watched as nineteen of them reached out and grabbed the wand. Immediately the sword sank into the pedestal, disappearing completely. Only one grabbed the sword and let the wand withdraw. As the wand disappeared, she threw her head back in a silent scream. She hunched over and grabbed her stomach as if in pain and dropped the sword. She collapsed to the ground, and her picture vanished.

"Great," I muttered. Ace had already warned me that it didn't like to be touched, I just didn't think it hated it that bad. I shoved my hands through my hair and pulled hard, staring at the wand and sword.

If I took just the wand, I wouldn't get hurt and Red Queen would be Queen again. Then Oz would keep going in circles and Ace would stay a slave. Or maybe he would truly give up, which would be even worse.

But I completely believed that the Vorpal Blade needed to come out. Not because of White Wizard's threat, but because it was the only thing that was strong enough to stand up to him. Maybe. That is, if Ace could actually do it. White Wizard had kept Ace so broken.

I believed that he could. I was going to have to bet my life—and all of Oz—on it.

If I was wrong, then hopefully White Wizard wouldn't get the sword. Since the Vorpal Blade was part of Oz, I was sure he could use it, just like he used the ice power Oz gave him. That meant that Red Queen could too. But truth be told, I wasn't willing to test that theory unless absolutely necessary.

I took a breath and studied the objects. Oz had just given me a warning, by showing me the pictures of the previous Alices. To get both items, I could only guess I'd have to grab them simultaneously, so neither object disappeared.

My hands came out and stopped an inch from the sword and wand. I licked my lips. "I hope this is the right thing to do." Not only in grabbing both, but touching the sword at all. I had a hunch this wasn't going to be pleasant, judging by the angry aura around the sword. I sucked in a breath.

"Three, two, one," I whispered, and grabbed them both.

The sword vibrated in my hand, sending electric shocks up my arm and filling my body with pain. I gasped. *It was trying to kill me.* This sword was death for anyone who touched it. Anyone but Ace. It wanted Ace, demanded him.

Thoughts of him flooded my mind so strongly that my surroundings blacked out and he was all I could see.

At the same time, the wand reacted. It felt my pain and responded by glowing red. Relief and healing flowed up my left arm, swirling around my body and fixing what Blood was doing. It would prefer to be held by Red Queen, but it was content to stay in my hand.

The two personalities collided in me and sparked with dislike.

I was dying and healing at the same time. They were yin and yang. Life and death. It was clear they were never meant to be held by the same person. Certainly not by someone who wasn't chosen by Oz. It was only because the wand was sympathetic that I was alive. If not, the power of their battle inside me would have shredded my body.

A constant tide of electric pricks covered my body, and my head felt like it was splitting apart. Like a bad ear infection, needles of pain stabbed at my ear and eyes from the inside, numbing my thoughts and senses. Ringing started in my ears and my peripheral vision seemed to narrow.

I turned around and began to stumble through the castle, every step a shot of pain and relief. All the pictures were gone from the walls, leaving just the glowing green hues. I didn't need them to find my way out, but the distraction would have been wonderful. Instead all I could think about was the magic that mingled and collided inside me.

My breath came out in huffs. The Vorpal Blade was so heavy, it was like trying to lift a dumbbell with one hand, but I didn't dare put my hands together. I didn't know what would happen if the sword and wand touched, but I wasn't about to find out now. My muscles screamed as I held the sword up by the handle so it didn't touch the ground as it continued to send painful currents through my already exhausted arms. As soon as my arm would painfully lower, the wand would send a wave of balm through my body and I could go on. The constant high and low was disorienting.

I had to blink repeatedly to keep my eyes focused. My feet tripped over themselves. I couldn't let go of the sword and wand. I didn't know what would happen if I did. What if they both disappeared and everything I'd done was for nothing? How many more Alice Games would it take for another girl to finally understand Oz and Ace?

I staggered around a corner and paused.

The front door to Oz was right there, just down this hall, a dark hole surrounded by the emerald green walls. On the other side of that door was Red Queen. But more importantly, Ace. Then I could give him the sword and see if I was right about him.

Or if my mistake would cost Oz—and me—everything.

CHAPTER TWENTY-ONE

I LEANED against the frame of the castle door, my breathing labored, and looked out at the world on the other side of the floating drawbridge. While I was inside, the mist had lifted, revealing the entire Game Board like a giant chessboard. In the dim light of False Dawn, three groups, all stained green from the Emerald Castle's light, were stationed around the white and black square. Red Queen and her army lined the right side. Ahead of me milled a ragtag bunch of people with Hatter in the lead. On the left side White Wizard stood with his arms folded, staring in my direction. Thousands of humanoid ice monsters stood behind him, created by his power. They shifted around him, gnashing their jaws together and leaving frost wherever they stepped.

The other two armies kept looking from the ice monsters to the Emerald Castle, then back to the monsters.

Ace was nowhere to be seen. Finding him in all those people was going to be hard enough. Was I really going to have to do it in the semi-dark too? I didn't have time to worry about that, not with the Vorpal Blade assaulting me like this.

This was it. Time to find out if I was right, or if I just *really* messed up everyone's life.

First, I had to get past the horrible floating bridge. Since this was my second time, it should have been easier, only it wasn't. I could barely stay upright, and every time my staggered steps took me out of the middle of the bridge and closer to the edge, my stomach twisted painfully and it was all I could do to not puke. My boots beat across the wooden planks as heavy as my heart. With each step, the sky around me grew lighter and lighter as normal colors returned to the world, opposite of when I first walked into the castle. It was the only positive thing that was happening to me. The wind whipped my clothes and hair around, blowing my face and making it harder to see.

Worst of all, it tugged at the slight wand in my hand, threatening to pull it away. But if I lost the wand now, the Vorpal blade would kill me.

Three feet left.

Two feet and then I would be on solid ground.

One more step. The sun was completely out.

I sighed and hunched over as I stumbled across the wonderful black and white dirt. I made it. I got them both out. Now all I had to do was get the sword to Ace and the wand to Red Queen. In that order.

A sudden roar of voices filled my pain-clogged ears like a tidal wave. I jolted and looked around, blinking continually to keep things in focus.

White Wizard tossed his head back and laughed maliciously as his monsters clicked their jaws with fervor. "It's mine! Finally!"

“Get the Alice!” Hatter squealed harshly, over his hoard as they screeched animal noises.

“Ali!”

Red Queen’s scream was almost drowned out by Lional roaring, “Protect the Alice! Defend the true Queen of Oz!”

All at once, thousands of people and ice monsters rushed at me.

I gasped in horror and started to hobble towards Red Queen. Adrenaline helped, but I still wasn’t moving that fast. *Go faster*, I thought, *go faster*! I might not be able to give her wand back yet, but I would at least be safe with her until I could. “Ace!” I yelled, but my voice was breathy and weak, easily washed out by the noise around me.

As the armies collided on all sides, fighting broke out in the three-way war. Men and women paired up to take on the nine-foot-tall ice monsters. Red Queen’s men encountered Hatter’s men and they attacked each other with weapons on hand. Ice monsters swung their arms and stepped on people as they went. Yells of rage, screams of pain, and puffs of dust filled the air.

My heart sank even more as Red Queen, and Hareson at her side, vanished from sight as the taller people in her army ran past her. Leading the charge was Lional, golden armor gleaming and a drawn sword as sharp as the danger in his eyes. His golden hair bounced with every step. He was heading right to me.

I half turned from him. “Don’t touch it!” I yelled. “Don’t touch the sword!” He wasn’t the Knight. If he—or any of the people around me—touched the Vorpal Blade, they’d die.

He must not have heard because he continued to charge full steam at me.

Lional was only feet away now.

"No!" I yelled and hugged the sword to my chest and hunched over it.

He sped right past me with a howl and lifted his sword high.

My eyes widened. I turned just as he brought his sword heavily down at White Wizard's head. He was only ten feet behind me.

White Wizard blocked the blow with a sword made of ice, needing two hands to absorb the power of Lional's attack. He let go of the hilt with one of his hands and thrust it out, shooting sharp ice crystals at Lional. Lional dodged out of the way. The crystals hit the people behind, causing several of them to explode into dust. Lional and White Wizard didn't even notice, they were too focused on each other.

"Get out of my way," White Wizard ordered coolly and lifted his chin in command.

"I only take orders from my Queen," Lional growled back.

With a yell of fury, White Wizard attacked Lional with his sword.

It felt so good physically to simply stand there, but I didn't have time for that. As much as I hated to leave Lional alone, the only way I could help him was to get the sword to Ace.

"Ace!" I yelled pathetically. "Red Queen! Where are you?"

I heard a horrible clicking noise behind me. I turned my head just in time to see an ice monster stomp up to me. Its movements were slow on the dirt, its feet freezing to the ground with every step, forcing the monster to pull its feet free every time. It clicked its jaw together, hollow eyes glowing, and reached out a huge hand for me.

I gasped, not sure how I was going to get away. Even with its slow movement, it was still faster than I was.

A Munchkin came out of the crowd next to me, with long arms like an ape and dressed in red. He gave a war cry and charged the monster, brandishing his hoe like an axe. He smacked the monster's hand with all his might. His blow did little, chipping just a tiny chunk of ice off the back of the monster's hand, but it pushed the ice monster's hand off course.

The monster's fingers touched the Vorpal Blade.

The sword pulsed in anger, causing me to huff out a yell.

Suddenly, the ice monster exploded into snow, drifting out in all directions.

The Munchkin's mouth dropped open. "I did that?" he whispered. Then he tightened his hold on his hoe and ran back into the crowd, determined to find another enemy.

I kept limping on, weaving around people so I didn't accidently touch them with the Vorpal Blade. With each step, it was getting harder and harder to see straight as images blurred and overlapped each other.

The wand could feel that Red Queen was close. It pulled toward her, wanted her, and the more it began focusing on her, the less it healed me.

The anger pulsing from the Vorpal Blade grew more intense, like a thousand bees stinging every inch of my body.

I gasped and bent over, panting as my vision blurred. I was dying. Truly dying. I didn't know if I was going to make it to Red Queen or Ace. The knowledge sent a shock of panic through my mind and caused my already laboring heart to stutter. I gulped at the air, needing the coolness in my overly warm body.

If I just let it go, put the Vorpal Blade down, this terrible sensation would go away. Even with it being so distracted, the wand would still heal me in seconds. All I had to do was let go of the sword. I could leave it here, go get Ace and bring him back to it.

I couldn't. The realization was almost worse than the pain. If I put it down, what would happen? What if someone else touched it? What if that person was White Wizard? Everything would be for nothing.

"Ali!"

Red Queen's voice broke through my frantic thoughts.

I blinked away the tunnel vision creeping in and looked around.

There she was, holding a shield, with Hareson right behind her fending off one of Hatter's men. She was so close, just twenty or so feet away, but there were dozens of people between us, fighting with each other. They moved and exchanged blows, blocking my view of her.

Still, just the sight of her elated me. Half my job was done—the latter half, but she was still here. I could almost give her the wand. I gave a relieved smile and stumbled towards her.

"Ali! Ali! Where are you?"

It was *his* voice. Ace's. He was somewhere behind me, close enough I could hear him.

My eyes widened. Longing for him welled up in me, rivaling the sudden similar surge from Blood as it flooded my mind with more images of him. Ace. He could make it all better. Take away the pain of the sword, make White Wizard go away, and I knew that with one hug, I would finally feel safe again.

I turned, looking to where his voice came from. "Ace!" I

yelled for all I was worth. It was like a newborn kitten's mew.

"Ali!" Red Queen's voice was getting louder behind me. "Where are you going?"

I shook my head, throwing off the guilt of walking away from her and stumbled forward. I heard him. I know I heard him. Where is he? There were so many people, moving and shifting that my blurry eyes couldn't focus on anything. "Ace!"

"Ali!" A hand grabbed my shirt from behind and pulled me to a stop. Red Queen hurried in front of me and gasped, staring at the sword.

The wand immediately started to vibrate in my hand, like the humming of a happy child.

I yelped and stepped away from her. "No! Not yet! Not yet! Don't touch it!" In the Emerald Castle, I might have considered giving her the sword, but there was no way I was going to hand it to her now, knowing the pain it inflicts. And if she took her wand now, that would be the worst thing possible.

Oddly enough, as soon as she was by me, the painful pulse the sword gave off lessened. Slightly. It was just enough for me to finally take a real breath, though I still winced, it finally felt like the air was getting to my lungs.

Her eyes widened with horror and she paled. "What are you doing?! Why do you have the Vorpal Blade? That's why White Wizard is still here, isn't it?" She gripped the rim of her small red shield until her knuckles were white.

"I have the wand too, but I need to keep using it a little longer. I'm sorry." I assured her quickly, and swayed. "But first I need to find Ace." The surge of energy his voice had given me was wearing off. I couldn't hear him anymore. Was he getting farther away? How long was I going to have to carry this thing? I didn't know how much longer I could last.

"Ace?" Red Queen squeaked in disbelief. "What is going on? You have to let go of the Vorpal Blade! It will kill you!" She bit her lip with fear, but still reached up to take it away.

I staggered back, horrified myself. She was willingly trying to touch it? Just for me, an Alice? As much as I didn't want to die—badly didn't want to die—I was replaceable to the Game. Red Queen was not.

"I know. Believe me, I know," I moaned. "That's why you can't touch. I don't know if my theory about you is correct or not. Please, I need Ace."

She shook her head. "You're not making any sense." She waved her shield in the air.

Movement from the corner of my eye caused me to look over just as Hatter broke out of the fighting. He was dressed in a tarnished suit of armor that didn't fit well over his round belly. On top of his helmet was a black top hat with his dingy crown around it.

He looked at me. "Oh, the Alice! You were so stubborn this morning, I didn't think you'd be such a good girl and bring them to me," he squealed gleefully, like Red Queen wasn't even there.

"What?" Red Queen gaped at him then looked at me in complete alarm.

I shook my head at him. "Do you, like ... are you even sane?" I finally asked, even though I already knew the answer. But seriously, all this was going on around us—his people were turning into dust while ice monsters were crashing around like giants—and he thought I was doing it for him?

He held out his arms and motioned with his fingers.

"Come now, come now." He giggled and squirmed with uncontained excitement. When I didn't move, he snapped fast as a dry twig. "Give it to me!" His face contorted into a ghoulish mask of rage.

I shook my head slowly, his moods throwing me off. "No."

Red Queen glared at him. She held out her petite arm and positioned the shield in front of me then took a couple steps forward, asserting herself in a way that finally made Hatter look at her. She lifted her chin, full of royal disapproval. "Lord Hatter, if you continue with these traitorous acts, steps will be taken against you." She might have been tiny, but in that moment she seemed like she was ten feet tall.

His eyes widened and his eyes shifted away from hers, cowed under her royal aura.

My brows rose, surprised at how powerful she came across just then.

"Ali!" Ace's voice echoed from somewhere close again.

My heart hitched painfully and I looked around, desperate. I still couldn't see him.

My movement triggered something in Hatter. He gave a grating snarl and lunged at us, hands out like claws. "I am the true Queen!"

Red Queen gasped and stepped back, causing me to almost fall as I wrenched the sword away from her. Hatter missed completely and landed on his knees, sputtering in shock.

"His hat!" I gasped. Hatter's closeness sent Blood into a new fit of rage. I gasped and bent over with a moan. My insides suddenly felt like they were on fire.

At first I didn't think she'd understand, but she gave a slight nod. She swung her shield out and smacked his ridiculous hat right off his helmet with a bell-like ring. The hat flew to the side, and the crown flung off as it tumbled through the air. It flopped onto a black square, upside down, as the crown skittered across the ground, only to be crushed under the foot of an ice monster.

Hatter screamed and grabbed his head. "HAT! HAT! HAT! HAT!" His eyes widened so big, it was amazing they didn't pop out. He clawed at his head, screaming and frantic.

Red Queen stumbled back from him, startled as he writhed like a madman.

But I could barely move from the electric pain causing my body to go numb. My right knee buckled and I wobbled, almost dropping to the ground, but I was able to put my weight onto my left in time to stay up. But not for much longer. Someone was calling my name, I thought, but it was hard to hear over the ringing in my ears. I stared up through blurry eyes at Red Queen as her mouth moved and she hurried to me, but I had no idea what she said.

Ace. It was the only clear thought in my foggy mind. *Need Ace.*

My feet shifted to the side and I wobbled like a frail old lady as I desperately looked around. It was hard to understand what was happening around me because everything was blurred with double images overlapping each other as all the color bled out.

All at once, the ground exploded into whiteness.

Simultaneously, the Vorpal Blade and the wand reacted, vibrating in anger together. A yellow shield appeared in front of me, created by one item—or both. I was protected from the piercing of the whiteness, but the ice crystal thrust into the shield with enough force that I was thrown from my feet. I hit someone small behind me and we were both taken out. We both screamed as we fell. She exhaled with a painful gasp when I landed full on her. I steamrolled over her and tumbled several more times across the ground before coming to a stop face down.

It was all I could do to huff breath in and out with my face pressed flat against the ground. The smell of dirt filled my nose and dried out my open mouth with its gritty texture. Even so, I just wanted to lie here forever.

My whole body hurt. It tingled painfully from the torture of the Vorpal Blade. My back was bruised from the fall, and my head felt like it was in a vise from hitting the ground somewhere. The only thing that didn't hurt was my left hand. It was warm and so oddly not in pain that it didn't seem like it belonged to my body. Like the soothing water of a warm shower, the wand continued to send healing pulses to my body, the soothing sensation creeping up inch by inch.

It felt so nice, as if the angry attack of the Vorpal Blade didn't exist anymore. I felt only the high, never the low.

A chilling warning clicked somewhere in the back of my hazing mind. I flexed my right fingers. There was nothing but dirt in my fist.

The Vorpal Blade was gone.

CHAPTER TWENTY-TWO

PANICKED ADRENALINE OPENED MY EYES. With a moan, I pushed up to my elbows and looked around, the stretch feeling good on my sore back and stomach muscles. Slowly my eyes came into focus.

Five feet in front of me, Red Queen lay on her back, unmoving, with her face turned away from me.

She was the one I'd flattened? I tried to jump to my feet, but my body wasn't ready to move yet. I sagged back to the ground, muscles like jelly. Desperately, I clawed at the dirt, trying to get to her. Get the wand to her. How badly was she hurt? I didn't kill her, did I? She would have turned into dust, right? But what if she had been touched by the Vorpal Blade?

Horrified anew, I looked around.

There it was. The sword lay so innocently five feet ahead of Red Queen, right next to a pile of dust and a cluster of sharp ice crystals poking out of the ground. It took a second to process that that's where I'd originally stood. And the pile of dust was Hatter.

It took a second longer to realize that no one was

moving. It wasn't that my ears were clogged up, there was a stilled hush in the air. Everyone on the entire Game Board was standing motionless, weapons lowered and staring as if waiting to see what would happen next. At me and Red Queen.

That's when movement drew my attention and I gasped. I was wrong. There was someone moving on the Game Board.

White Wizard walked confidently across the checkered ground, leaving icy footprints in his wake. He barely even looked like he'd been battling at all. There were a couple wrinkles and maybe three dirt smudges on his white clothes, but not even a lock of white-blond hair was out of place. His chiseled face was tight, his pale eyes wide and intense. And fixated on Red Queen.

Barely visible behind him was Lional, on the ground and covered in ice from the waist down. His sword was gone and one arm was limp at his side. With his other hand, he desperately hacked at the ice around his legs with a short sword.

But I didn't have time to focus on Lional. White Wizard was getting closer. He was almost at the Vorpal Blade. I took it out of the Emerald Castle. If he got it now, then I as good as killed Red Queen. I pushed up to my hands and knees. They were shaky but I was at least able to stay up now. Unfortunately, my knees buckled painfully when I tried to stand. I gasped and collapsed back to the ground.

Come on wand, I begged. *Help me!*

Hareson pushed his way out of the crowd on my right. He was bent over, left arm wrapped around his middle, his long, thin sword gripped in his right hand. Even from here, his breathing was visibly labored and there were cuts in his clothing. Still, he gritted his teeth and pointed his sword at White Wizard. "Ozians, gather—"

"Silence!" White Wizard yelled and stomped a foot on the ground. Frost exploded from him and spread across the ground like white ants, covering everything it touched.

People scampered out of the way in terror, but no one gave a peep.

Hareson was left alone, unmoving. He gasped as frost climbed up his legs and solidified into a chunk of ice encapsulating his feet and sword.

White Wizard scathed Hareson with a look. "I'll take care of you animals later. But first, there's something I've been waiting for, for a very long time." He turned back to his goals.

The Vorpal Blade had repelled the frost, causing it to divide around it, coincidently protecting Red Queen and me from the frost as well. That was something, right? It seemed like everything that had to do with White Wizard repulsed it. So it wouldn't let White Wizard use it. Right? It was a desperate, and probably vain, hope.

I pushed up and staggered to my feet, legs shaking and head spinning. I only made it a couple steps before I collapsed to the ground again. If only I could make the wand work, do something with it, instead of waiting for it to heal me. Frustrated, I bit my lip until I tasted blood. No, this wasn't happening. White Wizard couldn't get the Vorpal Blade. What had I done?

My muscles protested all the more, but I tried to stand again and fell right next to the unconscious Red Queen. I pushed the wand into her hand and closed her fingers around it. In any other game, this would have locked White Wizard up, but since the Vorpal Blade was out, it was essentially anyone's game now. I just hoped that the wand healed Red Queen fast enough.

"Are you actually trying to resist me, Alice?" White Wizard asked coolly. "And here, I was trying to figure out if I should reward you for bringing me the Vorpal Blade, or punish you for not coming when I called your name." He might have been talking to me, but he didn't take his eyes off the sword vibrating on the ground.

He'd called me? I'd never heard him. There must have been too much noise going on for my compromised ears to hear. It's not like I would have come anyway.

I glared at him and tried to retaliate, but my voice was too raw for proper words.

White Wizard stopped in front of the Vorpal Blade and stared down at it, eyes like frigid flames. "You *will* obey me," he ordered it. The aura that pulsed from him was threatening and belittling. It might have been aimed at the sword, but even the people backed away even more.

The sword vibrated harder on the ground as if it was fighting White Wizard's will. It rocked and shook on the ground, like it was caught between opposing magnets. Then slowly, the vibrating stopped. It lay on the ground, a beautiful, blood-stained but ordinary sword.

My last shred of hope died. I never found Ace. Red Queen was hurt too much to use her wand. And now the Vorpal Blade has given in. It was all my fault because I thought I knew better.

I was wrong.

White Wizard reached for the sword. A silver flash shot in front of his hand, blocking his path. White Wizard's hand jumped back up to his chest, fingers curling with anger and he made an annoyed sound low in his throat.

With a thud, a familiar blue and silver throwing knife sank into the ground next to the Vorpal Blade.

I gasped.

Ace materialized, crouching low over the Vorpal Blade. His hand wrapped possessively around the hilt and he stood up, stepping away from White Wizard. His eyes were wide in an almost childlike way, ears flat against his skull, almost disappearing entirely in his orange hair.

The crowd shifted and bumped into each other, but their terrified noises never rose higher than a murmur.

"*Cheshire Cat*," White Wizard spat the name in annoyance. "What are you doing?"

Ace opened his mouth, paused and closed it. Almost like he didn't know what he was doing yet. His gaze slid away from White Wizard's until he stared at the ground, shoulders bowed. Even so, his hand fisted on the Vorpal Blade, thumb rubbing along the hilt affectionately.

White Wizard gave a dismissive sound and waved a hand. "Nevermind. We'll address this later. Well, now that you have the Vorpal Blade, Cheshire Cat, kill the Red girl."

Ace flinched and looked at her. All emotions slid away from his face until it was nothing but stone cold.

"No." My voice was barely audible to my own ears.

Just then, Red Queen moaned and stirred. Her eyes drifted open and blinked into focus. Confused, she looked around then gasped up at Ace, holding the Vorpal Blade and staring at her. "Ace?" she mouthed, what color was left draining from her face.

"Kill her!" White Wizard's yell echoed in the still air.

Red Queen flinched.

Ace looked at me, his usual laughing eyes dead except for one emotion. Shame. Standing in front of me, being ordered to do what he was, he was ashamed. It was like he was saying, *This is what I really am. I'm sorry.*

It broke my heart. Slowly, I shook my head. "Don't listen to him."

He looked back at the ground, face contorted in confusion.

"I told you to kill her!" White Wizard pointing at Red Queen.

She gasped and scooted back into me, almost crawling into my lap and knocking me over. It wasn't Ace that scared her like this, it was White Wizard. She might have her wand now, but being this close to him, she'd lost her nerve.

Slowly the confusion cleared on Ace's face, replaced with bitter resolve. "No."

White Wizard froze, eyes wide with shock. In a flash, he lunged forward, grabbed Ace's hair and shoved him face first into the dirt. "You do not say that word to me!" Ice crystals formed around his hand, seeping onto Ace's hair.

Ace didn't fight, just lay there as if knowing what was going to happen and accepting it.

My stomach twisted, seeing the scene play out. Ace had already warned me about the abuse, but it was still jarring to see it firsthand.

Red Queen gasped and slapped a hand over her mouth. "Don't!"

"Stop it!" I yelled at the same time, but our voices were overpowered by White Wizard's.

"You don't have the right to ever tell me no. You are nothing. You have always been nothing. If it wasn't for me, you would still be nothing. I *made* you. And you are my slave," White Wizard drove his words into Ace by grinding his face into the dirt.

Angry now, I pushed Red Queen off and stood up. My

legs were still shaking, but I stood anyway. "You're wrong!" I yelled with all I was worth.

White Wizard looked at me, furious. It wasn't hard to understand what was going on in his mind. Just like his father subjugated him, White Wizard was obsessed with making sure that Ace was below him. It was a need that went deeper than even his desire to kill Red Queen.

Ace turned his head, alarm bright in his eyes. Funny, when he was dealing with White Wizard, his face was like a stone, but as soon as I or Red Queen was involved, he showed emotion. He showed what was in his heart. He didn't care that he was hurt, but every time White Wizard looked at us, he'd panic.

"He's not nothing." My hands fisted, nails biting into my palm. For the first time, it didn't matter that everyone was staring at me. There was only one person that mattered. I didn't do all this for him to keep being tortured like this. My voice was quiet, but it still carried because there was nothing to compete with. "He's not you and you aren't your father. You might have tried your best to crush him, but he isn't poisoned like you. He may be 'cursed' and have all those skills you forced on him. And own the Vorpal Blade. But it just made him better at his true Role. The Knight of Oz."

There were gasps all around.

I lowered my chin and glared at White Wizard. "I know you know his Role. You know exactly what he can do. That's one of the reasons why you're so obsessed with keeping him down."

Ace was staring at me, eyes wide and hanging onto my every word. Like it was the first time the idea had occurred to him. Slowly, the dead expression in his eyes melted away, leaving wonder.

White Wizard's fury turned to loathing. "It was *you*," he seethed. His tone went from hot to deadly cold, that frigid concentration that took him from scary to terrifying. "You're the reason he defies me. You're trying to take away my slave." He let go of Ace and stood up slowly, tilted his head back and to the side so he could look down on me, eyes white with hate. "Here I thought you were a smart Alice. I'll teach you to touch my things." A sword made out of ice appeared in his hand.

The blood drained from my face, leaving me light headed in fear.

Red Queen's tiny hand grabbed mine and she pulled me back, trying to make me run.

White Wizard thrust out his hand.

Ice wrapped around our feet, freezing all the way up the ankles. We wobbled, mid-motion. I gasped at the sudden biting cold, and goosebumps covered my body.

"No, no." White Wizard tsked. "You can't go anywhere. Not until you're made an example of. I was going to use that stupid lion and the stuffy hare first, but I think you would make a much better example." He took a step forward.

Ace appeared in front of him. White Wizard was just barely fast enough to bring his sword up and block Ace's thrust with the Vorpal Blade. There were still ice chunks in Ace's hair, making the orange locks stick out in places, but all the muscles in his back and arms strained as he put a lot of pressure into his attack.

Gasps and echoes of shock echoed around us.

White Wizard's eyes were wide. "How dare you attack me?" He grunted with the effort of fending off Ace's attack.

"Don't touch my Ali." Ace's voice was hard and strong, the same voice I heard when he was the Cheshire Cat. But for the first time, it didn't scare me.

My eyes widened as a gentle burning fire lit in my heart and masked the discomfort of my feet. Too many emotions tightened my chest, actually seeing him face off against White Wizard. The way that he said 'my Ali' made me feel so special, like no other title had. Like I was one of a kind, irreplaceable. I was also so proud of him for standing up to his demon, the man who had been tormenting him for centuries. Those emotions were battling with the gut-wrenching fear that he could get hurt.

"Ace," Red Queen whispered beside me in shock, as if she was seeing a whole new side to him.

"Everything in Oz belongs to me." White Wizard glared at Ace, his betrayal adding a new light of hatred in White Wizard's eyes. "You, the Alice, the Vorpal Blade. *Oz belongs to me*. I'll take great pleasure in reminding you of that as you watch helplessly."

Ice grew over Ace's feet, but before it fully solidified, Ace vanished and materialized behind White Wizard, who had to turn and block another attack.

"Not anymore." Ace attacked again, this time forcing White Wizard back a step. A chip appeared in the ice blade where it touched the Vorpal Blade.

With a furious yell, White Wizard went on the offensive. Ace blocked, grunting under the attack, and shifted his weight, forcing White Wizard past him. Ace swung, aiming at White Wizard's side, but a block of ice appeared between them and the Vorpal Blade sank into it. Ace stilled, ears perked up, and disappeared, sword and all, just as jagged ice spears thrust out of the ice block. But White Wizard didn't have long to relax, since Ace was at him again, seconds later.

It was like watching a game of chess. Every time one man made a move, the other had a solution to it. White Wizard was an amazing swordsman, his movements fast and precise. Any weaknesses he had were covered by his magic, the ice blocks or spears appearing—or disappearing—as needed.

Ace was just as skilled. Any form deficiency he had was covered up with his speed and cat reflexes, his ears perked forward and flicking around, as if able to sense when ice was coming a second before it hit. It didn't matter how much ice White Wizard threw at him, he was always able to disappear just in time and come back for the follow-up attack.

"Ali!" Red Queen grabbed my arm, pulling my attention from the fight and down to her. She motioned to the ice sticking us to the ground. "We've got to get you back to the Emerald Castle. Maybe that will end this madness."

I blinked, the reminder of the ice bringing back the biting cold and woke up my mind. The Emerald Castle. The portal between the worlds and my way home. Would it even work until a Queen was chosen? It was worth a try.

"Oh, right." I crouched down, almost lost my balance but managed to wobble back into place. I pushed at the ice, but my attention was shattered every time the sound of a sword thudding on ice reached my ears.

Thud. Male grunt.

Concentrate, I ordered my mind, *concentrate on the problem at hand.* Find a solution. Ace can take care of himself. My hands just slid over the damp ice. "This isn't—" thud "—working," I muttered.

Red Queen wiggled and moaned as she tried to get her feet loose. Her right hand slipped off, the wand brushing against the ice. It let out of shower of red sparks in protest. One of the sparks landed on the ice, melting away the ice until it disappeared.

"Did you see that?" I pointed. "The wand! Hold the tip against the ice."

Red Queen nodded. "Sorry," she whispered to the wand and pressed it against the ice around her feet. Sparks erupted from the tip, eroding away the ice wherever it touched. "It's working," she gasped and huffed some stray dark curls out of her face. "The wand spent so much magic on you and me, it's getting tired. I hope it can hold out a little longer." It wasn't long, but it seemed like forever before she was able to weaken the ice enough to pull her feet out, leaving a perfect print of the bottom of her boots behind.

She looked at me with success blazing in her eyes. "Okay, Ali, let's get you out." She pointed the wand at my feet.

The sparks were starting to come out in spurts, like a sparkler about to run out of gunpowder.

There was a yell of pain. I looked up in alarm, fear squeezing my throat closed.

It wasn't Ace. White Wizard fell toward us, a dirty boot print in the middle of his chest. He landed on the ground with a grunt only feet in front of us.

We gasped and stood up. With my feet stuck in place still, it was hard for me to keep balanced, but Red Queen grabbed my arm and helped me stay up.

Our movement drew White Wizard's attention and he turned murderous eyes on us. Ace leapt at him from behind, but White Wizard thrust a chunk of ice at him, forcing Ace to disappear to avoid it.

Frantically, I pulled on my legs, trying to get the ice to let go.

Red Queen clenched her teeth and stepped in front of me. She pointed her wand at White Wizard. "Step back!" Red sparks fizzled from her wand.

I don't know if she was bluffing or not. I thought her

wand was only able to heal and that it was almost out of magic.

White Wizard laughed at her. "Do you really think that tiny amount of magic can protect you?" He pulled his arm back, ready to attack.

"Red!" I yelled and grabbed her shoulders. She screamed as I threw her to the side as far as I could.

"No matter," he said with a cold smile of triumph and focused on me. White Wizard pulled back his arm in triumph and thrust forward.

I squeezed my eyes shut and flinched, waiting for the pain.

It never happened. Instead there was a male grunt.

My eyes popped open. "No!" I shrieked in horror.

Ace stood in front of me, Blood in one hand and the other hand around the ice sword extending from his stomach.

White Wizard breathed a huff of satisfaction. "I finally caught you, you stupid cat."

Ace grunted in pain. His breath was puffing in and out, but his voice was firm. "Me too." His ears flicked back as he thrust forward with a snarl.

White Wizard didn't have the time or mobility to react. The Vorpal Blade sliced through his ribs and into his heart. His mouth dropped open in pain.

Face to face, Ace glared at the man who had haunted him for so long. "You are a horrible person. And a terrible Queen."

White Wizard's mouth closed and opened again, but nothing came out. Instead, he froze. Literally. He turned into a perfect ice sculpture, shocked expression and all. A crack appeared at his heart and a second later, it erupted out until every surface was distorted. The bits started to come apart. Piece by piece, they rose into the air and dissolved into snow. In the warm air, the powder melted and disappeared.

Off in the distance, a similar thing was happening to the Diamond Castle.

The ice covering the field disappeared, and the ice monsters exploded into snow.

Around us people gave shouts of surprise. Like the snow melting in the sun, the animal parts that marked the people disappeared. They shifted, feeling their completely human bodies. A cheer of excitement echoed up, getting louder and louder until everyone was celebrating.

Freed from White Wizard, Blood's tip rose in the air. At first I thought Ace was lifting it, until it had risen so high he had to let go. The sword hovered in the air for a minute. In a flash of light, it exploded into nothing.

"Blood," Ace whispered in defeat, and crumpled backwards.

"Ace!" I caught him. His weight dragged me down until he lay on the ground with his head in my lap. I stared at him, seeing him in real life without cat ears for the first time.

My wide eyes stopped at the hole in his gut. So much blood came out of the wound. In all the time I'd spent in Oz, I hadn't seen anyone bleed. But now Ace's torso was covered in the red liquid.

Frantically, I bunched up the hem of Ace's shirt and pressed it over the hole. My mind raced over the first aid I'd learned. In case of a puncture wound, you shouldn't remove the object until on the operating table. But the ice disappeared with White Wizard. And there was no operating table waiting for Ace.

He groaned under my hands.

"It'll be okay, Ace." My voice was shallow and shook

with panic. "Just—just go to sleep. You'll be fine in the morning." Right? People who died in Oz just came back the next morning. Even the ones that bled. Right?

Amusement mingled with the pain in his face. "Even if it were true, I'm not sure I'd want to wake up tomorrow," he rasped.

"What do you mean, 'even if it were true?'?" My voice shook.

"You won't be there. I've been ... hollow for so long. I can't do it again." He looked up at the blue sky. "Blood. It's gone." His voice cracked with the loss. He took a long, pained breath. "Oz's indecision is gone. There's only one Queen ... and Oz can move forward now."

"So life can go on," I finished Ace's thought. "Birth and ... death."

In other words, he wasn't going to wake up tomorrow.

CHAPTER TWENTY-THREE

MY THROAT BURNED SO BADLY that nothing else would come out.

Red Queen stumbled up to us. She must have knocked her head again when I threw her because she was barely steady on her feet, mostly held up by the battered Hareson. Lional limped into view, holding his arm, open panic on his face until he saw that Red Queen was safe. Blood spots were starting to grow on the men where they'd been cut during the battle, but it didn't seem like they were gravely injured.

Red Queen dropped to her knees and stared at Ace, brows pulled up and tears in her eyes. "Don't worry, Ace. I'll heal you." She touched her wand to his chest.

I held my breath, waiting.

Nothing happened.

Red Queen made a sound of frustration. "No, don't run out now."

My chest tightened so painfully, I could barely breathe. I had to bite my lips to keep the moan of disappointment inside.

Ace put a sluggish hand over hers so that she'd look at his face. "It needs rest. And so do I ... I'm sorry," he said softly. "I'm so sorry for everything. I hope I finally made up for it. Fixed everything I did wrong."

Large crystal tears left clean trails down her smudged cheeks. "No, I'm the one who's sorry. I confused you so much with my selfishness that you couldn't understand your own task. And now, I don't even have the strength to make it right."

"It is right." He gasped. "Right now, it's right."

Tears pricked at my eyes and trickled down my cheeks, blurring my vision.

Ace turned to me and flashed a weak smile. "You're a funny Ali. After everything that's happened to you, now you cry? Over someone like me?" His hand lifted. It shook with the effort but was still gentle as he brushed the tears away. "Don't cry. I'm fine with this."

"Why? I'm not!"

"You won't even remember us when you get back," Ace said. "But I will never forget you, Ali. After all, I waited twenty-six Alices for you." He sucked in a breath and hacked out some air. "I'd rather die than ache for you for the rest of my life."

Red Queen looked at Ace with mixed emotions. "Your heart is no longer alone. You finally found your queen, haven't you?"

A ghost of a smile touched his face. "She'd make a ... horrible Queen for Oz." His halted voice grew faint. "But she's my queen."

More tears streamed down my face.

His breath stopped. He didn't turn into dust, like when people normally died in Oz. His corpse just lay there, still and horrible.

"Ace?" I shook him. "Ace!" My head dropped down until our foreheads touched. I felt the remaining warmth leave his body, and despair filled me. "No!" This couldn't be happening. My fingers desperately searched for a pulse on his neck, but there was none.

Lional chose that time to speak. "I don't know why you're so worked up. No one wanted him anyway." His words were hard, though his voice was soft.

My eyes widened. No matter how much Lional hated Ace, he shouldn't insult him over his body. I turned and glared at Lional. "I want him."

Lional frowned and looked away.

I did not do all this, work so hard to clear his name and fix Oz, just to have the man I loved die on me. Ace had already paid the price for his mistake; he shouldn't have to give his life too. I looked at Red Queen fiercely. "Bring him back."

She peered through her tears at me. "What?"

"Bring him back! You have the power, don't you? You said you have the power to heal people. Heal him. Bring him back to me!" My voice was strong through the tears.

Her expression crumpled with pain and guilt, head tilting to the side. "I can't. Not until Oz recovers. White Wizard and I used too much of its magic in the fight. It wouldn't help now anyway. No one in Oz has ever had the ability to revive the dead."

It was like cold water was poured over my head and dripped down to my toes, numbing my muscles and mind. He couldn't die. He couldn't. But there was no way I could stop it. No one in Oz could. My eyes widened. Oz.

I carefully moved Ace's head off my lap and stood up. I looked at the sky and yelled, "Oz! I know you can hear me!"

Out of the corner of my eye, I saw Lional look at Hareson like I'd gone crazy.

I ignored them. "Give him back!" I demanded to the clouds, so innocently white and fluffy in the blue sky. "Ace did everything you asked him to do. So reward him! Bring him back!"

Red Queen grabbed my arms. "Ali!"

I shook her off and kept yelling. "If you can't bring yourself to reward him, then reward me! I played your game. I figured it out and helped Ace do what you wanted. So reward me and give him back. If you can't bring him back to Oz, then send him to my world. I want him! So reward me!" I begged at the top of my voice, fresh tears rolling down my cheeks. My voice cracked to a whisper. "Reward *me*."

"Ali!" Red Queen grabbed my face and forced me to look down at her. "That's enough. It's not going to work. Ace is gone. Oz couldn't send him to your world anyway." I shook my head. "No, if Oz can bring me here, it can send Ace there. He's already been to the In-Between."

Red Queen glanced behind me, frowned, and then focused on me again. Her hands dropped to mine. She squeezed them as her eyes pooled with more tears. "Thank you, Ali," she said. "When you first came to Oz, I was a little worried. You were so odd, I didn't know what to think. Then the next morning you met Ace, I thought for sure White Wizard was going to win this Alice Games." She hugged me. "But I'm thankful you came. I really am. I'd never cared much for the Alices before, but I love you. I'm glad I met you, and I'm glad you met Ace."

I stared at her in surprise. "What? What are you talking about?"

"The Game is over," Red Queen said simply.

Hareson nudged Lional on the shoulder and pointed at

something over my head. "Look. That's never happened before."

There was a movement in the corner of my eye, and I turned, following Hareson's finger.

The Emerald Castle was disappearing. Its green walls were turning into glitter and wafting away with every puff of updraft from the cliff. A physical indicator that the portal between the worlds was closing. Forever.

"Wait!" I protested. A breeze touched my hair and tore at my clothes, tossing it around and growing in strength. No one else was affected by it; just me in my own personal dust devil.

Red Queen smiled big, a single tear etching down her cheek. "Goodbye, Ali of Alice." Her hands slid out of mine.

The wind intensified into a tornado, forcing my eyes closed and cutting off all sounds.

EPILOGUE

FROWNING, I glanced around, searching for a clue as to what was going on. I was in the Milstein Hall at the top of some stairs. Two flights below, the sounds of students talking and working reached up and echoed off the curved cement ceiling above me.

I knew I was on a tour of Cornell's campus, but how did I get to the top of the stairs? And why did my heart hurt so badly that I wanted to cry? Wasn't I doing something a moment ago? Something ... important?

I tried forcing my mind to snap out of it. I had to catch up with my group. I turned and smacked straight into someone walking the other way.

My papers slipped out of my hands, and I lost my balance. For a sickening moment, I tipped toward the open stairway.

"Whoa!" His quick hands caught my arms and pulled me away from the edge.

"I'm so sorry!" Mortified and still a little scared, I barely glanced at the tall young man. I dropped to the floor to collect my stuff. I couldn't believe I'd done that! I'm never that oblivious to my surroundings!

He knelt down too. "It's okay. You're not hurt, are you?" He picked up some papers and offered them to me.

"No, I'm—" I glanced up and froze, hand outstretched to take the papers. Wow, he was hot.

His full lips were cocked in a half smile, and his deep brown eyes gleamed with perpetual laughter. His hair was, well, orange, cut short and spiked up. There were so many emotions in his handsome face. Affection, relief, warmth, and others I couldn't identify. It was the first time anyone had ever looked at me like that. Like I was the most important person in the world.

Suddenly my eyes were swimming in water. I blinked in surprise and looked away. What was wrong with me? I run into a gorgeous guy, and he's nice enough to help me pick my things up, then I burst into tears? Missing some of the tour was not worth this humiliation.

He glanced down at the papers in his hand. "So it's Alice Liddell?"

I glanced at him. He was still talking to me? The weird girl that plowed into him? "Ah, it's Ali, actually."

"Oh, really?" He rocked back on his heels and watched me with interest.

"Yeah, my mom's name is Alice too, so I go by Ali." Ah, I sounded so lame. My face went up in flames. Why was I blushing so badly? Was it because I was fighting an insane urge to throw my arms around him? I was seriously going crazy. Why now? I swallowed and tried to calm my nerves. "And you are ...?"

He flashed a smile. For a second, he reminded me of a teasing cat. "I'm Ace Harte."

Ace. Something tickled at the back of my mind. But what?

Ace glanced at the papers again, fingering the botany program flyer on top. "So you're in Becca's tour group? And you're going into the botany program?"

"Ah, yeah." Right, that's what her name was. I'd forgotten. My hand jumped to my hair and tugged. It was a relief that he knew what botany was.

He nodded. "What's your favorite flower?"

My mouth opened to answer, then I paused. Yesterday I would have said the orchid, but a different flower popped into my mind. "Water lilies," I said softly. I looked down, frowning. "I don't know why. They just seem ... magical." Like knights and rainbows that came out of flowers. An embarrassed smile spread over my face, and I waved it away. "Sorry, that sounds silly." I glanced up at him and the air evaporated from my lungs.

He was smiling at me. Just smiling. His eyes were so tender. There was happiness and sadness there too, making my heart squeeze tight. I wanted to reach out and touch him. Soothe away the sadness until there was only laughter on his face.

My gaze lowered. What was I thinking? I'd just met him! I motioned to the dog tags hanging from his neck. "What about you? What are you majoring in?" I needed to change the subject before I freaked him out.

He blinked, the expression disappearing to a playful smile. "I'm majoring in English, but I'm also in the ROTC." His head bobbed to the side. He stood up and held out his hand.

I took it and let him pull me to my feet, heart going a million miles per hour. I smiled. "That's pretty admirable. Really." I was reluctant to let go, but I made my fingers slide out of his. Instantly I wanted to grab his hand back. Instead I accepted the papers he offered. My cheeks burned when his fingers brushed mine.

I cleared my throat. "So, your class right now is in Milstein Hall?" Did he need to go? It was a depressing thought, thinking that he had to go and I'd never see him again.

He waved a hand. "Actually, I heard Becca had another large group. We're buds, so I thought I'd come and help. I do that sometimes." He stuck his thumbs in his back pockets and rocked back on his heels. He glanced away, then cleared his throat. After a second, he looked back at me. "Hey, I know this is sudden, but I could give you the rest of the tour. At least one more catered to you, not the whole group. The botanical garden is in bloom right now. And the library is amazing. Like, right out of a dream. Want to check it out? Then we could meet up with your group for dinner. Or I could buy you something as a 'welcome to Cornell' thing."

My eyes widened. I wasn't being charming enough to merit a date. And the last thing I planned on finding at Cornell was romance. I wanted to plow through school as fast as I could, not linger and get bogged down with ties. But there was something about this man, a feeling that I never wanted to leave him again—even though I'd never left him to begin with.

He rushed on. "I'm not a bad person." His hand came up in a vow. "I'd been told before that I have a thing for being the knight in shining armor. You can trust me, I promise."

I did. I didn't know why, but I trusted him. Completely. A smile bloomed across my face.

Ace held out his hand, grinning. “Come on. Just you and me?”

“Okay.” My hand slid into his.

A Note to You!

Thank you so much for joining me and Ali on this journey. It was a lot of fun to discover the world of Oz, and come to understand and love the characters that live there. There's a special place in my heart for Ace! Leave a review and let me know who your favorite character was.

I hope that you will continue to join me on my journey as an author. I learned a lot in the making of this book, and I hope to only improve in the future. Keep a look out for my other titles!

Thanks again!

Michelle R Reid

ABOUT THE AUTHOR

Stories have always been important in my life. From the skits I made up for my friends while jumping on the trampoline (Moon Prism Power!), to my first full length novel I wrote in 8th grade choir against my teacher's wishes.

I am married to a wonderful man and we have three very active kids that keep me on my toes. In college, I studied Zoology, Biology, Art, and English. I drove my counselor nuts. I finally settled on wanting to be an author like my mom. (Alysia S Knight-check her out!)

'Curiosity killed the cat' is a good saying for me. I love to figure out how all the pieces of the puzzles fit—whether it be in a book, movie, or real life situation. I like to take what I've learned and weave it into my books.

ALSO BY MICHELLE R REID

YA Books:

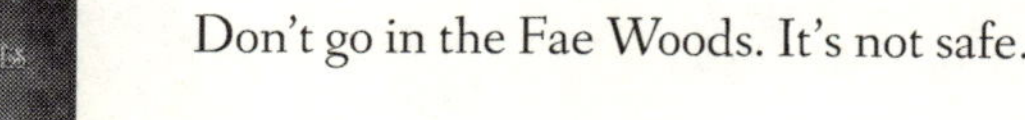

Don't go in the Fae Woods. It's not safe.

Don't go in the Fae Woods. It's not safe.

…e secrets are too dangerous to be left unsaid.

Fantasy Sweet Romance

She thought he was just a man in her paintings ...

until they met in real life.

Made in the USA
Middletown, DE
05 February 2025